PRAISE FOR AMY CLIPSTON

"Amy Clipston writes a sweet and tender romance filled with a beautiful look at how love brings healing to broken hearts. This small-town romance, with an adorable little girl and cat to boot, is a great addition to your TBR list."

—PEPPER BASHAM, AUTHOR OF *THE MISTLETOE COUNTESS*
AND THE MITCHELL'S CROSSROADS SERIES

"Grieving and brokenhearted, novelist Maya Reynolds moves to Coral Cove, the place where she felt happiest as a child. An old family secret upends Maya's plan for a fresh start, as does her longing to love and be loved. *The View from Coral Cove* is Amy Clipston at her best—a tender story of hope, healing, and a love that's meant to be."

—SUZANNE WOODS FISHER, BESTSELLING
AUTHOR OF *ON A SUMMER TIDE*

"*The Heart of Splendid Lake* offers a welcome escape in the form of a sympathetic heroine and her struggling lakeside resort. Clipston proficiently explores love and loss, family and friendship in a touching, small-town romance that I devoured in a single day!"

—DENISE HUNTER, BESTSELLING AUTHOR OF THE BLUEBELL INN SERIES

"A touching story of grief, love, and life carrying on, *The Heart of Splendid Lake* engaged my heart from the very first page. Sometimes the feelings we run from lead us to the hope we can't escape, and that's a beautiful thing to see through the eyes of these winning characters. Amy Clipston deftly guides readers on an emotionally satisfying journey that will appeal to fans of Denise Hunter and Becky Wade."

—BETHANY TURNER, AWARD-WINNING AUTHOR OF *PLOT TWIST*

THE VIEW FROM CORAL COVE

OTHER BOOKS BY AMY CLIPSTON

CONTEMPORARY ROMANCE

The Heart of Splendid Lake

AN AMISH LEGACY SERIES

Foundation of Love

Building a Future (available

August 2022)

THE AMISH MARKETPLACE SERIES

The Bake Shop

The Farm Stand

The Coffee Corner

The Jam and Jelly Nook

THE AMISH HOMESTEAD SERIES

A Place at Our Table

Room on the Porch Swing

A Seat by the Hearth

A Welcome at Our Door

THE AMISH HEIRLOOM SERIES

The Forgotten Recipe

The Courtship Basket

The Cherished Quilt

The Beloved Hope Chest

THE HEARTS OF THE LANCASTER GRAND HOTEL SERIES

A Hopeful Heart

A Mother's Secret

A Dream of Home

A Simple Prayer

THE KAUFFMAN AMISH BAKERY SERIES

A Gift of Grace

A Promise of Hope

A Place of Peace

A Life of Joy

A Season of Love

YOUNG ADULT

Roadside Assistance

Reckless Heart

Destination Unknown

Miles from Nowhere

STORY COLLECTIONS

Amish Sweethearts

Seasons of an Amish Garden

An Amish Singing

THE VIEW
from
CORAL COVE

AMY CLIPSTON

THOMAS NELSON
Since 1798

Published in Nashville, Tennessee, by Thomas Nelson. Thomas Nelson is a registered trademark of HarperCollins Christian Publishing, Inc.

Thomas Nelson titles may be purchased in bulk for educational, business, fundraising, or sales promotional use. For information, please email SpecialMarkets@ThomasNelson.com.

Library of Congress Cataloging-in-Publication Data

Names: Clipston, Amy, author.
Title: The view from Coral Cove / Amy Clipston.
Description: Nashville, Tennessee : Thomas Nelson, [2022] | Summary: "When a jilted romance novelist returns to the small beach town she once loved, she discovers not only inspiration but also a romance to call her own"-- Provided by publisher.
Identifiers: LCCN 2021047919 (print) | LCCN 2021047920 (ebook) | ISBN 9780785252931 (trade paper) | ISBN 9780785252948 (ebook) | ISBN 9780785252955 (downloadable audio)
Subjects: LCGFT: Novels.
Classification: LCC PS3603.L58 V34 2022 (print) | LCC PS3603.L58 (ebook) | DDC 813/.6--dc23
LC record available at https://lccn.loc.gov/2021047919
LC ebook record available at https://lccn.loc.gov/2021047920

Printed in the United States of America
22 23 24 25 26 LSC 5 4 3 2 1

For my super-awesome husband, Joe, with love and appreciation. Here's to the summer we met and our wonderful memories of driving around Sandbridge Beach and taking day trips to the Outer Banks. When I think of the beach, I remember some of our happiest times. I love you and this amazing life we've built together!

Prologue

Maya giggled as she raced down the beach to the ocean waves, breathing in the salty air and enjoying the feel of hot sand between her toes. Oh how she loved spending summers with her great-aunt in Coral Cove. This was her favorite time of year.

"Maya! Slow down!" Mom called from behind her.

But Maya simply threw her hands up into the air and ran faster. "Last one in is a rotten egg!"

When she reached the water, she jumped in with both feet and yelped with delight. Then, facing her mother and Aunt CeCe, she plopped onto her stomach and stared up at them. They were both standing where the sea barely touched their toes. What were they waiting for?

"Look! I'm a mermaid!" Maya announced as she splashed around. "My tail magically appears in salty water."

Aunt CeCe chuckled as she turned toward Mom. "Don't you love the imagination of an eight-year-old?"

"I wish I could bottle her energy," Mom said, shaking her head.

Glad she had energy, Maya screeched as a wave rumbled toward her, then carried her toward the beach. She was floating! When she sank to the bottom again, she laughed, then popped to her feet, spun in the water, and pretended to be a pinwheel. Once she stopped spinning, she dizzily stumbled backward and dropped onto the sand, flat on her back.

Looking up at her two favorite people in the whole world, Maya grinned. Oh, she didn't have a father, and sometimes that made her feel bad, but Mom told her what really counted. *You have a wonderful family, Maya. That's because Aunt CeCe and I both love you so very much. We'll always want the best for you, and we'll always be here for you. No matter what.*

"Come into the water with me!" She bounced up, then took her aunt's hand in hers and gave it a gentle tug. "Let's go!"

"Okay, but I can't run and jump like you do." She touched Maya's nose. "I'm not so old for a great-aunt, but my knees are beginning to complain about *their* age."

"I promise I'll just walk, then."

Maya grasped her mother's hand next. "You come too, Mom."

Her mother smiled down at her. "Of course I will."

Maya guided them into the North Carolina–coast water, and another wave of happiness washed over her as though it were the summer-warmed ocean itself. When she looked up to see seagulls fluttering above them in the bright blue sky, the sun's rays kissed her cheeks. That's how Mom always said it—"Kissed."

Maya gave her mother's and Aunt CeCe's hands a squeeze. "Isn't this the best time?"

"Yes, it is, sweet girl." Her aunt smiled. "I love playing with you, honey."

"Can we visit the dolls in your store after we swim for a while?"

"Of course." Aunt CeCe looked at Mom. "What do you think about pizza tonight, Vickie? I'll order it from our favorite place."

Mom's face lit up. She was so pretty! "Oh yes! That sounds delicious."

"Yay!" Maya sang as she released their hands. "I love pizza! But for now, let's swim like mermaids!"

This is my special place, she thought as she dove under the water. *I hope we come here forever—even when I'm a grown-up. I never ever want to stop spending summers in Coral Cove.*

Chapter 1

TWENTY-ONE YEARS LATER

The June sunlight streaming in through the windshield seemed to mock Maya's somber mood as she steered her bright metallic blue Toyota 4Runner onto Fourth Avenue, then passed some of the quaint little stores lining the streets of her favorite place in the world. She'd never tire of Coral Cove. It was her favorite place in all of North Carolina.

She tried to concentrate on the pop music serenading her through the vehicle's speakers, but her mind kept spinning with the reality of what just happened—she'd buried her beloved great-aunt CeCe, her last living relative.

As Maya's eyes filled with tears again, she tried to dismiss them. She was strong. She would pick herself up and move on. Besides, what choice did she have?

When her phone rang through the speakers, she saw her best friend's number on the screen. She hit the answer button on the steering wheel as she slowed to a stop at a red light.

"Hi, Kiana." Maya peered out the window. Saturday shoppers

moved in and out of the flea market, clothing store, and gift shop in this section of the block.

"How'd it go, My?"

"The service at Aunt CeCe's church was beautiful, and the words the pastor spoke at the gravesite were especially meaningful. Then a group of her church friends hosted a really nice potluck lunch. There was so much food, Key. You wouldn't have believed it. Anyway, I got through it better than I expected."

The light turned green, and Maya accelerated through the intersection, passing Coral Cove's single movie theater and her favorite ice cream parlor. She loved this little town that had been her great-aunt's home and Maya's special place to visit every summer.

"I'm glad, My." Kiana sighed. "But I'm also sorry. I wanted to drive down and be there for you. If only I could have switched with one of the other nurses today, but none of them were available. I would have rather been there to hold your hand than working here in Charlotte. You know that, right?"

"It's okay. I already told you I didn't expect you to come all the way down here for the funeral."

"But I could've helped you finish unpacking and making sure the store is ready to reopen on Monday."

Maya merged onto Laskin Road and then turned left onto Third Avenue. As she motored past the Best Friends Pet Shop, she spotted a big white tent near the store's side parking lot. Quite the crowd had congregated there.

She focused her eyes out the windshield again as CeCe's Toy Chest came into view across the street. A fresh wave of emotion pummeled her chest. Gayle, her great-aunt's best friend, had called her just over a week ago to tell her CeCe had suffered a massive heart attack and passed away. Gayle found her when she arrived at the store for work that morning.

Not even waiting until after the funeral, Maya had immediately packed up everything she owned, found movers who fortunately had a slot in their schedule, and given the keys to her apartment to the landlord. Then she headed down to Coral Cove to run Aunt CeCe's store and start a new life. As she knew she would, she'd inherited not only the business but the whole building, which included her aunt's apartment on the second floor. Its rooms weren't especially large, but it did have three bedrooms and two bathrooms, more than enough space for one person.

"I promise you I'm fine, Key. And you're always there for me. In fact, you're the only person I can count on, especially after . . . well, you know." Maya couldn't bring herself to say her former fiancé's name. Today had been painful enough.

"Don't even mention He-Who-Shall-Remain-Nameless. He's not worth your breath. I'm glad he's in Europe and out of your life. You deserve so much better."

Maya frowned. If only she could get Kyle out of her mind!

She steered her SUV into the driveway that led to the small parking lot behind the two-story brick building that had housed the toy store since before Maya was born, nearly thirty years ago.

She parked by the back door. "Thanks, Key. I'm really tired. It's been a long day, and I'm finally home. I just want to get out of these clothes and put up my feet. I'm going to let you go, okay?"

"Of course. I just wanted to check on you. Love you."

"Love you too. Bye."

Maya disconnected the call and stared at the back door that led not only to the store but to the stairs up to the apartment her aunt CeCe had lived in for so long. Maya and her mother had lived there, too, until they'd moved to Charlotte when Maya was four. Then Maya had spent her summers there throughout most of her childhood.

But now this whole place was hers—the store, the apartment, the entire building plus a garage. Aunt CeCe had even left her some money. And with Kyle breaking their engagement and moving an ocean away, she'd quickly decided starting fresh in Coral Cove was the best thing to do. Kiana and a few other friends lived in Charlotte, but other than that, no ties kept her there.

If only she knew how to start fresh with no family.

She climbed out of the driver's seat, then found her purse and the huge shopping bag bulging with disposable containers of leftover food. She had no idea what she was supposed to do with it all.

Once inside, she mounted the steep steps up to the apartment, wondering how her seventy-six-year-old aunt had managed them, especially with an armload of groceries. But CeCe had been strong, hardworking, and independent, which she'd proved daily by running her own business with only Gayle's part-time help.

Maya walked through the family room to the kitchen and stowed the leftovers. Then she moved to the master bedroom and surveyed the boxes and bags she'd already filled with CeCe's clothes and most of her accessories. She'd donate them sometime next week.

She stripped off her short-sleeved black dress and black pumps before stepping into a pair of jean shorts, a yellow T-shirt, and her favorite pink Birkenstocks.

Now that the funeral was over, she could ease into her new life in Coral Cove. But she couldn't shake this newest grief that followed her like a shadow. She'd always been close to her great-aunt, but after she'd lost her mother three years ago, CeCe had become even more important to her.

And now they were both gone.

Maya trudged back into the kitchen and found a can of Diet Coke in the refrigerator. Then she stood in the doorway to the second bedroom, always ready for guests. She hoped Kiana would visit often—and soon.

This room had been her and her mother's when they lived there. It was also where Maya had stayed as an adult when she visited her precious aunt every summer. They worked together in the store during the day, and Maya spent the evenings writing.

She moved to the smaller, third bedroom. Like CeCe had, she'd use it as an office, but it would take some work. Leaning on the doorjamb, she scanned the rolls of wrapping paper, containers of yarn and ribbon, piles of old quilts, and boxes of books, magazines, photo albums, and mementos Aunt CeCe had collected over the years. And then there were the books and office supplies Maya had brought with her. She'd never be able to concentrate with so much clutter staring at her!

She swallowed a groan as she considered the romance novel she'd yet to fully plot. Its deadline loomed over her like a dark cloud.

When Kyle told her he'd accepted the job of a lifetime overseas, he also said she couldn't go with him and not to wait for him. She was about to suggest they simply postpone their wedding if that was what he needed when he asked for his ring back. That request relieved her of any notions of romance right then and there.

Thankfully, her editor agreed to extend her deadline to July. Since then, Maya had only tinkered with the general outline. She hadn't managed to come up with any ideas to flesh it out. At least not any good ideas.

Then when Aunt CeCe passed away a week ago, she'd been dragged into a new undertow of shock, grief, and confusion. Her patient editor agreed to extend the deadline again—until mid-September. That still didn't seem like enough time, but she had to make it work. After all, writing was a career she loved. At least she had loved it before her own love life was destroyed.

She'd decide what to donate, toss, or move to the attic, then bring in a bookcase from the garage and organize what was left. Surely that and a new start in Coral Cove would help.

Maya turned toward the family room. The truth was, she had her first case of writer's block, and she had no idea how to overcome it. Her novels had always come fairly easily. For one thing, Kyle had inspired a lot of the creativity she needed to fuel her sweet romances. But now where would she get inspiration?

She'd worry about finding it later. After burying her dear aunt today, she was too emotionally distraught to think about the office. She just wanted to lose herself in memories—joyful memories. And so many of them were made in her great-aunt's store.

As she walked through the family room, her eyes scanned the cluster of family photos on a large table behind the sofa. They featured CeCe, Maya's mother, the maternal grandparents she'd never known, and Maya herself. Then she moved past the wall of photos of her from kindergarten to braces to high school and college graduations. She was grinning in every one of them.

She sprinted down the stairs, then opened the back door, allowing the comforting scent of the ocean to calm her battered heart. Memories of playing on the beach with her aunt and mother filled her mind, making her smile.

The ocean breeze reminded her she much preferred the sticky summer humidity to the cold, unrelenting hum of central air. Since the store was closed until Monday morning, she could enjoy the quiet with the back door open and the air conditioning turned off.

Maya walked down the short hall, past the two storerooms, a breakroom with a kitchenette, and a small bathroom. Then she opened the door leading into the large, cheerful toy store where she'd played as a child. She slipped behind the counter and picked up the framed photo of Aunt CeCe, Mom, and her taken five years ago, two years before her mother succumbed to complications from kidney failure.

Maya ran her fingers over the glass, tracing her mother's beautiful face. Maya stood between the two women on the boardwalk, and as the waves rolled onto the shore behind them, their smiles were nearly as bright as the afternoon sun.

Maya desperately ached for her family, the only family she'd ever known.

"I miss you both," she whispered, her voice hoarse.

Maya set the photo back on the counter and then ambled up and down the aisles, running her fingers along the displays of baby dolls, doll clothes, board games, stuffed animals, trains, cars, and action figures.

When she came to the aisle filled with Barbie dolls, she recalled the summers she and Aunt CeCe spent hours playing with Barbies and making up stories about them. That had inspired her love of writing.

Her eyes stung, and she sucked in a breath. She had to keep her mind busy to stop those pesky tears.

Maya snapped her fingers when she remembered the large box behind the counter. When she'd opened it yesterday, she'd found it full of Barbie clothes, shoes, purses, and other tiny items. Stocking the Barbie accessory display was exactly what she needed to keep her mind occupied on this quiet Saturday afternoon. Then before returning to the apartment, she'd look for anything else that needed to be done.

She pulled both a stool and the box from behind the counter and over to the display, then sat down and began hanging the accessory packs. She smiled as she took in one with a pink dress, matching pumps, and a purse. She hung another packet with a purple blouse, a coordinating skirt and headband, and fun shoes. She worked in silence for several minutes, then considered some musical company. Aunt CeCe had an old turntable on a wall shelf behind the counter so she could play some of her priceless vinyl records as she worked. Listening to some of her later Beatles music would certainly bring back memories.

But just as Maya reached into the box and lifted the last accessory packet, a strange noise sounded from nearby. She froze and listened, taking in a whining or squeaking that seemed to be coming closer.

She turned just as a calico kitten raced toward her and then jumped into her lap. Laughing as she dipped her chin, Maya said, "Why, hello there, little one."

The kitten rubbed its nose on hers.

"Aww," Maya cooed. "It's nice to meet you too."

The kitten meowed as it plopped down on her lap. Noting it was a girl, Maya touched her head and took in her pretty little face. Golden eyes sparkled in the light of the fluorescents above them, and her fur was an adorable combination of orange, brown, and white with some tabby stripes mixed in. Stripes also rimmed her eyes, reminding Maya of Cleopatra makeup. They made her gorgeous golden orbs even more prominent.

"Are you lost?" she asked the feline as she rubbed her head.

The kitten responded with a loud purr reminiscent of a small engine.

"Aren't you the sweetest? I'm sorry, but I don't sell kitty toys here. I think you meant to go to the pet store across the street." Maya rubbed the cat's chin, and the purring grew louder.

"Here, kitty, kitty!" a child's voice suddenly called. "Hello? Is anyone here? I lost a kitten." The voice sounded as if it were only an aisle or two away.

"I believe I found her," Maya called. "We're on aisle four—with the Barbie dolls."

A little girl Maya guessed was about eight or nine years old— dressed in pink shorts, a pink shirt featuring a black cat and the words *Bea's Cat Rescue*, pink socks, and a pair of pink Converse low-top sneakers—appeared at the end of the aisle. Her long, dark brown hair was pulled back in a ponytail adorned with a pink ribbon. Maya couldn't decide who was cuter—the kitten or the kitten's seeker.

The little girl pointed at the kitten. "She likes you."

Maya opened her mouth to respond, but her words were cut off by a man's hollering.

"Ashlyn!" He sounded frantic. "Ashlyn Beatrice Tanner! Where are you?"

"Over here, Dad! In the Barbie aisle."

A tall man with short brown hair a shade darker than the girl's came to the same end of the aisle. Maya guessed he was in his midthirties, and she couldn't help but notice his striking pearl-blue eyes, perfectly proportioned nose, and strong jaw. His blue shirt, sporting a black-and-white cat and the same *Bea's Cat Rescue*, fit him well over his wide chest, and his khaki shorts boasted muscular legs and a trim waist.

"Pardon the intrusion," he told Maya before he looked at the girl. "You nearly scared the life out of me when you ran across the street. Didn't you see those cars coming?"

The girl's brow pinched. "I was trying to find the kitten." Then she smiled and nodded toward Maya. "But look, Dad. I think she's found her new owner."

"What do you mean?" Maya asked.

The dad's face lit up with a handsome smile, and a dimple appeared on his chin. "I see that. She seems to have adopted you, miss."

"Me?" Maya shook her head. "Oh no, no, no. I'm not looking for a pet. I just moved in here, and I have so much to do. I can't possibly add caring for a kitten to my list."

The girl walked over to Maya and leaned down. When she rubbed the kitten's chin, she purred louder in approval. "But cats are easy. You don't have to walk them like you do dogs. They pretty much take care of themselves. You just have to feed them, give them water, and scoop out their litter box. Right, Dad?"

"That's true." The man joined his daughter. He had to be at least six feet tall.

Considering their similar T-shirts, Maya recalled the tent and crowd outside the pet store, and the pieces came together for her. "Are you running a cat adoption day at the pet store?" she asked him.

"Yes, we are." He held out his hand. "I'm Brody Tanner, and this is my daughter, Ashlyn."

Maya shook his hand. "Maya Reynolds."

"My dad's a vet, and he runs the Coral Cove Veterinary Clinic and Bea's Cat Rescue." Ashlyn pointed to her shirt. "Bea was my nana, but she passed away four years ago. I was only four then."

Maya picked up the kitten, who continued to purr in her arms as if she belonged there, and stood. "It's nice to meet you both."

"Did you know Miss CeCe?" Ashlyn gestured around the aisle.

"She was my great-aunt."

Ashlyn's nose wrinkled. "What's a great-aunt?"

"She was my grandmother's sister. So if your nana had a sister, she would be your great-aunt."

"Oh." Ashlyn nodded.

"We heard Miss CeCe passed away. I'm sorry for your loss," Dr. Tanner said.

"Thank you."

Ashlyn turned toward the display of Barbie accessories and began sifting through them. "We come here all the time, don't we, Dad?"

"We do." Dr. Tanner's expression warmed as he watched his daughter.

Ashlyn spun to face Maya, her expression full of worry. "You're going to keep the store open, aren't you?"

"Yes. We'll be open bright and early Monday morning. Miss Gayle and I will run it together."

"That's great," Dr. Tanner said as he folded his arms over that wide chest.

Ashlyn pointed toward the ceiling. "So now you live in Miss CeCe's apartment upstairs?"

"I do."

"Where are you from?" Dr. Tanner asked.

"Charlotte." The cat shifted in Maya's arms, and she tried to readjust her without being sliced by her tiny claws. She held the cat out toward the little girl. "She's obviously had enough of me. I think you should take her."

Ashlyn took the cat with a frown. "But I really think she likes you. You should adopt her. She was found behind the supermarket with her mama and three brothers and sisters. The rest found homes, but she still needs one."

"Like I said earlier, I really have too much going on right now. I'm trying to get a handle on running the store, and I have to get the apartment organized too."

"She'll help you. My kitties like to play with my pencil while I do my homework. Right, Dad?"

Dr. Tanner chuckled. "Yes. But you know it's Miss Reynolds's decision whether to adopt this cat. We never nag the people who come to the rescue shelter, and we won't nag her either."

"I know, but this kitty loves her."

Ashlyn's voice held a hint of concern, and Maya found her resolve fading a bit. "It's been a long time since I've had a pet. Is she already litter trained?"

"Yes," Dr. Tanner said, chiming in.

Ashlyn nodded with emphasis. "All your customers will like her too." She pointed toward the display window. "You could put up a big sign that says *Don't let the cat out* so they won't let her escape."

Maya glanced at Dr. Tanner, and he grinned. He certainly was handsome, but she scolded herself for even thinking about that. He was a married man with a child! She ought to be ashamed.

"I bet you'll even get more customers because of the cat," Ashlyn continued. "Stores with cats are the best ones."

Maya's lips twisted as she considered the girl's words. It would be nice to have a companion now, and Ashlyn was right. A cat was an easy pet. She took the kitten back, and when she rubbed her ear, a loud purr sounded once again. "Does she still need her shots and surgery?"

Ashlyn's brown eyes twinkled. "No. My dad takes care of all the shots and the surgery before the cats are ready for adoption."

"So I just need to pay the adoption fee and buy her supplies?"

"That's right."

"How much is the fee, Ashlyn?"

"It's thirty dollars, and you can get cat supplies at the pet store. I'll help you pick them out if you want."

Maya hesitated. Was taking on a pet too much when she already felt so overwhelmed? She examined the kitten's cute little face. "I don't know . . . What would I even name her?"

Ashlyn turned to the Disney-inspired Barbies on the shelf behind her. Not even a second passed before she had an answer. "Tinker Bell!"

"Tinker Bell, huh?" Maya smiled as she lifted the kitten's face to hers. "Does it suit you, little one?"

"Dad! There's that Barbie camper I told you about!" Ashlyn scooted down the aisle and pointed to her find.

"I told you to save your allowance for that, Ashlyn." Dr. Tanner shook his head as he took a step toward Maya, then lowered his voice. "Please don't feel pressured to adopt the kitten. Ashlyn is passionate about animals, but I don't want you to feel obligated to take on a pet if you're not comfortable with it."

Maya looked at Dr. Tanner's daughter, who now stood on her tiptoes browsing the Barbie dolls and playsets. "She made some good points, though."

"I always tell her she'll make a great sales professional someday."

Maya laughed as she met his gaze, and they shared a smile. But when she felt her cheeks warm, she cast her eyes down toward the kitten.

"Ooh, Dad! Look at this purple Barbie car. Isn't it cool? The package says it's 'off-road.' I think I saw it on a commercial at Tessie's house."

Dr. Tanner sighed. "Ash, we need to get back to the pet store to help with the adoptions."

"Okay." But Ashlyn still looked concerned.

Dr. Tanner reached for the wiggling kitten. "We should get going. It was nice meeting you, Miss Reynolds."

"Wait." Maya took a step back. "I'll adopt the cat, and I do think I'll call her Tinker Bell."

Ashlyn clapped her hands as she rushed down the aisle. "Yay! I just knew you'd take her."

"You sure?" Dr. Tanner asked.

Maya nodded and then met Ashlyn's eager gaze. "Let me get my purse and my aunt's shopping cart, and then after I take care of the adoption and bring Tinker Bell back here, you *will* have to help me pick out supplies at the pet store. Deal?"

"Deal!"

Chapter 2

Thank you for giving Oscar a good home, Mrs. Anderson." Brody handed her a receipt. He'd heard she'd recently become a widow, and he suspected she was lonely. "I'm sure you two will get along just wonderfully."

Mrs. Anderson looked into the pet carrier and beamed at the two-year-old tuxedo cat blinking at her. "I'm so excited. I haven't had a cat for years, but when I drove by and saw your adoption event, I just knew I had to stop. We're going to have so much fun, Oscar." She looked at Brody again as she slipped the receipt into her purse. "Thank you, Dr. Tanner. I'll be sure to bring him to your clinic whenever he needs care."

"You're welcome. And thank you for your confidence." Brody waved goodbye as she lifted the carrier and walked away. Then he glanced around the tent, where volunteers from his cat rescue and a couple of the employees from his veterinary clinic milled around, talking to folks who'd stopped by to see what cats were ready for adoption. This was his second event in a year, and he was pleased to see so many potential adopters in attendance.

His heart lifted as he glanced at his volunteers' Bea's Cat Rescue shirts. He'd started the rescue in his mother's memory, and he hoped she'd be proud. The charity meant so much to him, and he wanted it to be her family's legacy.

"So far we've adopted out four cats."

He turned as Kim Banks, his veterinary technician, sidled up to him. "Four? Already?"

"That's right." She pushed a lock of her long hair over her shoulder and smiled. "This event has already been more successful than the last. I'm sure the advertising campaign you ran in the paper and the local radio stations helped."

Kim lingered beside him. With her bright blue eyes, high cheekbones, trim figure, and long, golden hair, she was attractive. But even though he sometimes got the impression she wanted more, Brody wasn't interested in anything but a working relationship. He wasn't really interested in dating anyone after his horrendous breakup four years ago. It still haunted him. He'd been certain that Courtney was the love of his life, which was why he'd proposed.

But then she decided she didn't want an instant family. And ever since then, rather than worry about navigating a risky relationship, he'd focused on his daughter, his clinic, and the cat rescue.

"I saw Ashlyn go into the pet store with a dark-haired woman. Who is she?"

"She's the new owner of CeCe's Toy Chest, Maya Reynolds. That little calico that managed to wiggle out of Ashlyn's arms ran over to her store. When we found the kitten with her, Ashlyn convinced her to adopt it and then offered to help her pick out supplies."

Kim's smile widened, and she fluttered her long eyelashes. "Ashlyn is a great helper. She always offers to give me a hand around the clinic."

"I don't know what I'd do without her." Ashlyn was the light of his life.

A young couple, probably in their twenties, approached the table where Brody and Kim stood.

"Hi," the woman said. "Do you have any white kittens? The one we have now is black."

Kim slipped around the table. "We do. Follow me."

Brody turned toward the entrance of the store just as Maya and Ashlyn emerged. They seemed engrossed in conversation as Maya pushed her shopping cart, packed full of supplies. When she reached the crosswalk, she said something to Ashlyn and then watched as his daughter made a beeline for him. Meeting his gaze, Maya waved.

He returned the smile and wave before she pushed the cart into the crosswalk. Maya Reynolds certainly was attractive with her long, dark hair, chestnut-colored eyes, and outgoing personality. Curiosity filled him as he considered their brief conversation. She hadn't mentioned a man in her life—

"Dad!" Ashlyn called as she approached. "I helped Miss Maya pick out everything she needed for Tinker Bell." She began counting the items on her fingers. "Toys, food, bowls, a litter box—"

Brody touched his daughter's cute little nose. "I'm sure she appreciated that."

"She did." Ashlyn tilted her head. "Maybe I could visit her and Tinker Bell sometime."

"We'll see." He turned his attention to a group that looked like a mom and a dad, a young son, and a slightly younger daughter about Ashlyn's age. "Good afternoon. May we help you find a cat?"

"Yes," the little girl said. "Do you have any orange ones?"

Ashlyn beamed. "Yes! I'll show you."

Brody grinned as he watched his daughter lead the family to the two tabbies available for adoption. What would he do without her?

That evening Maya sat on the family room carpet and took what seemed like her hundredth photo of Tinker Bell. Then she opened her phone's texting app, sent her favorite dozen photos to Kiana, and waited for her best friend to call. Just as she'd expected, her phone soon rang with Kiana's name on the screen. "Hi, Key."

"You got a kitten?" Kiana nearly screamed.

"I did."

"She's precious. Where did you find her?"

"Funny tale, no pun intended. She actually found me." While Maya shared the story, she held up a stick with a bird hanging from a string. Tinker Bell ran and leaped, trying her best to capture the bird.

"So let me get this straight," Kiana began. "This kitten ran into the store and jumped into your lap and then an adorable little girl and her super-hot veterinarian father appeared and became your new friends as you adopted the homeless kitten."

"Exactly."

"That's the cutest thing I've ever heard."

"I think I made a mistake, though." Maya smiled as she touched the kitten's nose and then rubbed her little belly.

"Why?"

"Because I have so much to do around here—boxes to unpack,

items to donate, an office to set up, and a book to write. But I'm not getting any of it done because this little girl is too cute. I can't stop playing with her."

"That could be a good thing. You've been through so much lately. Maybe this little kitty is just what you need to find a muse again."

Tinker Bell smacked Maya's hand and then ran toward the kitchen before skidding, spinning, and scampering back to her.

Maya laughed. "Oh, Kiana, she's so cute! I wish you were here to see her. I'll probably be up all night playing with her."

"Enjoy her. You can always write tomorrow."

Maya frowned and turned toward the doorway that led to the disaster that would someday be a workable office. But perhaps Kiana was right. Maybe she did deserve a break.

Still, that deadline was looming. She just hoped this change of scenery and new life really would provide the inspiration she needed to get her career back on track.

"So did you get his phone number?" Kiana asked.

"Whose phone number?"

"The handsome vet, silly."

Maya snorted. "No, of course not. He has an eight-year-old daughter. That usually means a man's married."

"Not always," Kiana sang. "Did you see a ring on his finger?"

Maya considered that question as she waved the bird and Tinker Bell leaped and peeped, trying to catch it. "I honestly didn't notice, but when Ashlyn helped me pick out the supplies in the pet store, she mentioned her mom loves cats."

"So he probably is married. That's a shame."

"I'm not interested. I'm still licking my wounds after losing Kyle. Right now I need to stay focused on running my aunt's store and writing this novel before my publisher dumps me."

"They aren't going to dump you after five bestselling novels, My."

"We'll see." She picked up the kitten and started toward the bedroom. "I'm going to try to get some sleep."

Maya heard a yawn. "I didn't realize it was after ten. My bed is calling me. Sleep well."

"You too. Good night."

"'Night. Kiss Tinker Bell for me."

"I will. Talk to you soon." Maya disconnected the call and set the kitten on her bed. "Okay, Tink. Let's see if we can get some sleep."

Later, when Tinker Bell attacked her toes under the sheets, Maya shook her head and laughed. *I have a feeling this will be a long night.*

Monday morning Maya flipped the store's front-door sign from Closed to Open and then turned to the kitten sitting on the pine wood floor behind her. "Now remember, Tink. You have to stay in the store, okay? No running outside."

The cat blinked up at her.

"I made a sign asking the customers not to let you out." She held up a large card featuring a photo of the kitten with the words *My name is Tinker Bell, and I live in the store. Please don't let me out—no matter what I tell you. Thank you.* "Now, you need to promise me you'll behave, or I'll have to put you back upstairs."

Before Maya could finish her sentence, Tinker Bell took off, scuttling toward the back of the store where the baby doll strollers and high chairs, play kitchenette sets, bikes, skates, and skateboards were all on display.

With a sigh, Maya hung the two-sided sign where customers would see it in the window by the door, one side facing out and the other facing in. She taped up a few more of the notices around the store and then unlocked the register on the store's checkout counter.

The door leading to the back hallway opened, and Gayle entered holding a pink pastry box, a purse and tote bag slung over her slight shoulder. "Good morning," she called. "I brought fresh donuts for breakfast!"

"Hi, Miss Gayle." Maya came around the counter to meet her and breathed in the aroma of delicious treats. "They smell wonderful. Thank you."

Gayle frowned as she eyed Maya. "What have I told you about calling me Miss Gayle? You're almost thirty, Maya. It's time for you to—" She gasped when Tinker Bell scrambled over her black sneakers before bouncing toward the stuffed animal aisle. "What was that?" she nearly shrieked, her sky-blue eyes wide. "Did a chipmunk get into the store again?"

"That's my new kitten, Tinker Bell, and I've never heard the chipmunk story. You need to fill me in on that one." Maya walked to the stuffed animal aisle and found it empty. "Tinker Bell? Where are you?"

A teddy bear near the end of the aisle shifted, but the cat remained hidden. Perhaps bringing her into the store had been a bad idea.

"Please come here, Tink," Maya said, pleading. "You need to

meet Miss—I mean, you need to meet Gayle." She sighed and looked back toward the counter.

"When did you decide getting a cat would be a good idea?" Gayle set everything she'd carried in on the counter.

"Tinker Bell adopted me on Saturday."

Gayle pushed a lock of hair back from her thin face and then opened the box. She chose a chocolate-iced donut. "Did you go over to the pet shop after the luncheon on Saturday? I heard another adoption event was coming."

"No, I didn't go over there. Tinker Bell came to me. I was working on a stool in here with the back door open. She ran in and decided to leap into my lap."

"No kidding." Gayle grinned before biting into the donut. She moaned and closed her eyes as she chewed, then swallowed. "You need to come get one of these. I'm sure you remember that Joe's Donut Hut has the best in Coral Cove."

Maya chose a vanilla-iced donut with sprinkles. "I do remember that. Aunt CeCe loved them."

"So tell me about this new kitten I need to get used to. Who came up with the name Tinker Bell?"

Maya smiled. She'd always loved her aunt CeCe's best friend. While her shoulder-length gray hair did nothing to hide that she was in her midseventies, it was still nice and thick, and her bright eyes, dry sense of humor, and nearly wrinkle-free skin made her seem decades younger.

They enjoyed their first donut and then a second while Maya once again shared how she came to adopt Tinker Bell—plus who named her.

"That Dr. Tanner is a looker, isn't he?" Gayle quipped as she wiped her fingers with a paper napkin.

Maya nodded, then peered down the stuffed animal aisle. But her kitten was nowhere to be found. "He's not hard to look at, and he seems like a good father too." She peeked behind a row of teddy bears and then moved on to the stuffed cats and dogs. Tinker Bell sure knew how to hide.

After a few moments, Maya returned to the counter. "I have no idea where she is."

"If that thing bites or scratches me, you can be sure I'll file a workers' comp claim," Gayle snipped as she reached under the counter and pulled out a microfiber duster.

Maya shook her head. "She's very sweet. I'm sure she won't hurt you."

"Famous last words." Gayle began dusting the boxes of action figures.

Maya snickered as she put some cat treats in the food bowl behind the counter. The kitten came running, peeping and mewing, before sticking her little head into the bowl and practically inhaling one. Maya took the opportunity to pet her soft fur, and Tinker Bell purred.

"Did you get any writing done like you planned? Or did you play with your new kitten all weekend?"

Maya also appreciated how Gayle never minced words, which meant Maya never had to wonder what the woman was truly thinking or feeling. "I opened the document and stared at my cursor for a little bit yesterday afternoon, but no, I haven't accomplished a thing since I got here." She poured water from a bottle into the water dish while Tinker Bell continued to noisily chomp on her treat.

"What's your new book about?" Gayle asked from somewhere in the action figure aisle.

Maya straightened a stack of toy catalogs sitting beside the cash register. "It's another romance novel."

Gayle appeared at the end of the aisle, her expression incredulous. "Well, that doesn't tell me much. What's the story about? How does the couple meet? Do they like each other at first or hate each other? Do they live in a castle or on a ranch?"

"I haven't figured that out yet." Maya leaned forward on her elbows at the counter, resting her chin on one palm. "I had an idea back when I started plotting it in February, but then I lost my inspiration when, well, you know. I can't write a romance when I don't remember what it's like to have romance in my life."

Gayle's pretty face clouded with a frown as she wagged the duster at Maya. "Don't let that good-for-nothing poor excuse for a man ruin your ability to write amazing books and advance your career. He's not worth it, sweetie. I'm sure he's not across the ocean worrying about you."

Maya nodded and sighed. Last night she'd almost emailed Kyle. She still had so many questions. Why couldn't she have gone with him? They could have tried to work things out. But he said no. A flat-out no. And then he made it clear he didn't want to marry her.

The only explanation was that he'd never loved her, at least not enough to marry her. In the following days, she'd realized he *had* seemed less interested in their wedding plans, but she'd chalked it up to his being a man, ready to just get on with it. And then when he ended their relationship, he hadn't actually explained what his thought process had been, and she was too stunned to demand he tell her. He'd just insisted there was no one else, took the ring, and jetted off the next day!

Taking the job overseas was probably just an opportunity to get out of marrying her—although he had always cared a lot about advancing in his career, especially when a promotion included a big salary increase.

"It's just difficult, Gayle. When we lost Aunt CeCe, I was still reeling from the humiliating pain Kyle inflicted on me. It's all cut me to the bone, and now I've forgotten how to tell a story, let alone dream one up."

Setting the duster on a shelf stocked with boxes of candy, Gayle joined her at the counter. "I miss CeCe, too, but she would want you to keep writing. She was so proud of you. She encouraged all her customers to buy your books, and she always made sure Callie Lewis displayed your new releases in the front window over at Beach Reads. She wanted the whole world to know her niece was a successful author."

Maya sniffed, and her eyes stung. "Really?"

Gayle took Maya's hands in hers. "Yes, really. And she never liked that bozo Kyle. She told me he wasn't good enough for you, and she was right."

"She didn't like him?" Confused, Maya blinked. "She never said that. She was always positive and encouraging when I talked about him, and she sounded excited when I told her he'd proposed."

Gayle released Maya's hands and shook her head with emphasis. "She was fibbing, Maya. She didn't want to hurt your feelings.

Besides, she was afraid if she admitted the truth to you, you'd cut her off and never tell her anything. But she told me she always prayed you'd find a nicer man, one who put you first, not his career."

Why had she never realized Kyle cared more about his career than he cared about her? Well, she did now.

"Maya, I dated plenty of frogs before I met my Rodney, and even though he drives me nuts when he fails to get out another roll of toilet paper or put his snack dishes in the dishwasher, I wouldn't trade him or our family for the world." She touched Maya's arm. "Don't give up. You'll find your prince. And maybe you'll even find a man who knows how to find toilet paper and actually use a dishwasher." Gayle threw up her arms. "Imagine that! What a concept!"

She picked up the duster and pointed it at Maya. "Don't give up on love because of Kyle." She made a sweeping flourish with the duster and then headed down the game and craft aisle. "Get back to writing and keep the faith. You'll find the right guy when you least expect it."

Maya shook her head as that familiar heartache hit her. Certain that she and Kyle would build a home and family together, she'd been blindsided when he dumped her. And now, no matter what Gayle said, she was afraid she'd never find a "prince" or any man who'd want to marry her. After all, she was almost thirty, and she'd always hoped to be married by now with the promise of mother-hood on the horizon. But as her November birthday loomed, she was alone with no prospects.

She looked down at Tinker Bell and found her happily batting around a toy she'd pulled from the small basket Maya had brought

31

into the store. She took out a second duster and headed to the baby doll aisle.

"Are you going to participate in the Fourth of July parade this year?" Gayle's question floated from a nearby aisle.

"I hadn't thought about it."

"Well, July 4 is only a month way. You know it's a CeCe's Toy Chest tradition to have a float."

Memories of the Fourth spent with her aunt took over Maya's mind—waving from the float, tossing candy to children, riding in the passenger seat of CeCe's old 1955 Ford pickup truck painted purple. Those were some of her best memories. CeCe had been like her grandmother—or really, more like a second mother. For a moment, she couldn't catch her breath because of the grief packed around her heart.

The bell above the door chimed, and a woman entered with two preteen boys in tow. Her hair was obviously dyed—Maya could see her black roots under the golden-blond.

"Welcome to CeCe's Toy Chest," Maya announced as she approached them.

The woman's face darkened with a deep frown, and she suddenly looked vaguely familiar. Perhaps she'd been a frequent customer.

"Oh, Maya." She clucked her tongue. "I was so sorry to hear about your sweet aunt. She was such a lovely lady. And she seemed so healthy! To just have a massive heart attack like that . . ."

Maya swallowed back a new wave of emotion. "Thank you."

The two boys moved past her, mumbling, "Excuse me," before disappearing into the action figure aisle. The woman, however, continued to look distraught, shaking her head as she studied Maya. "I know you two were close. I remember you helping her in the store from the time you could barely see over the counter. You were so cute following her around and helping her stock the shelves. You must be devastated."

Maya's lower lip trembled, and tears threatened. She opened her mouth to respond, but no words formed.

A hand on her shoulder caused her to jump. "Maya, dear," Gayle began, her words measured, "a new box of sand toys needs to be unpacked. Our display is low. Why don't you get it. I'll handle things out here."

Maya nodded. "Right."

She headed down the back hall but then sprinted past the storerooms before pushing open the heavy back door. Thick, humid air hit her like a wall, but she welcomed it. Glancing up at the cloudless sky, she crossed the gravel parking lot to the three-bay garage housing the old pickup truck, parade float, and furniture Maya wasn't sure she would keep.

Realizing she might have to go back inside for the key, she turned the side door knob anyway and found it unlocked. She must have forgotten to secure it when she'd deposited a box in there yesterday afternoon.

After stepping inside, she flipped on the overhead lights and took in the purple pickup with *CeCe's Toy Chest* stenciled in white on the doors. The long, flat parade float sat beside it, only a naked purple stage. The oversize flat wooden teddy bear, toy train, ball, and doll that had sat on it for years were stored in the rafters above her.

She climbed onto the float and then sat down on the end with her legs dangling over one side. Last year CeCe told her she wanted a new theme for the float this year, and Maya tried to imagine creating one without her aunt, then running the store without her aunt and enjoying the boardwalk and beach without her aunt. It all seemed so wrong.

A few minutes later she pushed herself off the float and padded out of the garage. Once in the storeroom where they kept new deliveries, she searched until she found the sand toys. Then, squaring her shoulders, she lifted the box and made her way back into the store—her store. Again, she was strong, just like CeCe, and she would face this day with a smile and make her aunt and mother proud.

At closing time, Gayle flipped the sign in the front window from Open to Closed and locked the door. "What did you think of your first day as manager and owner?"

Maya set the contents of the register into a zippered bag for Gayle to take to the bank on her way home, an errand she insisted she didn't mind. "It was good. I felt more confident as the day went on, and hearing people talk about my aunt was a little easier by the end of the day."

Gayle swiftly gathered her belongings and the money bag. "Good. I went part-time so I could help my grandkids with their little ones, but if you need me to go back full-time temporarily, I can."

"I'll manage. See you Wednesday."

"Okay. But remember, just because Tuesday is my day off, that doesn't mean you can't call me if you need me. I just might need to bring one of the kids with me."

Gayle started for the back door, then stopped when Tinker Bell scrambled over, slid to a stop, and blinked up at her. "I'll see you Wednesday, too, stinker." She craned her neck and looked back at Maya. "You might want to put a bell on this one. She startled an old lady looking at a water pistol, and I was afraid the woman was going to pass out."

Maya laughed. "That's a really great idea. I'll run over to the pet shop after I eat something. A few days ago I noticed they're open until eight."

When Gayle left out the back door, Maya picked up Tinker Bell, who wiggled in protest with the loudest mewing yet.

"I guess you like all the attention from customers down here, but it's time to go upstairs. I'll give you a snack in the bathroom so I can eat in peace without you getting into trouble, okay?" She shook her head. "Why am I negotiating with a kitten?"

Maya turned off the lights and climbed the steps to the apartment. After depositing Tinker Bell in the bathroom with treats and fresh water, she rummaged through the leftovers still in the refrigerator. When nothing appealed to her, she closed the door.

"That settles it," she muttered. "It's pizza night."

Chapter 3

Maya strolled to A Slice of Heaven next to the pet shop and pulled open the door. The savory aromas that hit her caused her stomach to gurgle, reminding her she'd grabbed only a quick lunch more than six hours earlier.

The walls were lined with photos of mouthwatering pizzas, breadsticks, and calzones as well as beach landscapes. The black-and-white tile floor was worn, evidence of the family-owned restaurant's longevity—here since well before Maya lived in Coral Cove as a little girl. Aunt CeCe had always bought her pizzas from this place.

On her way to the ordering counter, she noticed several families gathered around the tables and sitting in booths. Some of the folks boasted bright red skin, no doubt after spending time in the sun without a sufficient amount of sunblock. They had to be vacationers, because locals knew better.

Maya took a spot in line and pulled her phone from the back pocket of her jeans, then scrolled through her emails in search of something to read while she waited for her chance to order. She'd settled on a gigantic slice of pepperoni pizza. When she thought she heard someone call her name, her head popped up and she glanced around.

"Miss Maya! Miss Maya!"

She pivoted and found Ashlyn waving to her from a booth in a back corner. Dr. Tanner lifted his hand and beckoned her to join them. Slipping her phone back into her pocket, Maya wove through the sea of tables, nodding hello to familiar faces until she came to where Ashlyn and her father sat across from each other. A large pizza perched on a pedestal between them. She wondered where Ashlyn's mother was. In the restroom? But no third place setting sat on the table. Maybe she was still at work.

Her eyes snapped to Dr. Tanner's left hand of their own accord. His ring finger was naked. Was he divorced? Not necessarily. Her friend Vanessa's husband worried a wedding ring might get caught on the engines he rebuilt at the auto repair shop where he worked, so he rarely wore his. But as a vet, Dr. Tanner didn't have that same job risk.

"Hi," Maya said, adjusting her purse strap on the shoulder of her orange T-shirt. "What a nice surprise."

And didn't Dr. Tanner look great in that light blue collared shirt that made his eyes seem an even brighter blue? But she had to stop noticing the man's looks! Chances were he really was married.

"Ashlyn got excited when she spotted you," he said.

"Fancy meeting her here, right, Dad?" Ashlyn giggled as her father nodded with a grin. "We're laughing because we come here all the time too!" Then the girl pointed to the small bag in Maya's hand. "What's in there?"

"Ashlyn. That's rude." Dr. Tanner's tone held a warning.

The girl's cheeks flushed bright pink. "Sorry."

"It's okay." Maya held the bag out to her. "I bought Tinker Bell a collar with a bell on it so I can find her in the store. Take a look. With a name like Tinker Bell, it makes sense for her to have one anyway."

Ashlyn took the bag and pulled out the pink collar with a matching bell. She smiled as she shook it and the bell rang. "It's my favorite color, and it matches my shirt." She held the collar up to her pink shirt, featuring a white heart in the center, before she dropped it back into the bag and handed it to Maya.

"How did Tinker Bell do in the store today?" Dr. Tanner asked.

"She startled a few people, and sometimes I didn't know where she was. But I never saw her run for the door, and she always showed up after a while. Hopefully the bell will help me keep a better watch over her."

Ashlyn pointed to the pedestal. "You can have some of our pizza!"

Maya took a step back. "Oh no. I don't want to impose."

"Don't be silly." Dr. Tanner pointed at his daughter. "We can never finish our pizza here because this one always insists we order a large. But her eyes are bigger than her stomach."

Maya chuckled as Ashlyn slid over on the seat.

"Sit by me, Miss Maya."

"All right. Thank you."

Maya slipped onto the well-worn, red-vinyl bench seat and dropped the bag and her purse between Ashlyn and her. A young woman approached their table wearing a red T-shirt with the store's logo and a name tag that read *Zoey*. "Would you like an extra plate for your guest?" she asked.

"Yes, please," Dr. Tanner said.

Zoey looked at Maya with her striking hazel eyes—perfect with her gorgeous dark skin and braided black hair. "What would you like to drink?"

"Diet Coke, please."

"Coming right up." Zoey wrote on her notepad before hurrying off.

"Do you like pepperoni, Miss Maya?" Ashlyn asked.

Maya angled her body toward the little girl, who was sliding a piece onto her paper plate. "I do. It's my favorite."

"So that's something else we have in common. We both like cats and pepperoni pizza." Ashlyn held up one palm, and Maya gave her a high five and a smile.

Maya glanced at Dr. Tanner, who was grinning at his daughter as he lifted his plastic cup. He obviously enjoyed her company.

Zoey returned with a paper plate, plastic utensils, a napkin, and a cup of soda, setting it all in front of Maya. "Do you need anything else?" She swept a look around the table.

When they all said no, she left.

Dr. Tanner indicated Maya should help herself to the pizza. "So aside from chasing after your new four-legged employee today, how were things at the toy shop?"

Maya chose a piece and pulled it onto her plate. "We stayed busy all day. How about at your clinic?"

"Not too bad for a Monday. I even got out earlier than I thought I would tonight, which is why Ash isn't still at day camp. But they do offer extended hours when parents need them—except for weekends. They're closed on Saturday and Sunday."

He jammed his thumb in the direction of the restrooms.

"Excuse me. I'll be right back. I just realized I need to wash my hands again. I think I grabbed a sticky collar at the clinic." He slid out of the booth and left.

Maya turned her attention to Ashlyn. "When you were in the toy store Saturday afternoon, I noticed you like Barbie dolls."

"Uh-huh." The girl's expression brightened.

Maya leaned in closer. "Do you want to know a secret?"

"Yes! I love secrets."

"I like Barbies too. They're my favorite dolls."

Ashlyn's eyes narrowed. "You're teasing me."

"I promise you I'm not. Cross my heart! I lived here until I was about four, and then I started staying with my aunt CeCe every summer. We used to play with Barbies together, and I've loved them ever since."

"Do you have a favorite Barbie?"

"Yes. It's the one my mom told me was hers when she was little. She's called Western Barbie. She has on a cowgirl outfit, a hat, boots, and bright blue eye makeup. And if you push on her back, she winks."

Ashlyn cackled with delight. "That's so funny!"

"She has a horse named Dallas too."

"Do you still have them?"

Maya nodded. "They're somewhere in my aunt's attic."

"When you find them, will you show them to me?"

"Sure." Maya smiled. "Do you have a favorite Barbie?"

"I do. It's from my mom too. It's a cheerleader Barbie. She has a pink uniform and pink pom-poms. She's so cute. She even has brown hair and brown eyes like my mom and me have."

"How fun."

"I lost one of the pom-poms, but then I found it in the basket with the cats' toys." Ashlyn laughed, and Maya joined in. "Tomorrow night I'm going to a sleepover at my best friend Tessie's house."

Maya picked up her drink. "What do you do at sleepovers?"

"We play with our dolls and play games. Sometimes we build forts with blankets and tell ghost stories. We also have tea parties."

"Tea parties?" Maya pivoted on the bench seat to face her. "Tell me more about them."

Ashlyn's darling face lit up again. "Oh, they're so fun, Miss Maya! We set up a little table with a tea set and tiny sandwiches. Then we put on our best dresses and sometimes hats and we have tea." She took on a serious look. "It's a very formal event, you know."

"Really?" Maya tried not to grin, but it was hard. "And all your friends like tea parties?"

"Uh-huh." Ashlyn looked down at the table. "My mom loves them too. We do it all the time when she's not too tired from working at the hospital. She's a nurse and helps people."

"That's so nice." Maya nodded. *That's probably where she is, then.*

Ashlyn fingered her napkin while keeping her eyes focused on the table. "We play dolls too. My mom likes to play with my baby dolls, not just my Barbies. We have so much fun."

"That's really sweet." Maya looked up as Brody rejoined them.

"What did I miss?" he asked as he took a piece of pizza.

"We were just discussing—"

"Maya Reynolds! Is that really you?"

Turning, Maya spotted Callie Lewis rushing to their table. She was owner and manager of Beach Reads, and with short-cropped

AMY CLIPSTON

brown hair, large red glasses, and a distinctive voice, she always reminded Maya of Annie Potts's character in the original *Ghostbusters* movie. That had been one of her mother's favorite childhood films. "Hi, Callie."

Ashlyn waved to Callie. "Hi, Miss Lewis!"

"Hello there, Ashlyn. That pizza looks awfully yummy." Callie turned to Ashlyn's father. "Good to see you, Dr. Tanner."

He nodded. "Good to see you too."

When Callie's expression grew somber, Maya braced herself for the condolences she'd heard from customers throughout the day.

"Oh, sweetie." Callie clucked her tongue and patted Maya's shoulder. "I was so shocked to hear about your aunt. Every time she came into the bookstore she'd stand by the checkout and tell everyone in line they should try your books. She just adored you."

Maya swallowed. "Thank you."

Ashlyn gasped. "You write books?"

"Yes. I do." When she realized Dr. Tanner was watching her with interest, heat crawled up her neck.

"You didn't know, Ashlyn?" Callie quickly fetched a chair from the empty table across from them and sank onto it. "Maya is a well-known author. She's written five books now, and they're all bestsellers."

Ashlyn's eyes grew wide. "Wow."

"Is that right?" Dr. Tanner tilted his head before taking a bite.

Ashlyn tapped Maya's arm. "Do you write children's books?"

Maya shook her head. "No. I write—"

"Romance books." Callie shot a look at Dr. Tanner. "And they're very wholesome. Nothing inappropriate at all." Callie turned her attention back to Maya. "You should have a book signing at my store sometime soon. You haven't had one here since last summer, and you've had two more books release since then."

"Thank you for the offer, but it will be a while before I can do that. I'll be really busy running the store and writing at the same time."

Callie clasped her hands together. "Are you staying in Coral Cove permanently?"

"I am." Out of the corner of her eye, Maya could see Dr. Tanner still watching her, and a new insecurity rolled over her. This was worse than the few times her publisher had talked her into giving interviews.

She pushed a thick lock of hair behind her ear and kept her eyes focused on Callie. Why did this man have such an effect on her? And again, he was probably married! Ashlyn didn't say her parents were divorced—not even a hint.

Callie touched Maya's hand. "That's wonderful! We definitely need to get together. When is your sixth novel coming out? I know I've ordered it. I just can't remember the release date."

"September." *The same month I've got to turn in the manuscript for my new one!*

"And what will the next one be about?"

"Uh, well . . ." Maya was reluctant to admit she was floundering. One question might lead to another, and soon she'd be admitting her love life was in shambles, causing a severe lack of inspiration. Dr. Tanner didn't need to know that.

Zoey appeared beside Callie, saving the day. "Would you like a plate, Miss Lewis?"

"Oh, no thanks, Zoey. I'll get my calzone to go." Callie stood. "Well, I should get going. It was great seeing you, Maya. Stop by the store, and we'll talk about scheduling a book signing as soon as you're free. But don't make me wait too long."

Before Maya could respond, Callie had waved goodbye to Ashlyn and Dr. Tanner. Then she dragged her chair to its proper place before traipsing to the counter, greeting a few locals along the way.

"You should write children's books," Ashlyn said. "Then I could read them."

Maya chuckled and glanced at Dr. Tanner, who responded with a warm smile. "Thank you, Ashlyn, but I'd have to take a class."

"Why? You already know how to write books." Ashlyn scrunched her nose.

"I don't know how to write children's books. They're different from the books I write."

Dr. Tanner lifted another piece of pizza. "How long have you been writing?"

"My first book was published four years ago. I thought it was a fluke, but it sold well and got good reviews. My publisher has kept me pretty busy with contracts since then, and I've committed to writing two each year."

"I'll have to check them out."

"Oh no." Maya shook her head. "Don't feel obligated."

"You're working on one now?" He lifted the pizza to his mouth and took a bite.

Maya shrugged and swished the straw in her cup. "Sort of."

He lifted his dark eyebrows.

"I've been a bit distracted, so I'm not as far along as I'd like to be."

He gave a somber nod. "That makes sense. I'm sorry."

An awkward silence fell over the table as they all took a bite.

Maya looked at Ashlyn once she'd swallowed. "So tell me about your favorite books. What do you like to read? What authors do you like?"

Ashlyn gushed about her favorites until the pizza was gone. She was quite the reader, reminding Maya of herself as a girl.

When Zoey brought the check, Dr. Tanner pulled his wallet from the back pocket of his trousers.

"Let me give you some money." Maya opened her purse to take out her own wallet.

"That's not necessary. Ashlyn and I are just glad you could join us. Right, Ash?"

Ashlyn nodded. "Uh-huh."

Zoey returned with Dr. Tanner's card and charge slip. "Be sure to come back soon."

"Oh, we will!" Ashlyn told her.

Dr. Tanner signed one copy of the slip and then slid the other one and his card into his wallet. The man was not only handsome and loving to his daughter but generous too. If he was married, his wife was a lucky woman.

Maya breathed in the warm night air as they stepped outside. "Thank you for the pizza. It was delicious."

"You're welcome," the doctor said as he threaded his fingers with his daughter's. "Good night."

Ashlyn happily waved before Dr. Tanner led her down the

street, and a thought dropped into Maya's heart. *If only I'd had a father when I was a little girl. A father who wanted me.* But that was an old dream, and she was a grown woman who'd had the best mother and aunt a girl could ever want. That and a chance for a new life right here in Coral Cove was enough.

Then another thought hit her. Dr. Tanner hadn't mentioned Ashlyn's mother—not even once.

Chapter 4

Maya walked to her building, unlocked the back door, and loped up the steps into the apartment, where she found Tinker Bell squeaking and mewing in the bathroom as loud as any kitten could.

"Hey, little one," Maya sang as she opened the apparent prison door. "Did you miss me?"

The kitten screeched and then ran into the family room, straight toward her apartment toy basket.

"I'll take that as a yes." Maya snickered before following her charge and putting on her new collar and bell. "Why don't we start getting the office organized?"

She scooped up the kitten and carried her into the workspace, where she sat her down with a toy mouse. Tinker Bell raced around the room, her bell tinkling away.

While Maya sorted through her aunt's things, her mind wandered back to her meal with Dr. Tanner and Ashlyn. Maya was still curious about how the girl's mother fit into their lives. And if she was married to the man, wasn't it strange that he hadn't said a word about her?

Maya pushed a box full of yarn to the side and walked over to the desk. When she sat down and moved a stack of books, a photo slipped out from between two of them before fluttering to the floor. She picked it up, and her chest squeezed. She and Kyle were standing on Coral Cove's beach, grinning at the camera, a car show right behind them. He looked so attractive in the black swim trunks that complemented his tan skin, dark hair, dark eyes, and dazzling smile. And she had some fond memories of their visits to car shows in and around Charlotte. He'd taught her everything she knew about cars—old and new.

He'd driven down to visit her that weekend and had been so attentive, bringing a dozen pink roses for Aunt CeCe and a dozen red for Maya. Then he'd insisted on taking them both to the most expensive restaurant in Coral Cove.

Maya had been so blind then—a fool to believe Kyle truly loved her after dating men who seemed completely uninterested in a meaningful relationship. When he finally proposed at Christmas after they'd dated for more than two years, she'd been certain they would be together for the rest of their lives. But he'd shattered her world only a few months later.

She missed his companionship. The way he'd hold her hand as they walked together and discussed their hopes and dreams for the future. Their late-night talks. His warm hugs that seemed to make any problem she had evaporate.

Maybe . . .

Powering up her laptop, Maya clicked her way to her email and opened a new message. But then she stilled. While she longed to know exactly why Kyle left her behind, she shook her head. No, she had to remain strong and not reach out to him. He'd made himself clear.

She opened the top desk drawer to stow the photo and found a logbook she needed. Good. Although over the years she'd learned how to keep up on the latest trends in toys and games, order and track product, and generally run her aunt's day-to-day business, she definitely had some things to learn about the store's finances.

She pulled out the book, then flipped to the pages for the last year, taking in the monthly sales numbers for CeCe's Toy Chest. They'd been consistent throughout last summer, but then, even with the usual busy weeks leading up to Christmas, they'd dropped off during the fall and winter. While they'd come back up in the last couple of months, sales had been higher last spring than this spring.

Maya went back a few pages and soon realized sales had been dropping for more than two years. Not severely, but enough to be a concern.

She studied the logbook for several more minutes before her eyes started burning with exhaustion. She set it on the desk and picked up Tinker Bell, who squealed in protest and kicked her legs like a turtle turned upside down on its shell.

"It's bedtime, little one. You can play again tomorrow."

Tinker Bell squirmed until Maya set her on the master bedroom floor. Then Maya changed into a clean tank top and shorts from a little pile of clean clothes on the only chair in the room, too tired to find pajamas let alone put the clothes away. She'd have to do more laundry before long anyway . . . and this time get it all in drawers.

She brushed her teeth in the adjoining bathroom and then climbed into bed while Tinker Bell curled into a ball in the upholstered chair.

Rolling to her side, Maya contemplated the financial picture she'd found. She had to find a way to bring the sales numbers up at the store. It was her job to keep her great-aunt's legacy going.

But how? It might take her a while to figure out the why, but that shouldn't stop her from—

An idea suddenly filled her mind, and her heart leaped. She stared down through the dark to where the cat had settled. "Tink, I think I just came up with a great way to increase both traffic and sales in the store. I'll text Gayle in the morning and tell her I have something exciting to talk over with her."

The cat responded with a purr as Maya sat up. She turned on the light, then grabbed a notebook and began sketching.

<hr />

"So what's this brilliant idea?" Gayle asked the following morning as Maya flipped the sign from Closed to Open.

Maya turned toward Gayle as the woman leaned against the counter. "I told you I didn't expect you to come in on your day off to discuss it." She crossed the store and stood in front of her.

"It's fine. My grandson decided to take the day off today, so I have time. Now, what's going on?"

"Last night I found my aunt's logbook where she recorded the store's monthly sales. Did you know they've been declining the last couple of years?"

"Yes. CeCe mentioned it a few times. That's why she added the video game section, skateboards, and an entire aisle of action fig-ures." Gayle tilted her head and seemed to study Maya. "You were here last summer. So didn't you know that already?"

Maya came around the counter and hopped up on a stool. "I noticed the store seemed less busy, but I didn't realize sales had consistently declined." She hesitated and took a deep breath. "I have a crazy idea I think might bring more business into the store."

"I'm listening."

"Brody and Ashlyn Tanner shared a pizza with me last night, and Ashlyn gave me the idea."

Gayle shook her head. "That girl is something else. Such a cute little chatterbox."

"She's brilliant is what she is. She told me she's going to a sleepover tonight, and I asked her what she did at sleepovers. She mentioned having tea parties. When I asked her about them, she said she and her friends dress up and make little sandwiches and have tea. And then it hit me last night."

Maya jumped down from the stool as a fresh buzz of excitement zapped through her. "What if we clean out the smaller storeroom and host tea party birthday parties for little girls? We'll paint the room and buy princess paper products and then partner with the bakery down the street for cakes and talk to Callie about offering books as party favors. We can charge like ten dollars per child or something. I'll just have to make sure I cover costs and make a profit."

Maya clasped her hands together. "What do you think?" She sucked in a breath as Gayle lifted her chin and frowned.

But then Gayle smiled. "I love it!"

"Yay!" Maya pulled out the drawing she'd created last night. "So here's how I imagine the room. Little tables in the center with the birthday girl over here. Then maybe a buffet to keep all the paper products and serving platters in. We can also put up a border with princesses on it or maybe posters. We can figure that out later."

She flipped the drawing over and revealed a list. "I wrote down what we'll need. Let's see. Paint, paper products, serving trays, teapots, saucers, teacups—"

Gayle lifted her eyebrows. "Let me guess, Maya. You drew and made a list instead of working on your novel. Am I guessing correctly?"

"I was just excited to get started." Maya shrugged.

"Uh-huh," Gayle deadpanned. "Sounds more like procrastinating to me."

Maya waved off the comment. "Yeah, I know. But you like the idea?"

"I do." Gayle opened her mouth to say something more but then jumped and yelped. She glared down as the kitten rushed by, her collar's bell ringing in her wake. "Silly cat! I'm going to start calling you Stinker Bell because you're a stinker!"

A bark of laughter escaped Maya's mouth.

"Don't try to change the subject, Maya. You need to get back to writing."

"I know, I know. But right now I'm focused on the store and making my aunt proud."

Gayle rubbed her shoulder. "I told you. Your aunt is already proud of you. I love your idea for the store, and we'll make it happen. But promise me you'll work on your book too."

"I'll try." She rubbed her hands together. "I want to run my idea past Ashlyn and see what she thinks. I need to know if her friends will actually want to have their birthday parties here."

"They will." Gayle shook her head. "That Brody is a good man with the way he took Ashlyn in. She's a lucky girl to have him for her father."

Maya blinked. "Brody took—"

The bell over the door rang as a group of preteen boys walked into the store.

"Do you have any new video games?" one of them asked.

As Maya directed them to the correct aisle, she hoped Gayle would finish that story sooner rather than later. But when she returned to the counter, Gayle was gone. She'd have to wait until tomorrow.

Chapter 5

I like Miss Maya," Ashlyn announced as Brody steered his pickup truck toward the location of her latest sleepover. "I had fun eating pizza with her last night."

He'd been thinking about how much he liked his four-door Chevrolet pickup, but now he gave Ashlyn a sideways glance. "I did too."

He'd been delighted when Maya agreed to join them. Conversation with her was easy, and he enjoyed witnessing the friendship that seemed to be blossoming between her and his daughter. They were in some kind of deep conversation when he returned from washing his hands.

Not only was Maya sweet, but like the day the kitten found her, she hadn't been wearing any makeup—at least as far as he could tell. She was effortlessly beautiful. She also had a gorgeous smile. Plus, he'd never met a published author before, and he was curious about her books. He'd have to get to Beach Reads soon and buy one.

"Right, Dad?"

"What's that?" he asked as he braked at a stop sign, then slapped on his right blinker.

Ashlyn huffed. "Aren't you listening to me?"

His lips twitched as he bit back a smile. "I'm sorry. What were you saying?"

"I said we should have dinner with Miss Maya again."

"Maybe we will." As he turned onto the street with Tessie's house, he continued contemplating their new friend. Maya seemed so humble, almost embarrassed as she talked about her career, yet Callie said she was a bestselling author. Surely a woman as successful and gorgeous as she was had a serious boyfriend or even a fiancé. But he hadn't spotted a diamond on her finger. Nor had she mentioned anyone else moving to Coral Cove.

Not that he was interested.

Brody motored into the Gillespies' driveway, shifted into Park, and cut the engine. "Now, you remember your manners, okay?"

"Yes, Dad." Ashlyn rolled her eyes. "You don't have to tell me that every time."

He chuckled and gently pulled a lock of her hair. "Stinker."

Brody climbed out of the truck and retrieved Ashlyn's tote, sleeping bag, and pillow from the back seat. As they headed toward the front porch, he hoped Maya would enjoy Coral Cove enough to stay. It didn't hurt to have a woman like her in Ashlyn's life.

Brody parked his pickup in the garage under his beachfront home, and then instead of going up the indoor stairs to the first level, he just closed the garage door and jogged up the front steps to the front porch. One member of the family always waited by the window facing the street when he'd been left home alone, and Brody was eager to see him.

When he unlocked the front door and stepped into the foyer, his golden retriever greeted him with a happy bark and a tail wag.

"Hey, Rusty!" Brody leaned down and rubbed the dog's head. "Would you like to go for a walk?"

Rusty trotted to where his leash hung on the wall and barked again.

"Okay. Just let me get changed." He walked through the family room that stretched all the way to the back deck, recalling how pleased he'd been when the contractor and decorator he'd hired last summer finished with his newest renovations. The room had a nautical theme with paintings of lighthouses, beaches, and boardwalks on the walls. A light blue sectional sofa sat in the middle of the room alongside two matching recliners, all facing a large flatscreen television.

At the back of the house, they'd installed wide collapsible glass doors that led out to the huge back deck, allowing an unobstructed view across the line of dunes that reached out toward the magnificent Atlantic Ocean. Like the shoreline itself, the house was angled slightly to the north so they could not only see the sun rise but get an impressive glimpse of the sun setting in the west. When they turned their chairs toward the bay, they could see the entire sunset stretched across the sky. Very few buildings in Coral Cove stood higher than two stories.

He greeted the four cats lounging on the sofa as he crossed to the hallway that led to the three first-level bedrooms, then changed into khaki shorts, a faded concert T-shirt, and sandals. Once he'd hooked Rusty's leash onto his collar, the dog towed him through the large kitchen to the sliding glass door that also led to the deck that spanned the length of the house. Brody breathed in the warm saltwater air and looked up at the clear blue sky as he and his faithful companion descended the stairs to a lower-level deck with a walk that stretched across the dunes to the beach.

The crashing waves presented a sweet melody as Brody rambled down the beach, looking out at the water where families bobbed along, riding the waves, laughing and splashing. When he spotted a pretty brunette strolling along in jean shorts and a gray tank top, his heartbeat sped up. He picked up his pace as he headed toward her.

"Maya! Maya!"

A warm ocean breeze swept past him and blew a lock of dark hair in front of her face. She pushed the tendril behind her ear and stopped walking. Then as she faced him, he broke into a jog with Rusty keeping pace at his side.

"Dr. Tanner!" She waved and hustled toward him, her face breaking into a wide grin. "Hi!"

Brody grinned back. "I thought that was you."

"Who's this?" She dropped to her knees beside the panting dog and began rubbing his fur.

Brody knelt beside her. "This is Rusty."

"It's nice to meet you, Rusty." The dog responded by licking her cheek, and she chuckled.

"Rusty." Brody groaned as heat crawled up his neck. He pulled the dog away from her. "Rusty, we talked about this. You're embarrassing me. You can only lick Ashlyn and me."

Maya laughed as the dog's tongue lolled out of his mouth. He clearly seemed to be smiling as he divided a look between his master and a new friend.

"Oh, I don't mind, Rusty." Maya gave him another rub. "What brings you two out here this beautiful evening?"

Brody stood and wiped sand from his legs. "Just playing." He jammed his thumb behind him. "We live in that house over there. The one with two decks."

Maya's mouth dropped open. This wasn't the first time he'd witnessed such a reaction. The bright green, two-story beach house with its large windows, white shutters, and sweeping double deck *was* impressive.

She blinked. "Wow."

"It's ridiculously big for my family." Embarrassed, he grimaced as he raked his fingers through his hair. "It looks like the Brady Bunch should live there, right?"

"It's magnificent." She peered up at the house again and seemed to be lost in thought.

He held his breath, wondering if she was passing judgment. Lots of people would own such a place merely as a status symbol, but not him.

When she met his gaze again, he was relieved to see her expression was open, warm. "What do you call it? Beach houses always have creative names, like Rock 'n' Reel or Catch 'n' Relax or Absolute Beach."

He turned and pointed. "That's Sandy Feet Retreat."

"What a cute name!"

"Thanks, but I can't take credit for it. Honestly, I can't take credit for the house at all. My father built it a long time ago, and my mom named it. I inherited it when she passed away. It's not a vacation home; it's our family home. We made a lot of memories here."

"It's gorgeous. When I was a kid, I'd take long walks on the beach with my mother and great-aunt and imagine what it would be like to live in one of these amazing homes. I pretended I had a big family with several brothers and sisters. And I'd make up stories about our life. I'd imagine a giant decorated Christmas tree in a big front window and the family gathered around it opening gifts. And then I'd envision my birthday party with dozens of friends playing on the beach. It was the picture-perfect family in the picture-perfect house."

He couldn't stop a smile. She was adorable!

Her cheeks reddened, and she cleared her throat. "Anyway, I suppose that's why I became an author. I like to make up stories." She kicked at the sand with her toe. "Is Ashlyn at her sleepover tonight?"

"Yes. I dropped her off earlier and then decided to take this guy for a walk." He rubbed Rusty's neck. When Rusty tugged on his leash, Brody took a step in the direction of the boardwalk. "Would you like to walk with us?"

She seemed to hesitate for a moment, but then said, "I'd love to."

They started down the beach side by side just as the sun sent radiant colors across the horizon to the west. Evening waves crashed along the shoreline as Brody detected a hint of flowers in the fresh air. He assumed it was Maya's perfume or lotion, and his pulse ticked up. He wasn't immune to feminine delights; he was just cautious.

"How were things at the store today?"

"Interesting. I have an idea I want to run by Ashlyn the next time I see her. I need her opinion and possibly her help."

"I can bring her over." He turned toward her. "Can I do anything to help you in the meantime?"

"Actually, yes. I'd love to bounce the idea off you too. Gayle likes it, and it would be nice to get another adult's opinion."

They approached the boardwalk, and he pointed to an empty bench. "Would you like to sit awhile?"

"That would be nice."

They ascended the steps together, and when Maya sank onto it, he lowered himself beside her. Rusty plopped next to his feet, his tongue lolling as he peered at the beachgoers walking by. When Maya's leg brushed Brody's, he nearly jumped.

Okay. He had to admit it. He hadn't felt such a strong attraction to a woman since his failed relationship with Courtney.

He turned his attention to the sunset, which somehow seemed more brilliant with a companion. When he sneaked a peek at Maya and found her watching the sunset, too, he relaxed.

He rested his right ankle on his left knee and angled his body toward hers. "So what's your idea?"

"Well, last night I was trying to get my home office organized, and I found an accounting log of my aunt's for the toy store. I noticed the store seemed less busy when I was here last summer, but I was surprised to learn sales have been declining for a couple of years. The business isn't necessarily in trouble, but it might be if I don't do something to draw more traffic."

"Huh." He rubbed the stubble on his chin. "I'm surprised to hear that. It always seemed busy when I took Ashlyn there."

"I started trying to think of ways to bring in more business and realized Ashlyn had given me an idea."

"What did she say?"

"When we were alone at the table in the restaurant last night, she told me she liked to have tea parties with her friends. I asked her about the tea parties, and she said she and her friends get dressed up and have tea and little sandwiches. She even has tea parties with her mother. So I came up with the idea of hosting them for little girls' birthdays where they can dress up and even bring their dolls."

Brody's jaw clenched, and he stilled.

Maya stopped speaking, and her brow pinched. "Are you okay?"

"Ashlyn told you she has tea parties with her mother?"

Maya nodded, and confusion flashed over her face.

"What else has she told you about her mother?"

"Well, she said she likes cats and works long hours as a nurse helping people at a hospital." Maya picked at a loose piece of wood on the bench's seat.

Brody turned his eyes toward Rusty and sighed, scrubbing his hand down his face while he decided how much to share with Maya. Although he hadn't known her very long, he did trust her. Still, the truth was painful to admit.

"What's wrong, Dr. Tanner?" Maya looked as though she really cared.

When he met her gaze, he relaxed the muscles in his face. "First, the folks who bring their pets in to see me, my staff, strangers, and acquaintances all call me Dr. Tanner. But my friends call me Brody. I'd like you to call me Brody too."

"Okay, Brody." Her smile was warm.

"Second, Ashlyn's mother isn't in the picture."

"Oh."

"It's okay." He frowned. "Ashlyn has an overactive imagination sometimes."

"I see." Maya's expression seemed hesitant, and he wanted to assure her she'd said nothing wrong.

He crossed his arms over his chest and blew out a deep sigh. "Ashlyn's mother was an addict. I don't know how I'll ever tell her that when she believes her mother was an angel. Sometimes I think it's better if she lives in that fantasy forever. Who wants to learn their mother was an out-of-control addict who died in a car accident? The truth is she was out partying instead of taking care of her toddler."

"I'm—I'm sorry."

He closed his eyes for a moment before going on. "I wish I'd been there for her. I had no idea how bad it was. I blame myself for not paying more attention and being a better brother. But sometimes I think Mom hid the truth from me—"

Maya sat up straight. "Brother?"

Brody matched her body language. "Oh my gosh! Sorry! I completely forgot to mention the important detail that Ashlyn's mother was my sister."

Maya's eyebrows rose. "Oh! At first I thought you were married, and then I thought you might be divorced. Then earlier today Gayle commented how you're a good man for the way you took Ashlyn in, and I wondered what that meant. It all makes sense now."

"I've never been married." *Though I almost was.* He shook his head, hoping to dislodge the painful memory of his one and only serious relationship. "It's just not easy for me to tell people the truth about Julia. She was six years younger than me. Biologically, Ashlyn is my niece, but emotionally and legally, she's my daughter in every sense of the word."

Maya nodded.

"Julia was close to our dad, and when he died, she couldn't handle it. Just sixteen, she started running with a rough crowd, drinking, and eventually doing drugs. Then at nineteen, she got pregnant." He grimaced. "Julia went out with a different guy nearly every night, so I don't know if she knew who the father was. She told Mom it didn't matter."

He took in a deep breath through his nose. Leaning forward as if doing so could expel the pain, he wrapped his fingers around the edge of the seat. "She did clean up while she was pregnant, and Ashlyn was born healthy, not addicted to anything. Mom thought Julia would stay sober for good then, but she went right back to drugs and alcohol about six months after Ashlyn was born. Mom begged her to get help. She even staged an intervention with our pastor and some of Julia's former friends, but it didn't work. In fact, she got worse."

He paused and looked at the ocean as memories crashed through his mind like the waves pounding the shore. "One night when Ashlyn wasn't even two years old, Julia went to a party and never came home. Mom got a call in the middle of the night, telling her there'd been an accident. Julia was driving, and she and her passenger, a young man named Damon, were both high. She drove off a bridge and into a ravine. They drowned." His voice sounded rough, and he tried to clear his throat, but it felt as if it were full of sand.

"I'm so sorry, Brody," Maya whispered as she rested her hand on his.

Heat rushed to the spot where their skin touched, but he went on. "Mom took custody of Ashlyn after Julia died, and she felt it would be best for me to be co-guardian in case anything happened to her. By this time I was working in a clinic in Raleigh, but I returned home and helped as much as I could. Ashlyn was my mom's whole life. I'd even hear her slip and call her Julia."

Maya gave a deep exhale as her eyes filled with tears. He could feel her empathy, and it gave him the courage to continue.

"Then when Mom died four years ago, I became Ashlyn's only guardian. Until she was old enough for school, I had to put her in day care so I could work, and she heard all the other kids calling their fathers Daddy. She came home one day and called me Daddy, and I couldn't correct her. After all, I am her dad. I eventually adopted her, officially."

"And you're an amazing dad." She squeezed his hand.

He smiled down at their joined hands, and his chest swelled with admiration for this kind woman. "Thank you. Ash is my whole life. My goal is to give her everything she needs. Julia couldn't, and my mom didn't get the chance."

"I understand."

Maya withdrew her hand, and then silence stretched between them as the sunset faded and the cicadas sang the day into night. The light poles lining the boardwalk sent a warm yellow glow down the boardwalk.

He cleared his throat. "I'll talk to Ashlyn and remind her to stop telling fibs about her mother. We both wish her mother was here, but she's not." He met Maya's gaze and felt a rousing of his pulse as she smiled. "I'm sorry for interrupting you. I think your idea for the tea parties is great."

"You do?" Her lovely chestnut eyes sparkled. "I think I'll decorate one of the back rooms with a princess theme and set up little tables and chairs. But I want to get Ashlyn's opinion about it and see if she thinks her friends would like that idea for birthday parties."

He chuckled. "I'm sure she'll love it, and she and her friends love anything that has to do with princesses and dressing up. But I'll let her know you want to discuss it with her."

"Thank you."

They were silent again as several beachgoers strolled past them, bringing with them the smell of cocoa butter.

"I get the impression you were close to your great-aunt."

She smiled. "I was."

"I'm sure you miss her." He stretched his arm out on the back of the bench, careful not to touch her shoulders.

"All the time." She sighed. "My mom died three years ago after having uncontrolled diabetes for years. When her kidneys failed, she was dependent on dialysis, and then pneumonia took her. She was only forty-eight."

"I'm sorry. My mom wasn't much older."

She studied him. "What made you want to become a veterinarian?"

"Well, my dad was a cardiologist, and he always encouraged me to pursue a career in health care. To his dismay, I was more interested in taking care of animals than people, and he jokingly blamed my mom. After all, she started rescuing cats, and I loved helping her do it. I also volunteered with the vet who used to own my clinic." Brody leaned down and rubbed Rusty's neck. "This guy is the most patient dog around, putting up with six cats and Ashlyn. He's a saint."

Maya leaned over and scratched the dog's back. "Six cats? He sure is."

Brody turned toward her again. "You know, the Roast Shack accepts pets in their open-air section they use in warmer weather. I take Rusty there all the time. We could get a cup of decaf before calling it a night. What do you think?"

"Sounds perfect."

Chapter 6

After crossing the street next to the boardwalk, Brody and Maya stepped into the Roast Shack's open-air service area. The delicious aroma of coffee immediately filled Maya's senses.

They stood at the end of the line as Maya glanced around the restaurant, listening to all the customers chatting. One wall featured a gorgeous mural of the beach at sunrise, and the opposite wall had a matching mural of the beach at dusk. She smiled as she recalled her great-aunt sharing how she'd watched the artist work on the sunrise mural while she enjoyed a cup of coffee.

Maya reached into her pocket for her wallet but then groaned when she realized she'd left it at home.

Brody spun toward her. "What's wrong?"

"I took my phone and my keys when I left my apartment, but I forgot my wallet."

He lifted a dark eyebrow. "Did you think I would invite you out for coffee and then expect you to pay?"

She opened her mouth to protest but then closed it. He had a point.

Brody retrieved his wallet from his pocket as they approached the counter, where Karis O'Neill, who looked to be in her late sixties by now, grinned at him. The brunette with silver roots, bright hazel eyes, and a gap between her two front teeth had owned and operated the coffee shop with her husband, Ted, for as long as Maya could remember.

"Hello, Dr. Brody." Karis glanced at Maya and gasped. "Maya! Honey! It's so good to see you." Her smile faded. "I'm so sorry about your aunt. We'll all miss her."

"Thank you." Maya shifted her weight from one foot to the other, and Rusty licked her hand as if he knew Karis's sympathy had hit her square in the chest.

"What can I get for you two?"

Brody looked at Maya. "A decaf, right?"

"Yes, please."

"Make that two, Karis."

Once Karis had poured two coffees into disposable cups, she took Brody's cash. When she handed him his change, he dropped both bills and all the coins into the tip jar. Yes, the man was generous.

"You two enjoy your coffee." Karis winked at Maya before they walked away.

Maya gritted her teeth and hoped Karis—or any of the coffee shop's customers—wouldn't get the wrong idea about her and Brody. Not that he would ever be interested in her as more than a friend. Kyle had convinced her of that. What man would? Even her own father—

"So you like hard rock music?" she asked once they were seated at a table, Rusty sitting at her feet. She stirred sweetener and creamer into her cup.

Brody's brow furrowed for a split second and then recovered. "How'd you know that?"

She pointed to his shirt. "Carolina Rebellion."

"Oh." He looked down at his chest and laughed. "I forgot I threw this on before taking Rusty outside. Yeah, I do like hard rock."

"I've never been to one of those events, but I've heard it's a big deal—a three-day concert with a few dozen bands, right?"

"Right. I haven't been to one in a while, but I used to like to go. How about you?"

Maya took a sip of her coffee. "I like all kinds of music. My aunt always took me to the oldies concerts at the beach, and she has a great vinyl collection."

"I remember those concerts." He lifted his cup. "How's writing? Did you get any done last night?"

Maya sighed. "No. I'm pretty frustrated with myself right now. I feel like I've forgotten how to write, which is silly, but I'm more focused on the store."

"You need to give yourself a break. You're grieving, and grief is an unpredictable beast. It can sneak up and suck all the life out of you, including your creativity. It's emotionally paralyzing."

Maya's mouth dried as she took in his earnest expression.

"Grief is definitely a factor," she said. "But there's something else too."

Brody sipped his coffee. "Do you want to talk about it?"

Maya hesitated, then decided to trust him. After all, he'd shared the truth about Ashlyn's mother with her. "It's difficult to write romance after a bad breakup."

He cringed. "I'm sorry to hear that."

She didn't mean to make him feel uncomfortable. "Thanks." She reached down and rubbed Rusty's ear. "When will Ashlyn be home?"

"Hopefully she'll be ready to come home when I leave the clinic tomorrow. We're open half-days on Saturdays, and my partner and I alternate being there." Brody shook his head and gave her another embarrassed expression. "Even with Rusty and the cats, the house is too quiet when Ash is gone. I miss her constant questions and creative stories. Hey, maybe she'll be a writer someday."

The love for his daughter sparkling in his gorgeous blue eyes warmed something deep inside of her.

"Would you like me to bring her over Saturday to discuss your tea party idea?"

"I would love that."

When they'd finished their coffee, they walked out to the street and Maya glanced up at the bright stars winking down at them.

"How about Rusty and I walk you home?" Brody said as they started toward the corner together. "We could use some more exercise."

"Sure. By the way, does the clinic have a float in the Fourth of July parade?"

He looked at her. "We do. And your great-aunt always had one too. Are you planning on keeping that tradition?"

"I am. But I still have to figure out a theme for this year."

They talked about the holiday as they strolled the two blocks to her building.

"Thank you for a nice walk and the coffee," she told him when they reached her back door. "I had a great time."

Brody nodded toward his dog. "Rusty and I did too. Well, good night, Maya."

"Good night, Brody."

Once the two were out of sight, Maya climbed the back steps and unlocked her apartment door, where she was greeted by persistent mewing from the bathroom.

"I'm coming, Tink!" Maya sang as she hung her keys on a hook. When she opened the bathroom door, the kitten bounded out, squealing as she rushed toward the kitchen.

"All right. I'll feed you. Just calm down there, missy. I wasn't gone that long." Or was she? She'd lost track of time once she and Brody started talking.

Brody.

She smiled to herself as she lifted the kitten's food bowl. This new familiarity with him sent a strange thrill through her. She spooned stinky food into Tinker Bell's bowl and then read the words on the side of the can. "'Enjoy your salmon in savory gravy.' Yeah, it smells delightful." She placed the bowl next to the kitten, who was quick to start eating.

Shaking her head, Maya stepped into the office, then sank into the desk chair and powered up her laptop. The clock in the top right corner of the screen read 9:45. So she had been gone for quite a while.

She opened the document for her new novel, then pulled up a blank page and typed *Chapter 1*. Her conversation with Brody twirled through her mind as the cursor blinked at her, beckoning her to begin. Who needed a fully formed plot? She'd just start writing and see what happened.

But instead her eyes scanned the office and its sea of boxes—some her great-aunt's and others hers. Pushing herself from the chair, she crossed the room and sat down on the worn beige carpet beside a brown box with a lid. It was marked *Photo Albums*.

Right on top of the stack she found an album from when she was about Ashlyn's age. She flipped through and scanned several photos of herself on the beach in her favorite pink bathing suit, building sandcastles.

Moving on to the next section, she found photos of her and Aunt CeCe posing in the Barbie aisle of the store. She smiled as she took in her aunt's familiar dark hair and eyes that mirrored Maya's and her mother's, along with her bright, affable smile. She could almost hear her contagious laugh.

Maya leaned back on the equally worn brown sofa behind her and flipped to another section, now taking in photos of her mother and aunt. She smiled as she recalled her mother's voice and how beautiful she'd been before kidney failure had turned her skin yellow and the side effects from dialysis had caused her to lose so much weight that she was frail and gaunt.

When Maya reached the last page, she found a white letter-size, sealed envelope with her name written on the front in her aunt's beautiful penmanship. She turned it over in her hand, and her heart thudded as she opened the envelope and pulled out a sheet of plain notebook paper.

To my sweet Maya,

You know you mean the world to me. You're the granddaughter I never had, just as your mother was the daughter I never had. And today I'm writing to tell you about a mystery I know is very close to your heart—the facts surrounding your father. I plan to leave this letter where I'll be sure you'll find it after I'm gone.

You started asking about your father when you were a little girl, and your mother told you he left before you were born and nothing else. Not even his name. I know that's been hard on you, and that's one reason I've always wanted you to know the truth, at least ever since you were old enough to understand. But your mother asked me not to, and I promised I wouldn't.

Now, however, she's been gone for nearly two years, and I think you deserve to at least know once I'm gone as well. I'm sorry if my writing a letter strikes you as cowardly, but it does make it possible for me to explain everything succinctly. Just like you, I often organize my thoughts best when I write.

Do you remember when you accidentally learned your mother's last name was originally Sullivan and she'd legally changed it to Reynolds—my last name as well as her mother's maiden name? I thought she'd tell you the truth then, but she sidestepped your questions, and eventually you let it drop. The older you got, the more you realized your mother simply did not want to talk about her past.

Well, it's time you learned the truth.

It all started when Vickie was in college at Georgetown and worked at a café. Both her parents had recently died, and with very little inheritance even as an only child, she was putting herself through school. At the café she met a man nearly a decade her senior, and they struck up a friendship. He came in once a week, always sitting in her area.

Friendly, open, and handsome, he was also an attorney with a successful law firm in DC. She was attracted to him. As their friendship grew, he visited her at the café more often. One night he asked her out, and soon they were dating. Your mother fell hard for him. She told me she was completely blinded by love and believed he loved her too. And when he asked her to spend the night with him, she did.

You can figure out the rest. Pregnant, she believed everything would work out because they were in love. She thought he would ask her to marry him and then she'd drop out of school and become a wife and a mom to you.

Unfortunately, it wasn't that simple. When she told him she was pregnant, he said he loved her and never meant to lead her on, but he was married. He also mentioned his wife couldn't give him children.

Vickie was so crushed she didn't want to hear any more. He'd never worn a wedding ring, yet she felt so naive—so betrayed. She left him where he stood, unwilling to listen to more lies.

Keeping you was never in question, and she never contacted him again because she was afraid he might try to get custody of you in order to have a child in his life. As a successful family law attorney, he had the expertise, power, and means to do it. She was terrified he'd have her declared unfit because she was only twenty-one and had no real income and no home. I thought perhaps she should give him the chance to take care of you both, but she insisted she could never trust him.

She immediately dropped out of school and moved in with

me. She didn't want your father to find her, and between changing her name and realizing she'd never told him mine or exactly where I lived along the coast, she felt safe.

Now, I know this is a lot to digest. I wanted to share all this with you so many times. Your mother, however, was always afraid you'd be angry with her for keeping the truth from you. She was scared she might lose you, just as she was afraid she'd lose you to your father when you were born.

Maya, I'm begging you to forgive Vickie for not telling you.

I helped her both financially and emotionally when she entered the college closest to Coral Cove so she could commute and earn her marketing degree. You know which school; you've seen photos of her in her graduation cap and gown, you in pigtails at her side. I always did what I could for you and Vickie, and I've been so very blessed to have you both in my life. After she moved to Charlotte for a great professional opportunity, I was grateful she sent you to me every summer. You and your mother meant so much to me, and I wanted to stay a part of your lives.

I'm certain you're shocked and feel betrayed right now, but I need you to understand that your mother did what she did to protect you. Again, please forgive her. And forgive me.

Vickie told me your father's name was Quincy Hamill. I believe he also went by a nickname or maybe a middle name, but I can't remember what it was.

Maya, Vickie never gave your father the chance to say whether he wanted to be part of your life. Still, if you try to find him, remember that he did deceive her, and yes, he might have tried to take you away if your mother hadn't protected you. Be careful with your heart.

And don't forget how much your mother and I both loved you.

Aunt CeCe

Tears cascaded down Maya's face. As she read the letter over and over again, she felt as if the apartment walls were closing in on her. Anger, grief, and confusion all poured through her, and bile rose up in her throat. Her mother had *lied* to her for her entire life.

Lied!

Mom had always said her father left them, leading her to believe he'd made it clear he didn't want his own child. But that was a bald-faced lie! The shock rocked her to her core. The truth was her mother had hidden her from her father, and there was a distinct possibility that he'd wanted to be a part of her life. He just never had the chance.

She studied her father's name, mentally reciting it again and again.

"Who are you, Quincy Hamill?" she whispered. "Are you still alive somewhere? Did you want to be in my life?"

She closed her eyes and took a shuddering breath. Aunt CeCe had been right. Her mother had hidden her for a reason. This man had lied to her, betrayed her, misled her. And her aunt had pleaded with Maya—*begged* her—to forgive her mother. But how could she when she'd had plenty of opportunities to tell her daughter the truth?

Maya's hands trembled as she stared at her laptop. She could get on the internet right now and search his name, and her heart screamed for her to do it. Yet her aunt's warning rang through her head. Quincy Hamill was a stranger to her, and he could hurt her the same way he'd hurt her mother. For now at least, even though so many questions haunted her mind and heart, she'd just allow herself to digest the truth.

~·~

Maya pushed a box of Christmas decorations out of the smaller storeroom Saturday afternoon. Then she stood in the doorway and huffed out a breath. Although she'd been moving boxes between customers all morning, with only a quick sandwich for lunch, the room was still half full of them.

When the bell at the front of the shop dinged, she swiped one hand over her sweaty forehead and hurried back to the store. "Welcome to CeCe's Toy Chest," she called as she made a beeline for the front door.

"Miss Maya!" Ashlyn scurried toward her. Maya smiled to see her in a light purple shirt with a drawing of Rapunzel on it. "My dad said you need my . . . my . . . I remember! My expertise."

Maya managed not to laugh. "That's true. I do." She looked behind Ashlyn to Brody.

He was smiling, too, and as their gazes entangled, goose bumps chased each other up her arms. He looked so handsome and professional in those khaki chino trousers and a gray collared, short-sleeved shirt. She inwardly groaned as she touched the messy bun on top of her head, certain she looked like a train wreck! She hoped her mascara hadn't run. If only she'd worn something nicer than a pair of jean shorts and a T-shirt with the store's logo over the breast pocket. But not only did most of Coral Cove's shop owners and their employees keep it casual in this beach community, she'd known she'd be working in the storeroom.

Brody nodded toward his daughter. "Ashlyn's been itching to see you ever since I told her you wanted her opinion on something."

"That's right," Ashlyn said. "Dad and I came as soon as he finished working at the clinic and we ate some lunch." She glanced around the store. "Where's Tinker Bell?"

Maya pointed toward the ceiling. "She's upstairs. Since Miss Gayle doesn't work here on Saturdays, and I've been running in and out of a storeroom, I was afraid she might get lost."

"Oh." Ashlyn frowned but then brightened. "So what do you need to talk to me about?"

"You gave me an idea when we were out for pizza, and I want to know what you think of it."

Maya explained her proposal for hosting parties in the back room, detailing how she planned to decorate it and serve tea and cake.

Ashlyn's eyes rounded as Maya spoke, and then she clapped her hands. "That sounds amazing!"

"Does that mean you like the idea?"

"I love it!" Ashlyn spun to face her father and took hold of his hand. "Dad, can I have my birthday party here?"

"Yes, you *may*." Brody shrugged. "It's fine with me."

"When is this birthday?" Maya asked.

"The end of August," Brody told her.

Maya nodded. "That works. I just need to finish cleaning out the room and then paint it and decorate it. Right now it's still pretty full of boxes and supplies. I worked on it yesterday and a little bit today, but I haven't made much progress."

Ashlyn started toward the door leading to the hallway. "Let's go get it ready now."

"Whoa there, Ashlyn," Brody called, and she faced him. "Honey, it's up to Miss Maya when she works on the room." He stepped over to Maya and lowered his voice. "I'm sorry."

She smiled up at him. "It's fine. In fact, I'd be happy to pay her to help me."

"Really?" Ashlyn rushed back to her.

Brody shook his head. "Miss Maya doesn't need to pay us to help her move some boxes. And we do want to help her, don't we?"

"You do?" Maya asked. "But isn't there something I'd be preventing you from doing today?"

"We just have to check on the cats over at the rescue."

Ashlyn tapped her father's arm. "Why don't we help and then go to the rescue?"

"That works for me. What do you think, Maya?"

"I would greatly appreciate the help. It's time to close anyway." Glad she'd decided to keep the same Saturday hours Aunt CeCe had established, she walked to the front of the store, flipped the sign to Closed, and locked the door.

Ashlyn rubbed her hands together as they started toward the back of the store. "Let's get to work!"

Chapter 7

It's well after four already," Maya announced when she glanced at her watch.

Maya, Brody, and Ashlyn had moved what seemed like dozens of boxes both big and small, as well as other items, from the small storeroom into the larger one. But it was too crowded to leave them all there. So her helpers assisted Maya in organizing seasonal decorations, choosing unneeded items to throw into the trash or donate, setting aside stock to add to the store's displays, and marking a few boxes of mementos to take up to the attic.

At one point Maya thought, *Aunt CeCe, I love you dearly. But did you really have to not only keep everything but keep it in such a scramble?*

Brody came to stand beside her. "Is it really that late?" His lips lifted. "Time flies when you're having fun."

Her eyebrows flew up. "You and I have completely different ideas of what fun is."

He laughed, and she couldn't help laughing too.

"I need to let you get to the cat rescue."

Ashlyn joined them, holding a pink jewelry box decorated with bright purple, yellow, and green flowers. "Look what I found."

Maya gasped as she reached for it. "I haven't seen that in years. Where was it?"

Ashlyn handed her the box and then pointed toward a pile of cartons behind her. "At the top of that open box back there. There were some blankets over it."

Maya opened the jewelry box, taking in the ballerina, the little mirror, and the colorful rubber bracelets, beaded necklaces, and Hello Kitty watch inside. She lifted the watch and turned it over in her hands. "Oh my goodness. This was my mother's." She clucked her tongue. "I think it just needs a battery."

Ashlyn reached for it. "May I see it?"

"Of course."

When she gave Ashlyn the watch, the little girl examined it closely. "Wow. This is so cool."

"You think so?"

"Oh yeah. And those necklaces and bracelets are too."

Maya closed the jewelry box and gave it to Ashlyn. "It's all yours. Enjoy it."

"Really?" Ashlyn's dark eyes widened.

Brody rested his hand on Maya's shoulder. "That's not necessary."

"I know." Maya peered up at him, admitting she enjoyed the warmth of his hand on her shoulder. "But I have no use for the jewelry, and Ashlyn likes it. Consider it payment for the tea party idea and her hard work today."

Ashlyn set the box down on a folding chair before wrapping her arms around Maya's waist. "Thank you, Miss Maya!" Then she opened the jewelry box, pulled out the rubber bracelets, and shoved them onto her right wrist.

"You're welcome." Maya touched Ashlyn's hair. "Maybe your dad can find a battery for the watch."

Ashlyn looked up at Brody. "Can you, Dad?"

"I'm sure I can." Brody turned to Maya. "Would you like to come to the cat rescue with us?"

She gave him her best coy smile. "If you let me pick up supper for us on the way, since I owe you at least one meal."

"You win." He grinned as he lifted a forefinger. "But I'm driving."

"Perfect." Maya touched Ashlyn's arm. "So what would you like for supper?"

Ashlyn tapped her chin. "Um, pizza?"

"Okay." Maya chuckled. "Let's just check on Tinker Bell first, and then we can pick up the pizza on the way."

⁓•⁓

Brody maneuvered his pickup into the parking lot as his veterinary clinic came into view. He loved the long, one-story building painted bright blue and boasting a delightful mural with shadows of dogs and cats chasing colorful butterflies and bees in a field of cheerful flowers. Behind the building was the large fenced-in area where clients walked their dogs, and beyond it were the two large red barn-shaped buildings that served as the cat rescue.

Maya, seated beside him in the passenger seat, turned toward him as he steered the truck into a parking spot. "What does the *C* stand for?"

"The what?" Brody slipped the truck into Park and, puzzled, looked over at her.

Without missing a beat, Ashlyn leaned forward between the two front seats. "His middle name is Charles, after his grandfather."

"Oh. You're asking about the sign." Equally inviting, he thought, were the artistic signs at the road and on the building that read *Coral Cove Veterinary Clinic* and *Bea's Cat Rescue*. The names Brody C. Tanner, DVM, and Cameron J. Montgomery, DVM, sat at the bottom.

Brody turned toward his daughter and touched her nose. "You don't miss a thing, do you, Ash?"

Ashlyn lifted her chin. "You need to pay better attention, Dad."

Brody climbed out of the truck, then darted around it and reached for the large pizza box in Maya's lap. "Let me carry that."

"I can handle it." She nodded toward the clinic. "Just hold that door open for me."

He unlocked the clinic door, then held it open for Maya and Ashlyn before locking it behind them. "Welcome to the clinic. Obviously, this is the waiting room."

Maya glanced at the long wooden reception counter, the blue bench seats and chairs, and the colorful paintings of cats and dogs on the walls.

Brody breathed in the strong scent of cleaners, grateful that his staff took sanitizing seriously.

Ashlyn steered Maya behind the counter. "The rescue area is outside."

Brody slipped around them and pulled open a door. "I built the rescue buildings after my mom passed away. I thought we could eat in the breakroom and then go outside to see them."

As they walked down a hallway, Brody pointed out his and

Cam's offices, a restroom, examination rooms, a laboratory, an X-ray room, and an operating room.

"Our breakroom is back here." Brody took the pizza box from Maya's hand and then pushed open the last door.

Maya followed him into the room, which had a kitchenette with a sink set into a small counter, a stove, a microwave, a dishwasher, a refrigerator, and several cabinets. A rectangular oak table with six chairs sat in the middle of the room while a chocolate-brown sofa lined the far wall under a window.

Brody opened a cabinet. "I'll get some plates and napkins. Ash, would you please grab us some sodas from the fridge?"

"Diet for me, if you have it," Maya told her. Then she placed the pizza box in the middle of the table before washing her hands at the sink.

"May I eat with the cats?" Ashlyn asked, setting two cans of Coke and a Diet Coke on the table.

"Will you be careful? The last time you ate out there, you spilled an entire can of Coke on the floor, and we had a sticky mess. We have enough messes to clean up around here."

"I promise I won't spill this time." Ashlyn crossed her fingers over her heart.

"Fine," Brody finally said. "Here are the keys."

"I won't let you down, Daddy. Miss Maya, come and find me after you eat, okay?"

Maya, who'd been perusing a cluster of photos on the wall, glanced at Ashlyn over her shoulder. "I will."

A minute later, Ashlyn hurried out the door carrying a plate with two pieces of pepperoni pizza, a can of Coke tucked under her arm.

Brody turned to Maya, and she pointed to the photo behind her. "That has to be your mom."

Brody came around the table and sidled up to her, then took in the photo of his mother holding an orange tabby. She'd been in her fifties then, and her dark hair had just started to gray. But her blue eyes were still bright, her smile warm, her face glowing with happiness. "What gave it away?"

Maya looked up at him. Her expression was almost intense, and it jolted his heart. "You have her eyes."

"I've heard that before."

"She was beautiful."

"She was." He frowned. "She suffered an aneurysm in her sleep one night."

"I'm so sorry."

He gave a solemn nod. "I think about her every day." His lips formed a flat line. "Ashlyn and I miss her so much."

"I completely understand." Maya pointed to where another cluster of framed photos hung. They all featured Ashlyn, Brody, and volunteers posing with several cats. The red barns stood behind them. "This place is incredible. I'm sure she would be so proud of you and Ashlyn."

"Thank you." He made a sweeping gesture toward the table. "We should eat before the pizza gets cold."

"Good idea." Maya sat down across from Brody, and he passed her a plate and the can of Diet Coke before pushing the pizza box her way. She chose a slice and thanked him. "Did your mom run her cat rescue out here from the beginning?"

He shook his head. "No. Much to my father's dismay, she started it at home. Dad built the main level of our house with three en suite bedrooms for our family of four, a half-bath, a family room, a dining room, and, of course, a kitchen. The upper floor has two bedrooms and a bath he designed for guests. But Mom started keeping foster cats in one of the upstairs bedrooms, and then they took over the other one as well. Before we knew it, the whole floor was theirs."

He grinned. "Dad used to complain about it, but I could tell it didn't really bother him. He just wanted her to be happy." He lifted his drink. "She left instructions in her will asking me to keep the rescue going. I didn't expect to lose her so soon, but she once mentioned that she'd like me to keep the rescue in her memory. We're an officially approved charity, and we pay someone to run it for us part-time. We also have volunteers, but I'm definitely involved. It means a lot to me."

"When did you start this practice?"

"It hasn't always been mine. When I came home after my sister died, I first worked here for Dr. O'Reilly, the same vet I worked for when I was in high school. He was getting close to retirement and gave me the option of buying him out. My best friend, Cam, and his wife were considering getting out of Raleigh and coming to the coast. We'd gone through undergrad and vet school together and kept in touch despite the miles between us. I wanted to invest the money my father left me, and I convinced Cam to come and join me in the practice here. We pooled our resources, and the practice became ours five years ago."

As Maya chewed another bite of pizza, he took a drink of his soda and watched her. She looked like she was trying to put the pieces of a puzzle together.

"You look like you want to ask me something."

"When did you lose your father?"

"My father was a cardiologist. Ironically, he died of a heart attack when I was twenty-two. I can't believe it's been thirteen years."

"That's terrible. You must have been devastated."

"We all were."

"Were you close to him too?"

Brody nodded. "Oh, we had moments when we disagreed. And sometimes he was tough on me. But I knew he always had my back. I took it hard. I was finishing up my undergrad at NC State." He ran his fingers through the condensation on his can of Coke. "But my sister took it the worst. Like I told you before, she was only sixteen. Then she went down a bad road and never recovered."

"I'm sorry your family has been through so much heartache."

"Thank you."

They ate in silence for a few minutes, and he realized he and Maya had both been through tough times with their families—something they had in common.

"You mentioned your mom was a single mother. Do you know your father?"

She shook her head. "I've never met him. Mom told me he left us before I was born. But the other night I found out that isn't true."

"What do you mean?"

She explained the contents of her aunt's letter. "I'm still reeling from the truth."

"Are you going to look for him?"

She stared at her soda as she shrugged. "I'm not sure. Aunt CeCe warned me to be careful with my heart, and I'm not sure how I would handle it if he rejected me."

"But he might be excited to meet you."

She nodded. "That's true."

Just then the door burst open, and Ashlyn rushed in holding her empty plate and soda can. "Are you two coming to see the cats or what?"

Brody wiped his mouth with a napkin, then grinned at Maya. "I guess that means we need to finish eating and get to work, huh?"

After cleaning up, Brody and Maya followed Ashlyn out the back door into the large grassy area outlined with a chain-link fence. Brody wondered how everything looked through Maya's eyes. The two red barns had screened-in porches with chairs, cat trees, litter boxes, and woodchip floors. Several cats milled around the barn on the right.

As they stepped through the gate and into the second fenced-in area, Ashlyn took hold of Maya's hand. "Those are the cat houses over there. The one on the right is where the cats called feral cats live, and then the one on the left is where the cats that can be adopted live. The feral cats are allowed to come in and out of the houses through the cat doors, but we keep the tame cats inside since we want them to go to homes where they'll be kept inside." Ashlyn tugged Maya toward the barn. "Come on. Let's go."

"Ashlyn, slow down," Brody called after them.

When they reached the house on the left, Ashlyn placed her hand on the door's knob. "Now, don't let any of the cats out. These are the tame cats ready to go to homes."

Ashlyn pulled open the door, and a choir of colorful cats

approached Maya, meowing and purring. She sat down on the floor and began rubbing their heads and chins. "Oh my goodness! I want to take them all home."

Brody chuckled. "You might change your mind when you have to feed them all."

"I'll help you feed them and clean the boxes." Ashlyn held a small tortoiseshell cat who was happily batting her beaded necklaces.

"I appreciate the offer, but I think I should probably stick with Tinker Bell for now."

"Maybe later you can get a boy, too, and name him Flynn Rider. Dad says lots of cats like to have companions."

"Flynn Rider after Rapunzel's boyfriend, huh? I love it." Maya chuckled as a black cat rubbed its head against her arm. "This place is really amazing. I love how it's set up."

Brody watched as she scanned the carefully planned and supplied interior—the line of cabinets, the sink, a couple of paper towel dispensers, large bags of cat food, several cat trees and small litter boxes, and a flat-screen television mounted to the wall. A large plastic kiddie pool filled with sand sat in the middle of the floor, serving as a giant litter box.

"Oh, Brody. I love this photo of your mom." She pointed to the framed photo of his mother holding a calico cat. It hung by the door below the words *Bea's Rescue—in loving memory of Beatrice Lynn Tanner*. "It must take a lot of time and money to keep this place running."

"I'm grateful for our manager, our volunteers, and all the donations we receive." Brody opened a cabinet and pulled out a large bag of dry cat food. As soon as he began filling bowls, at least a dozen cats ran over. "Local stores donate bagged food with holes in them, and volunteers come to visit and feed the cats throughout the week. One of the volunteers coordinates trying to find homes for the ones we're able to adopt out. I provide this facility and medical care, and Ash and I take this time slot most Saturdays."

He looked up at the mini-split unit in the wall. "Both houses are heated and cooled. The cats live very happy lives here."

Maya stood. "Wow. Again, this is amazing." She pointed to a staircase on the opposite wall. "What's up there?"

"We have a couple of rooms for the cats that need to be separated from the rest. We put the pregnant cats up there or the new ones that still need to be quarantined while we make sure they're healthy. We also have some foster moms to help with the mama cats and babies."

"Put me to work." Maya raised her hand.

Ashlyn took it. "Come on. We'll feed the cats upstairs and scoop out their boxes."

After they finished caring for the tame cats, they moved on to the feral cat house, nearly identical to the first house. While most of the two dozen cats peered at Maya from a safe distance, a few were brave enough to smell her shoes. But they ran when she reached down to touch them.

"Dad says not to take it personally," Ashlyn said. "They don't like me either."

Brody found fresh dry and canned food while Maya set to work changing water bowls and Ashlyn dealt with the litter box. When they reached the second floor, the same jobs awaited them.

"I have an idea for your Fourth of July float," Brody said,

speaking over the ensemble of cats singing for their supper as he filled their bowls.

Maya set down a water bowl and faced him. "What is it?"

"What if you stage a tea party on it? You could even hang a banner inviting folks to schedule a tea party at your store." He turned to face her, leaning his hip against a counter with cabinets below.

"That's a great idea!" Ashlyn called from one corner of the room. "Then me, Tessie, Bailey, and Sammie can ride on the float."

Maya nodded slowly. "I love it. That's brilliant."

Brody made a production of blowing on his fingernails and then rubbing them on his chest, making Maya laugh. "Well then," he said, "we'd better get busy building your float."

"You want to help me with that too?"

"Why not?" He shrugged. "If my daughter will be one of your stars, the least I can do is help."

"Okay then. Let's make a plan." And when she blessed him with a sweet smile, his breathing paused.

That evening Maya sifted through a pile of books while Tinker Bell sat on a box by the office window and peered at traffic on the street below. Maya dropped several volumes into a box marked *Donations*. Then she arranged a handful of her favorite romance novels on the bottom shelf of the press-board bookcase she'd located in the garage and managed to maneuver up the stairs.

As she stared at one of the romance novels, her thoughts turned to Kyle. Her heart twisted as she recalled their plans—organizing a wedding, buying a house, having a family . . . She'd been so close to reaching her dreams, and now she was back at square one.

Suddenly determined, she slipped into the desk chair, then powered up her computer, opened her email program, and started a new message.

Dear Kyle,

How's London? Is the job everything you hoped for? Was it worth leaving me? Why didn't you take me with you? You know I can work anywhere. Why did you have to break our engagement? Did you ever really love me at all? You owe me an explanation for throwing our relationship away as though it meant nothing to you.

Email me back.

Maya

She groaned and covered her face with her hands. She sounded so pathetic!

When her phone rang, she was relieved to find Kiana's number on the screen. "Hi, Key."

"Hi! How are you?" The words were laced with excitement. She sounded as if she was bursting at the seams, dying to tell a secret.

"You're awfully chipper. What's new with you?"

"Well . . ." Kiana drew out the word. "I met someone."

Maya sat up straight. "Tell me everything."

"His name is Deacon. He teaches math at a middle school in Union County, and he's so handsome. He has sandy-blond hair and the most gorgeous brown eyes."

"How'd you meet?" Maya moved her chair to the window and rubbed Tinker Bell's ear. The kitten responded by rolling onto her side and purring.

"It's funny, really. You remember Jeannette, right? She's a nurse for one of the other pediatricians at the practice."

"She's the one with the pixie cut, right?"

"Exactly. She works for Dr. Washburn. Anyway, last night she had a surprise thirtieth birthday party for her boyfriend, and she invited everyone in the practice. Well, Deacon is her boyfriend's brother."

"Oh wow." Maya turned toward her kitten, who stood, stretched, yawned, and then jumped down onto the floor, where she found her toy mouse and attacked it.

"I went into the kitchen to get a drink and found a cooler full of sodas. When I reached in for one, the lid closed on my hand, and I yelped out in pain."

"Ouch!"

"Exactly. Deacon had just walked in, too, and he came to my rescue. He made me a little ice pack out of a zip-lock bag, and then we talked until the ice melted." She gave a dreamy sigh. "He's thirty-two. And we have so much in common. We like the same music, and we both love kids. We just clicked, you know? I really like this guy, My."

"I'm so happy for you." Maya leaned back in the creaky desk chair. "He sounds like a breath of fresh air."

"Oh, he is! Total opposite of the last guy I dated. Ugh. What a creep." Maya could hear the disgust in her tone. "Trace would have asked me to hurry up and get *him* a drink while I was at it."

Maya groaned. "You got that right. So did Deacon ask for your number?"

"Yes." Her voice took on a dreamy tone again. "He called me this morning, and we met for coffee. We sat in that coffee shop and talked for hours. He wants to get together again tomorrow for lunch. I know it's early, but I think he could be the one."

Maya smiled as Tinker Bell tossed the toy mouse into the air and then raced after it, bumping into a few boxes on her way across the room. "That's so wonderful."

"Now I want to hear your news. Have you seen that handsome veterinarian again?"

"As a matter of fact, I spent some time with him and his daughter today."

"Well, spill it! I want to know everything."

"So let me get this straight," Kiana began when Maya was finished. "Brody and Ashlyn are helping you get the party room ready *and* build your Fourth of July float?"

"That's what he said."

"He's totally into you."

"I don't know . . ."

"Why don't you think so?"

"It's just a vibe I get from him. I think he's only looking for friendship." Maya held up her hand as if Kiana could see it. "But that's okay. A friendship is way less risky than taking the chance I'll get my heart broken again."

"Listen to me. Don't let Kyle's stupidity ruin any chance of a relationship with a great guy. Brody sounds like he's a lot more mature and stable than Kyle could ever be. And by the way, I love the idea for the parties. They'll be a hit. You heard it here first."

Maya laughed. "Thank you. I hope you're right. I have something else to tell you." She took a deep breath and then told Kiana what she'd learned about her father.

"Wow," Kiana said when she was finished with that news. "So have you searched for him on the internet yet?"

"No. I'm not sure I want to." She explained her hesitancy. "But I have so many questions I'd like to ask him."

"That's a tough one. Do whatever you feel is the best for you."

"I will."

"Tell me more about this party room. What color are you going to paint the walls?"

"I was thinking about pink or purple. Those colors go well with a princess theme." Maya relaxed as she and Kiana discussed her new business idea. It felt so good to talk to her best friend.

When they ended the call, Maya returned to the desk and with a sigh stared at the email she'd written to Kyle. Kiana's words about him echoed through her mind, but in her heart, Maya struggled to let him go. It would be easier to forget him if she had some kind of closure, if she knew *why* he'd completely cut her off. Had he lied when he said there was no one else? She didn't think so, but she was tempted to grill his friend Austin. The guy would probably just cover for him, though.

She hovered her mouse over the Send button, bit her lower lip, and then hit it. The message disappeared, and she sucked in a breath. Maybe Kyle would tell her he'd made a mistake. Or he might delete her message and ignore her. She'd just have to wait and see.

Maya picked up Tinker Bell and carried her toward the bedroom. "It's bedtime, cutie."

As she readied for bed, though, she wondered if she would be able to sleep. What if she'd just given Kyle the opportunity to hurt her even more? He might tell her his mistake was thinking he could marry a woman he never truly loved. A woman who wasn't lovable after all.

Chapter 8

The following afternoon Maya opened a carton with a dozen eggs and inspected each one as she stood in the dairy aisle of the local grocery store. Finding them all intact, she set the carton in the child's seat of her grocery cart. Then she turned toward the milk case just as another cart wheeled beside her.

"I guess you need milk, too, Miss Maya!"

Maya spun toward Ashlyn and Brody, then placed her hands on her hips and gave the little girl a feigned frown. "Are you following me? Do I need to call the sheriff?"

Ashlyn giggled. "No."

Maya's heart lifted when she noticed the little girl was wearing the beaded necklaces and rubber bracelets she gave her.

"How's the writing going?" Brody asked. Today he wore a pair of khaki shorts and a gray T-shirt with the NC State logo on it—and he still looked really good.

"It's not." She sighed. "I was just staring at my laptop screen, so I decided to go grocery shopping. This is how I procrastinate. Last night I worked on organizing my office and talked to my best friend on the phone. When I'm stuck, I do anything but write."

He leaned forward on the cart and shook his head. "I'm sorry."

"Hey, Dad." Ashlyn touched his arm. "Are we going to invite her over for a cookout like we talked about in the truck? You said you wanted to next time you saw her, and here she is."

Brody laughed, and Maya was almost certain he was blushing as he eyed his daughter. "Yes, I was getting to that, Ash." He looked sheepish as he smiled at Maya. "Would you like to join us for a cookout this evening?"

Maya hesitated, not wanting to wear out her welcome with her new friends. "Are you sure?"

"Of course I am. Why don't you take your groceries home and then come over?" Brody pointed to the packages of ground beef, buns, and potato chips in his cart. "We have plenty of food. But we'll understand if you need to write instead."

"Actually, spending the evening at the beach might help me find some inspiration. The ocean always seemed like a good muse."

"That's wonderful. You remember my house, right?"

She nodded. "I do. And I'll bring dessert."

Maya nosed her SUV into the driveway at Sandy Feet Retreat. She could have walked, but she didn't want the ice cream she bought to melt.

She blew out a puff of air as she took in the huge home, thinking about how her apartment could fit inside the first level alone and still leave room. Then she parked and gathered her purse, keys, a tote bag with her bathing suit and flip-flops just in case, and a bag with the ice cream and several toppings.

As she climbed out and started up the driveway, one of the doors on the three-bay garage hummed as it opened, revealing Ashlyn. She was grinning as she rushed out. "Hi, Miss Maya!"

"Hi," Maya called.

"What did you bring?"

"Ice cream and all the fixings to make sundaes. I hope you like vanilla fudge swirl."

"Yum! It's my favorite. Come inside, and I'll show you my house."

Maya followed Ashlyn inside the garage to a doorway that revealed stairs that led up to the main level. She swallowed a gasp as they walked into a large family room that stretched the complete width of the house. "Your home is simply gorgeous, Ashlyn."

"Thank you."

When she felt something wet brush her thigh, Maya looked down at Rusty peering up at her. "Hi, Rusty."

"You've met our dog?" Ashlyn asked.

Maya leaned down and rubbed the dog's ear. "Yes. The night I saw your dad on the beach."

"You need to meet our cats too."

"Does Rusty get along with the cats?"

"He loves them, but they don't always love him. Dad says he tends to annoy them. Ariel and Jasmine are almost always in here." Ashlyn looked around. "There they are."

Maya followed her to where a tuxedo cat and a tabby snored together on a huge sectional. Ashlyn pointed to the tuxedo cat. "This is Ariel." Then she pointed to the tabby. "And this is Jasmine."

"So nice to make your acquaintances." Maya rubbed their

heads, and they each opened one eye before returning to their slumber.

Ashlyn gestured toward a larger tuxedo cat sitting under an end table. "Prince Eric is over there. And I think Aladdin is sleeping on my dad's bed. The other two are probably upstairs."

"Your cats have fabulous names. Do the other two have Disney names?"

"Mm-hmm. One's a boy, and one's a girl."

"Let me guess, then." Maya bit her lip and then snapped her fingers. "I know! Simba and Nala."

Ashlyn's brow pinched. "Did my dad tell you?"

"No. Honest." Maya chuckled. "Just a lucky guess."

"Maya, hi!" Brody walked in from the large open kitchen behind him. He gave her a smile that sent warmth sizzling through her veins.

She held up her bag. "I brought ice cream and toppings so we can make sundaes for dessert."

"Thank you." He took the bag and then gestured toward the deck, where a table with six chairs sat under a yellow umbrella beside a propane-powered grill. "The grill is ready. I can put the burgers on now."

"Ashlyn and I will set the table."

"That would be great."

Maya set her purse and tote on a chair in the family room and then followed Ashlyn into the enormous kitchen. "Show me where the plates and utensils are."

While Brody grilled and Maya and Ashlyn set out everything from place settings to fruit salad, condiments, buns, and chips,

Maya breathed in the savory fragrance of the cooking burgers mixed with the fresh ocean air.

After filling their glasses with iced tea, Maya looked at Brody and took in his attractive profile. That strong jaw and those high cheekbones. And those striking blue eyes and full lips. She wondered what it would be like to feel those lips brushing against hers, and her heartbeat stuttered.

Stop it! He's only a friend!

"Let's eat," Brody announced as he carried a platter to the table.

Ashlyn cheered. "My dad makes the best burgers!" She patted the chair beside her. "Sit by me, Miss Maya."

Maya shared a smile with Brody and felt a flush of heat as her eyes moved to his lips again. She sank down on the chair beside Ashlyn, and Brody took a seat across from them.

"Everything looks delicious. Thank you for inviting me."

Brody handed her the platter. "You're welcome."

Maya chose a burger and set it on a bun before adding a little of everything: cheese, lettuce, mayonnaise, honey mustard, a slice of tomato, and pickles. She looked out over the sand dunes and took in the beachgoers sunbathing and bobbing in the waves. Seagulls swooped overhead, calling to each other. She spotted a boat with a rainbow-colored sail moving over the water in the distance.

"I could get used to this view," Maya said before scooping fruit salad onto her plate and then scooting the serving dish toward Ashlyn.

Brody picked up his burger. "It never gets old."

"I love our house." Ashlyn smothered her burger in ketchup. Then she put on the top half of her bun and took a bite.

Maya bit into her own burger while watching a wave crash on the beach. She peeked at Brody. "Did you say your father built this house?"

Brody nodded as he wiped a mustard smear from his clean-shaven chin. "He did. My grandparents owned a little cottage they'd purchased on this double lot in the fifties. Dad knocked it down and built this house for my mother in the early eighties. I did some renovations a few years ago, and then a few more just last summer."

He pointed toward the upper floor. "I replaced the hardwood floors throughout the house. I also had the entire house repainted, inside and out."

"I love the green exterior!"

"So do I." He gestured toward the family room. "I bought some new furniture, too, and I updated the bathrooms and the kitchen."

She glanced back at the kitchen, silently admiring the honey-oak cabinets, light tan granite, blue backsplash tastefully decorated with shells, and stainless steel appliances. "The whole place is just gorgeous."

"Thank you." Brody popped a chip into his mouth. "Do you miss Charlotte?"

Maya shrugged. "Yes and no. I miss my best friend, but we keep in touch." She took another bite of her burger, enjoying its juicy goodness.

"What's your best friend's name?" Ashlyn asked before tossing a piece of her burger to Rusty. The dog easily caught it.

"Kiana. We went to high school and college together."

Ashlyn picked up a potato chip. "My best friend is Tessie. Well, her name is Tessa, but we call her Tessie."

"That's a nice name." Maya smiled at her.

"Where did you go to college?" Brody asked.

"UNC Charlotte. Kiana is a pediatric nurse. My degree is in English with a concentration in creative writing."

Brody swallowed. "Did you have a house in Charlotte?"

"No." Maya shook her head. "Not even when I lived with my mom. She always rented. Although we stayed in Charlotte—and thankfully in the same school district—she'd move us to a new neighborhood every couple of years. I once asked why she wouldn't buy a house or maybe a condo, and she said she was more comfortable renting and liked to decorate new places. I, on the other hand, always dreamt of owning a home. Anyway, I moved into her rented apartment when she got sick, and I stayed there after she passed away."

"That had to be difficult." He paused. "You mentioned she was in kidney failure and on dialysis. Was a transplant an option for her?"

"We thought so. I was about to be tested to see if I was a good match when she became so ill with the pneumonia that took her."

Brody shook his head. "I'm so sorry to hear that."

"Thank you." Maya swallowed her grief. "I'd quit my job as an office manager to care for her, and when I got my first book contract, I decided to write full-time. Mom left me a little money too. That's why it was so easy for me to pick up and move here. And I can write anywhere." She pointed to his T-shirt. "Tell me about NC State."

He picked up another chip, then shared a couple of stories about his time in undergrad. Ashlyn entertained herself with Rusty, no doubt familiar with most of her father's stories. She didn't seem to be upset after hearing about Maya's mother. She suspected Brody would have changed the subject if he thought it would upset Ashlyn. Of course, as a vet's daughter and an animal lover, she would know all about death. Not every pet could be saved.

When they'd finished eating, they stowed the leftover food before building ice cream sundaes, topping them with the caramel, fudge, and whipped cream Maya brought. Then while Maya and Ashlyn filled the dishwasher, Brody cleaned the grill.

"Did you bring your swimsuit?" Brody asked when he stepped into the kitchen.

Maya nodded. "I did. Just in case."

"Then would you like to enjoy the beach for a bit?"

"Oh yes, please!" Ashlyn clapped her hands.

"Sure," Maya said.

Ashlyn steered Maya to the half-bath in the hallway, where she changed into her low-back, sapphire-blue one-piece swimsuit and matching flip-flops. Then she fetched her favorite blue-and-white-striped beach towel and met Brody and Ashlyn on the deck. He was spraying sunblock on his daughter, who'd changed into a two-piece—pink, of course!

Maya tried her best to keep from staring at Brody, but he looked so attractive in his plain, dark blue swim trunks, and her eyes kept defying her resolve as they assessed his muscular chest, shoulders, and arms.

Brody held up the can. "Would you like some?"

"Yes, please, I forgot mine." Maya took the can and sprayed her arms, legs, neck, and feet.

When she handed the can back to Brody, he looked a little

uncomfortable. Then he said, "Uh, would you like me to spray your back?"

She nodded and tried to ignore the heat that rushed through every cell of her body as she turned her back and he lifted her long, thick braid. Brody touching her hair as he sprayed the cool mist was almost too much for her heart.

"Thank you," she mumbled when he was done.

"Let's go swim!" Ashlyn hollered before grabbing Rusty's leash and high-tailing it to the deck stairs.

Minutes later, Maya stood at the edge of the water, enjoying the feel of the sand beneath her feet as she tented one hand over her eyes and watched Ashlyn and Rusty frolicking in the waves.

She turned to Brody beside her. "I have a serious question for you."

"Okay . . ." He reached down and lifted a flat rock from the sand.

"It's obvious Ashlyn named your cats. Who named Rusty?"

Brody chuckled as he skimmed the rock, which bounced over the water three times before it sank into the sea below. "I did."

"I thought so." She grinned.

"He was a rescue. He was found in a home where an older man had just passed away, leaving Rusty's mother and a whole litter." Brody nodded toward the beach behind them. "Want to sit?"

"Yes."

They sank onto their towels, and Maya hugged her knees to her chest. When she turned toward Brody, she found him watching his daughter, a smile turning up his lips.

"Ashlyn is great, Brody. I really enjoy hanging out with her."

He glanced at her. "She enjoys spending time with you too. She's really bonded with you. I appreciate how patient you are with her and the gifts you've given her. Thank you for thinking of her."

"You're welcome, but you don't need to thank me. She's my little buddy."

They shared a smile, and Maya felt like an invisible magnet was pulling her to the man at her side. Was she imagining it? Or did she feel that way because he was attracted to her too?

Brody snapped his fingers. "That reminds me. I need to give you the phone numbers for Ash's friends' moms so you can talk to them about the tea party float."

"Oh, that'd be great. Thank you."

They both peered at the ocean again, and Maya relaxed while enjoying the rhythmic crashing of the waves.

Brody dug into the sand with his toes. "You must have a lot of happy memories of coming here as a kid."

"Absolutely. Aunt CeCe and I were just about always here whenever the store was closed."

"I was always with friends, and it seemed like all the kids hung out together. Of course, most everyone I knew eventually moved away." The skin between his eyes pinched. "I wonder why I never ran into you. I'm certain I would have remembered you."

"How old are you?"

"Thirty-five."

"Then you're six years older than I am, and I imagine we had different friends." Maya couldn't stop a grin.

He chuckled and shook his head, and that dimple of his came out to play. "That makes a lot of sense. So you're twenty-nine."

"Yes, I am." She picked up an orange-and-white shell and ran her thumb over its ridges, wondering why Brody was still single. Not only was he handsome and a loving father, but he was outgoing and funny. What woman wouldn't want to scoop him up?

"You said the ocean inspires you to write. How?"

She hesitated. "Well, it started when I was Ashlyn's age and pretended I was a mermaid princess."

"Really?" A grin lit up his face.

She laughed. "Yes. The ocean really did stimulate my imagination. At the store and with my aunt, I made up a lot of stories about Barbies. But here, I made up stories about me—how I was that mermaid princess or sometimes an explorer. More recently, as an adult here to visit CeCe every summer for a month, I took long walks on the beach, and it helped clear my head so I could keep writing. Something about this place helps me find my creativity."

He nodded slowly. "Have you talked to Callie since you saw her at the pizzeria?"

"No. Why?"

"I was just wondering if you'd given more thought to a book signing."

"I really don't have the time. I need to get this party business going, and I'm still struggling with even outlining my book."

"Oh." He shrugged, and something unreadable flickered across his face.

"You look like you have an opinion on this."

He rubbed his jaw.

"Please just say it."

"Well, a book signing might provide inspiration."

"How do you figure that?"

"I'm not an author, but I imagine seeing people excited to purchase and read your books is kind of thrilling. A book signing might remind you of one of the reasons you create stories."

"Huh."

His dark eyebrows lifted. "What?"

"You're pretty smart for a doctor."

Laughter escaped his lips, and her spirits lifted.

"So tell me about this book you're trying to write."

"You mean the bane of my existence." She tossed the shell onto the sand, then stretched out her legs and leaned back on her hands.

"Yes, that one. What is it supposed to be about?"

She looked up at the clear blue sky as a flock of seagulls flew by. "Originally, it was supposed to be about a young woman who planned to return to her small hometown only for her ten-year high school reunion. But then she's laid off from her big-time corporate job, and much to her dismay she has no choice but to stay there. Her best friend is married and still lives there.

"Then she realizes she's falling in love with her best friend's brother. But he's known her since she was in kindergarten, so of course he sees her only as his kid sister's friend. She tries to make him understand that she's grown up now, but by the time he discovers he loves her, she's moved on with someone else. So then he has to fight for her."

Maya turned toward Brody and found him watching her with an intensity that made her skin itch. She sat up and brushed the sand off her hands. "It sounds stupid when I say it out loud."

"Why? I could see that as one of those movies on the Hallmark Channel. My mother loved them."

"Maybe, but my agent and editor thought it needed some different twists and turns. I agreed and started amending my outline. But it's difficult to get even that far with a story about love when you've lost your faith in it."

He drew a circle in the sand with his finger. "What happened with your ex?"

She shrugged as if each thought of Kyle didn't send a wave of longing through her, especially since he hadn't responded to her pathetic email. "Kyle got this golden opportunity—he said it was his dream job—in the UK. He told me he didn't want me to go with him, that I didn't need to wait for him, and then he actually broke our engagement. It was as if the plans we made for our future didn't mean anything to him. He just erased them, then ran off to start a new life without me."

Brody looked sympathetic. "Maybe you wouldn't have been happy if you'd married him, not that it makes the breakup any easier. Breakups are always painful."

"Maybe it wasn't meant to be." She sighed. "Our wedding was set for this August. I had to cancel the church, the reception venue, the caterer, the flowers . . . At least the invitations hadn't gone out yet."

Brody wiped the sand off his legs. "I'm sorry."

Ashlyn ran toward them, Rusty trotting behind her and happily barking. "Can we all go home now and play a game?"

Brody looked at Maya. "Would you like to stay?"

"I'd love to."

After changing out of their bathing suits, the three of them sat on the deck and played Uno under its lights as the sun set. Maya took in the breathtaking view and wondered what it would be like to watch nature's show here every night.

When Ashlyn started yawning, Brody announced it was her bedtime.

"But—"

A look from Brody stopped her cold. "Thank you for spending time with us, Miss Maya," Ashlyn said before hugging her.

Maya rubbed her back. "I had fun." She gave Ashlyn a wave before Brody towed her indoors.

"I'll be right back," he said over his shoulder.

"Take your time." Maya entered the kitchen and unloaded the dishwasher. Then she stacked the clean dishes, platters, glasses, and utensils on the counter before putting them away. She just had to search to find the right place for the platters.

The two tuxedo cats came to sit in the doorway, scrutinizing her with their sparkling green eyes.

"Hi there," she said with a chuckle. "It's nice to see you again."

Both cats yawned and stretched before sauntering back into the family room.

Maya had just finished stowing the utensils when Brody joined her. "Did she bed down without complaint? I remember resisting bedtime when I was her age—especially when Aunt CeCe had friends over. I loved to hear adults tell their stories."

He leaned back on the counter. "She was asleep before I could finish her story. She still likes me to read to her."

"The sun and playing in the water wore her out."

"Exactly. Thank you for unloading the dishwasher. I didn't expect you to do that."

"You cooked. It's only proper that I put the kitchen back in order." She smiled and once again felt an almost magnetic connection to him. She took a step back. "Well, I should go try to get that outline in better shape."

"Thanks for coming over. Ashlyn and I like to entertain our friends. Let's do this again soon."

"I'd love that."

He pulled his phone from his pocket, then cleared his throat before cupping his hand to the back of his neck and giving her a shy smile. "Would it be all right if you gave me your number?"

"Of course it would." He was so adorable!

"Great." His cheeks flushed as his dimple made its grand appearance. "We'll exchange numbers, and then I'll send you the numbers for Ashlyn's friends."

Maya unlocked her phone and handed it to him. He programmed in his number and then sent himself a text message before handing her phone back to her.

"I'll send the numbers now." He pulled his phone from his pocket and sent them one by one, causing her phone to chime several times in response. "I'll let them know you'll be contacting them about the float."

"Thank you." She slipped her phone into her pocket and then gathered her purse and tote bag from the counter.

Brody gestured toward the front of the house. "I'll walk you out."

They walked downstairs and stood in the driveway. Above them, the stars twinkled from the dark blue sky. Maya relished the sound of waves coming from behind Brody's beautiful home.

She looked up at him and appreciated how those pearl-blue eyes sparkled in the moonlight. "I had a really nice time this evening."

"We're so glad you could come."

She unlocked her SUV. "See you soon."

"I look forward to it."

She climbed in, started her Toyota, and then rolled down the window and waved to Brody before backing out of the driveway. Then, glancing in her rearview mirror as she turned for home, she found him watching.

An image of Brody's eyes so filled with love for his daughter appeared in her mind. Suddenly, to the depth of her bones, she knew she was ready to find her father. She just hoped if and when she found him, he would care for her a fraction of the way Brody cared for Ashlyn.

Chapter 9

Maya's hands trembled as she sat in front of her computer and typed *Quincy Hamill* into the search bar. Tinker Bell purred at her feet. "Okay, Tink. Here we go." She sucked in a breath and hit the Search button.

Dozens of results appeared, but none of them matched the name her aunt gave her as she scrolled through them. Quincy Jones, Quincy Cleaners, Quincy's Restaurant, and other businesses featuring the name Quincy were no help.

Maya groaned and opened her Facebook page. After typing *Quincy Hamill* in the search bar there, she hit the button and was presented with a list of people with the first and last name Quincy but no Hamills. Then she tried Instagram, Twitter, and other social media platforms with the same results—no one named Quincy Hamill.

She heaved a frustrated sigh and retrieved her aunt's letter from the top drawer of the desk, where she'd put it to keep it safe. Then she reread the few sentences that had haunted her.

Your father's name was Quincy Hamill. I remember it because it was so unusual. I believe he also went by a nickname or maybe a middle name, but I can't remember what it was.

Maya leaned back in her chair and sighed. "Well, Tink, I don't think we're going to find him tonight. If only Aunt CeCe had remembered his other name . . ."

The cat opened one eye, yawned, and then closed it.

"Thanks for the encouragement," Maya muttered. "We'll try some other spellings for Hamill the next time. That might be the problem."

After turning off her computer, Maya scooped up the kitten and padded toward her bedroom. Her mind twirled with fantasies of finding her father, meeting him in person for the first time, and learning about any other long-lost relatives. But that all seemed like an impossible dream when she couldn't readily locate him in the cyber world.

Maya deposited the kitten and her beloved pink toy mouse on the bed. "But we're not going to give up on this yet, Tink. We'll keep searching, right?"

The cat blinked up at her, then jumped off the bed and wiggled her way under it.

Maya grabbed some pajamas and slipped into the bathroom, determined. She had to find her father. If she didn't, how would she ever rest?

The following Friday afternoon Maya finished sweeping the floor of her new tea-party room, then glanced around and breathed a sigh of relief. She'd managed to finally finish cleaning it out, and in the remaining storeroom, she'd also readied another half dozen boxes of her aunt's belongings for the attic. While her arms, neck, and back all ached, she felt as if she'd made enough progress to make her new business venture a reality.

Tinker Bell scampered in with Gayle in tow.

"I'm telling you that silly cat is going to be the death of me," Gayle grumbled. "Every time I turn around, she's there, watching me. I've almost tripped over her at least five times."

Maya smiled. "She likes you."

"A likely story, Stinker Bell." Gayle huffed at the cat, hands on hips. "I think she wants to get rid of me."

Maya shook her head. She had a feeling Gayle loved the kitten as much as she did.

"So you've been working hard on this room, huh?"

"I have." Maya swiped her forearm over her sweaty brow. "Thank you for covering for me in the store."

Gayle walked in and looked around. "I don't mind. It hasn't been any busier than usual, but I think this clever idea will help."

"I hope so. Now I need to decorate. After painting the walls pink or purple, I'm thinking of putting a border with princesses about halfway down. Or maybe I could get some of those stick-on images of Disney princesses. I should hire Ashlyn as my consultant." Maya felt a tug at her heart. She hadn't seen Ashlyn and Brody since Tuesday, and to her surprise, she missed them.

"Ashlyn Tanner, huh?" Gayle grinned. "You and Brody would make a cute couple."

"Oh no, no, no. We're just friends, and I enjoy spending time with his daughter."

"With just Ashlyn? Right." Gayle snorted. "And I have a bridge to sell you."

Maya waved off the comment. "Anyway, I'll go to the hardware store tomorrow for paint. I also need to find a few little table-and-chair sets. It will be cheaper to get used ones. I'll check Facebook Marketplace."

"I'll start closing the register."

"Thank you, Gayle. You're a lifesaver."

"And don't you forget it."

⌒•⌒

After Maya closed the store on Saturday afternoon, she pulled out her phone. She wanted to ask for Ashlyn's help, but she hoped texting Brody wouldn't seem like she was chasing him.

Stop being ridiculous! He's your friend! And he was the one who asked to exchange numbers.

She typed, Hi! I'm headed to the hardware store to buy paint for the party room. Is Ashlyn available to help me choose a color?

Conversation bubbles appeared almost immediately, followed by Brody's response: Sure! We're still at the clinic. The hardware store is across the street. Pick her up here?

Perfect! Be there in a few minutes.

I'll have her outside.

Thirty minutes later, Maya and Ashlyn stood at the paint supply counter in Coral Cove's only hardware store.

"Okay," Maya said. "We have the color of paint we chose all mixed, plus our supplies. Tape, drop cloths, sponges, paintbrushes, rollers, and trays. Good thing I didn't assume my aunt had any of that in her garage. I think that's everything. Now we just have to pay for it all and load up my SUV."

Ashlyn pointed behind her. "My dad is here. We're over here, Dad!"

Maya spun to face Brody. Today he wore black shorts, a green T-shirt with a muscle car on it, and sandals. She hoped he couldn't tell how happy she was to see him. "Hi. I didn't expect you here. I thought you still had patients."

"I finished up and changed. I keep some clothes at the clinic." Brody walked over to Ashlyn and touched her shoulder. "Were you helpful, Ash?"

"Oh yes. I told Miss Maya she should paint the room blue like the sky, and then paint puffy white clouds on the walls. Then she can stick on a picture of Cinderella's castle, the one at Disney World. Show my dad what you found on your phone, Miss Maya."

Maya pulled her phone from her back pocket and pulled up the images she'd captured from Etsy. Brody stepped over, and she breathed in a mixture of sandalwood soap and something that seemed uniquely him. His nearness made her senses spin.

"I found these images," she began, handing him her phone. "And I learned I can use sponges to add the white clouds. Then I'll look for a castle, maybe some birds, and even a few Disney princesses for the walls too. If you scroll, you'll see some different options."

He nodded as he scanned the photos. "This is fantastic. We can do this."

"You want to help me again?" She blinked at him.

Brody studied her. "Did you think we wouldn't want to?"

"You need us, Miss Maya. You said I have the best ideas, right?" Ashlyn asked.

"You do."

Ashlyn pointed to her chest. "That means you need me."

"We'll go home and change into old clothes, then meet you at the store," Brody said. "Did your aunt have a ladder?"

"I didn't find one."

"Then I'll grab my ladder too."

"Sounds like a plan. And I'll buy supper."

"Deal."

~⸰~

Maya scanned the boxes Brody had just helped her carry up from the storeroom, then nodded toward an empty corner of the attic. The large room had cartons and old furniture piled everywhere.

"We can set them over there. Thank you so much for your help. I'm not sure why Aunt CeCe had some of these things in the storeroom, especially her special linens. I can't bring myself to get rid of them, but I don't need them downstairs."

"I understand. I still have boxes of things that belonged to my sister and parents." He studied her, but his expression was unreadable.

"Is something on your mind?"

"Do you think you'll stay in Coral Cove?"

"I plan to. After all, my life began here. It seems only fitting to come back, especially since I'm the last Reynolds. Like me, my mother was an only child, and my grandmother was Aunt CeCe's only sibling."

"I feel the same way about living here."

"You don't have other family members?"

"I have some cousins in Hickory, but we're not close. I haven't seen them since my mom's funeral." He leaned back against the slanted wall behind him.

"I'm sorry."

He shrugged. "It's okay. Ashlyn is all I need."

"What are your best memories of your parents?" She found a sturdy old end table and sat on it.

"I'd say probably the holidays when my dad wasn't on call. Most of the time he was on the go, saving people. When I was a little boy, I resented it. But as I grew up, I came to understand what a skilled physician he was." His eyes were trained on an attic window as if he could see his father there. "He was a blessing to his patients. I'm proud of him, and I'm grateful to be his son. I just wish I'd had more time with him."

"That's beautiful, Brody."

He smiled. "My mom was the most loving, caring, nurturing person on the planet. Every memory of her is wonderful." He tilted his head. "What about your mom?"

Maya sighed. "I keep finding boxes of mementos she left here when we moved to Charlotte. The other night I found a photo of her from when she was in college, and I was struck by how young and healthy she looked. When I think about her now, I have a difficult time not remembering her as too thin and sickly."

"It had to be challenging watching her suffer like that."

"It was terrible. She tried home dialysis, but it didn't work for her. She had to go to a center three times a week, and she was so ill all the time. After her treatments, she would just crash and sleep the day away. The next day she'd be better, but then she'd crash again by the time she had to go back to the center. She was exhausted and irritable. I can't blame her, but I still feel like I lost her twice—first when she was so sick and then again when she passed away."

She found Brody's face full of warmth and empathy, making her feel their connection was growing stronger. "I'm sorry for being a downer, talking about such sad memories."

"You're not. It's refreshing to talk to someone who understands what it's like to lose the people you love the most."

Encouraged by his openness, Maya asked another question. "What are your hopes and dreams for the future, Brody?"

"Mine?" Brody rubbed a spot on his shoulder. "They aren't so much for me but for Ashlyn. I'm focused on being the best father I can for her. I want to get her through high school and college so she can have the most wonderful life possible. I want her to be happy and know she's loved no matter what."

Maya smiled. "You already are the best father. Every child should be as blessed as Ashlyn is to have a dad as loving as you. I always wondered what it would be like to have a father. A piece of my life always seemed to be missing." She hesitated and then felt compelled to share what was in her heart. "I started looking for mine."

"You did?" He closed the distance between them, his blue eyes dancing in the sunlight pouring through the attic windows.

She frowned. "I've searched the internet and social media, but I can't find anyone named Quincy Hamill. I'm not giving up, though. I need to check some alternative spellings in case Aunt CeCe got his last name wrong."

She looked down at her sandals. "I always felt like the strange one when I was a kid. I was the only little girl in Scouts who didn't have a daddy to take her to the father-daughter dance, so I didn't get to go. Another time, in third grade, we had to write about our family. The teacher made it clear that every family is different, but one boy still made fun of me when he found out I not only didn't have a father but didn't even know his name. When I asked my mother his name, she said, 'It doesn't matter. He left us, and he doesn't deserve to be part of your family story.'"

Her voice hitched and then recovered. "But it did matter. It *always* mattered, and it hurt so much that it cut me to the bone. And now to find out she lied . . ." She took a deep breath, trying to keep her tears at bay.

Brody walked over and touched her hand, causing a spark that danced up her arm. "If I can help you find him, I will. Just let me know how, okay?"

She nodded as she sniffed. "Thank you."

He paused. "What about your hopes and dreams?"

"Well, I wanted a husband and children, but I've given up on love—at least for now. I'll probably just follow in my great-aunt's footsteps and run the toy store. And hopefully, I'll still be an author too."

"Don't give up on love yet."

Something in his expression made her mouth dry, and she held her breath for a heartbeat as the air around them suddenly felt electrified. When Brody remained cemented in place, she wondered if she'd imagined it. "Thank you for carrying up those boxes."

"I didn't mind." He cleared his throat as they headed for the stairs. "Do you need me to bring up more?"

"Not from the storeroom. Maybe you can help me move some from the apartment later, but we should start painting now."

Down in the party room, Maya and Brody worked together to tape up the woodwork, then started painting on opposite walls. Maya concentrated on the lower part of her wall while Brody stood on the ladder and cut in the top of his.

"Have you ever been to Disney World, Miss Maya?" Ashlyn called from the remaining storeroom across the hall. Maya had set her to work sorting some additional decorations she'd found.

"I have," Maya called back. "How about you?"

Ashlyn came to the door. "My dad took me last Christmas."

"Oh, I bet it's beautiful at Christmastime." Maya dipped her roller in the paint tray.

"It's the best. When did you go?"

"I went with some friends in college on spring break. It was packed, but we had fun."

Brody looked down from the ladder. "What are your favorite rides?"

"That's a tough question. I suppose Pirates of the Caribbean and It's a Small World. How about you?"

"Space Mountain and Rock 'n' Roller Coaster."

"You like Big Thunder Mountain Railroad too," Ashlyn reminded him.

Brody grinned. "That's true."

"Oh! Oh!" Ashlyn threw her arms up into the air. "Don't forget the Jungle Cruise. You know our favorite line the skippers say: 'Presenting . . . the backside of water!'" She cackled, and Maya and Brody joined in.

"What are your favorite rides, Ashlyn?" Maya asked.

"Oh, so many." She began counting them off with her fingers. "Let's see. The Haunted Mansion, Slinky Dog Dash, Peter Pan, It's a Small World . . ."

Maya smiled. When she looked up at Brody, she found him watching her, and the sparkle in his blue eyes sent another wave of heat thrumming through her veins. If only she knew what that sparkle meant.

Walt Disney World remained the topic of conversation, and soon she and Brody had finished the first coat of paint.

"So," Maya began as she wiped her hands on a rag, "I'm getting hungry. What should I order for supper?"

"Pizza!" Ashlyn exclaimed.

"Uh, well . . ." Maya turned to Brody, who was rinsing their paintbrushes in the utility sink at the back of the room. She'd have to bring down that folding screen in the guest bedroom to hide the ugly thing during her parties.

He met her gaze, and understanding flashed over his handsome face before he looked at his daughter. "Ash, Maya may not want pizza again." Then he turned toward Maya. "What sounds good to you?"

"How about we order from Subs-N-More? They have salads, and I'm really in the mood for one with grilled chicken."

"Ooh! I love their sandwiches!" Ashlyn sounded more than pleased.

Brody nodded. "Perfect."

After they'd finished cleaning up, they retreated upstairs, where Ashlyn played with Tinker Bell in the family room and Maya placed their order for delivery on her laptop in the kitchen.

"Why don't you show me those heavy boxes and I'll take them up while we wait for the food," Brody said.

"Oh, thank you." Maya showed him the boxes of books in the office, then set the table while he worked.

Soon the back-door buzzer sounded, and she dashed down the stairs to grab the food. Then the three of them took a seat at her table.

"How's your salad, Miss Maya?" Ashlyn asked as she picked up half of her grilled chicken sandwich.

"Delicious, thank you." Maya forked some lettuce and shredded cheese. "How's your sandwich?"

Ashlyn gave a thumbs-up.

"Do you want to look for those wall decals while we eat?" Brody asked as he lifted a section of his ham and turkey sub.

"Great idea." Maya pulled her laptop from the edge of the table and soon found the decals she wanted to complete her princess theme. After ordering them, she found a notepad and started making another list of supplies. The one she'd started the night she got the idea for the tea parties had disappeared somewhere. "I need paper products, inexpensive tea sets, and table-and-chairs sets."

"Do you want to search for those now too?" Brody popped his last potato chip into his mouth.

Maya glanced at the clock on the microwave. "I was wondering if we could paint the second coat before you leave. I can look for the other things later."

"Sure." Brody gathered his trash and Ashlyn's. "Let me help you clean up first."

"Thank you, but I can do that later."

As Maya and Brody added another coat of blue paint to the walls, leaving Ashlyn in the apartment to keep Tinker Bell happy, they named all the musical concerts they'd attended. Maya silently marveled at how well she and Brody worked together. When she and Kyle tried working on a project at his house, they'd spent more time bickering than accomplishing their task. She and Brody were the total opposite as they chatted easily and worked seamlessly.

Ashlyn stepped into the party room. "Tinker Bell is sleeping. Is it okay if I leave her alone for now, Miss Maya?"

Maya craned her neck toward the little girl. "Sure. I've been thinking. You've been such a big help to me lately. How about you go into the store and pick out a toy?"

Ashlyn bit her lip and looked at her father. "Is that okay, Daddy?"

Brody climbed down the ladder, then set his jaw and took a step toward Maya. "I think you should set a price limit before you set a little girl free in your store."

Once they'd agreed on a limit, Maya told Ashlyn where the store's light switches were. Then she took off, and Maya turned to Brody. "Thank you."

"Why are you thanking me?"

"For letting me spend time with Ashlyn, for helping me, for being my friend."

She suddenly realized how corny her words sounded and felt the result of her embarrassment creep up her neck. But Brody didn't seem to mind. Instead, his expression brightened.

"I feel like I should be thanking you. You mean a lot to Ashlyn, and we both enjoy spending time with you. You're already a good friend."

There it was. A friend. Nothing else.

He gathered the paint rollers and brushes. "Let me know when the decals arrive, and I'll help you apply them and make the clouds. If you'd like help, that is."

"I never turn down a tall man with a tall ladder," she said, teasing him.

He laughed, and she enjoyed the warm, rich sound. And if friendship was all he wanted, she'd just have to be content with it. And get over her attraction to him.

They'd just finished cleaning up when Ashlyn reappeared with three Barbie accessory packs, each including an outfit with matching shoes and handbag.

"Those are perfect." Maya pulled Ashlyn over for a side hug. "I'd better let you two go home. It's getting late." She held the back door open while Brody carried the ladder outside and loaded it into his truck. Then she stood by the front passenger door as Ashlyn buckled her seat belt. "Thank you both again for all your hard work today."

Ashlyn held up the Barbie outfits. "Thank you for the presents. I love them."

"You're welcome. Talk to you soon." Maya stood by the back door and waved as Brody backed up the truck and then steered out of her parking lot.

When she returned upstairs, she cleaned the kitchen before sitting down at the table and opening her laptop. She accessed her email, half afraid and half hopeful she'd find a response to her message to Kyle. But she saw only a few ads from her favorite websites and a message from her agent. Her heart sank, but then she instantly felt guilty. She'd just had a wonderful time with Brody and Ashlyn. Why couldn't she stop letting Kyle spoil her life?

After responding to her agent, she searched for tea sets and children's table-and-chairs sets on Facebook Marketplace. She'd just finished messaging a few sellers when her phone rang with Kiana's name on the screen.

"Hey. What's new?" Maya asked as she answered.

"Oh my goodness. I was just on the most amazing date, My." Her friend was actually gushing.

"With Deacon?"

"Yes."

Maya recognized that dreamy tone again. "Give me the details." She'd continue searching Facebook Marketplace as she listened.

"Well, we've talked just about every day since we first met. He even brought me lunch at work yesterday. And then he said he wanted to take me on a proper date, so tonight we got dressed up and went to the Melting Pot for fondue."

"How romantic!" Maya truly was happy for her best friend. Although Kiana hadn't experienced a broken engagement, she had endured a couple of awful breakups and heartaches.

"I can't wait for you to meet him. We have so much fun. We never seem to run out of things to talk about, and I feel so comfortable with him." Kiana sighed. "So how are things at the beach?"

"Good. Busy." Maya updated Kiana on the progress with the party room. "I'm hoping to have it all up and running right after the Fourth of July."

"Brody and Ashlyn helped you do all that today? He's totally into you, My."

"You keep saying that, but we're just friends, and that's fine." At least she'd try to convince her heart that friendship was enough for her. She still craved a husband and family, but that didn't mean Brody would make that dream come true. She looked down at the floor just as Tinker Bell ran by with her toy mouse hanging out of her mouth.

"We need to find a time to get together," Kiana said. "I miss you."

"I miss you too. And I'm really happy for you. Deacon sounds amazing."

"Thank you. But we need to get Brody to ask you out. I don't believe either of you want to be just friends. Maybe you can drop some subtle hint. Say something like, 'Boy, it would be nice to have a date for the Fourth. Do you know any single guys?'"

When Kiana laughed, Maya joined her. "You're a mess."

"That's why you love me."

And it was.

Chapter 10

Brody rushed into the kitchen, where his cell phone sat ringing on the large island in the center of the room. When he spotted the answering service's number, his blood ran cold. Calls on weekends never boded well, and today he was the vet on duty.

"This is Dr. Tanner."

"Hello, Dr. Tanner. This is Laurie. I received a call from Jeremy Cavanaugh. His dog, Hershey, was just hit by a car. He said it looks bad, and he sounded pretty frantic."

Brody's eyes slammed shut as an image of the sweet chocolate Lab filled his mind. "Please tell him I'm on my way to the clinic."

He disconnected the call and peered into the family room. Ashlyn sat on the floor beside Rusty, hugging one of her dolls as she watched a favorite Disney movie. How many times had she seen *Brave*? He'd lost count.

He couldn't risk bringing her to the clinic. He wanted to shield his daughter whenever a tough case might not turn out for the best.

She usually stayed with Tessie, but that family was gone for the weekend, and he didn't feel comfortable calling the parents of any of her other friends on such short notice. He needed to find someone else he trusted.

Maya.

She answered his call immediately. "Brody. Hi. What are you up to this Sunday?" Her tone was chipper.

"Maya. I need your help." The words came out in a rush, but he kept his voice low so his daughter wouldn't hear. "I have an emergency at work, and I'd prefer not to take Ashlyn with me."

"Bring her over."

He blew out a relieved breath. "You're a lifesaver."

"You know I love spending time with her. I was just on my way to look at a few little tables and chairs. Is it all right if I take her with me? The sellers are local."

"Of course. We'll be right there." Brody ended the call and then stepped into the family room. "Ashlyn, I need to go to work. I'm taking you to see Maya, okay?"

"Yay!"

"Shut off the television while I get dressed."

After he'd changed into scrubs and called Kim to come in, sure he'd need her assistance, he steered Ashlyn out to his truck. Soon he was pulling into the gravel lot behind Maya's building. She hurried outside when he came to a stop. She must have been watching for them.

Brody rolled down his window, and Ashlyn hopped out of the passenger seat.

"Thank you so much, Maya," he said, then lowered his voice. "I think this will be a tough one. A dog was hit by a car, and it sounds bad."

"Oh no! Don't worry about us. We'll be fine."

"Hi, Miss Maya!" Ashlyn came around the front of the truck. "I heard we're going shopping."

"We are. And then we can get some dinner." She looked up at Brody. "Call or text me, and I'll bring her home for you."

"Thank you." He turned toward his daughter. "Have fun and remember your manners, Ash. See you later."

"Bye, Daddy!" Ashlyn waved as he backed out of the parking lot, and he steeled himself for whatever awaited him at the clinic.

~·~

Four hours later, Brody dragged himself into the shower at his house and allowed the warm water to pound his sore muscles. He felt as if he'd run twenty miles on the beach. Although the afternoon had been emotionally draining, he was grateful Cam was available to help him with the complicated surgery and sweet Hershey had pulled through in the end.

After drying and pulling on shorts and a T-shirt featuring the clinic's logo, Brody texted Maya. I'm home. Bring Ashlyn anytime. No rush. Thanks.

She quickly typed back. Okay. We're eating dinner at Pancake Palace right now. Want anything?

No, thanks.

See you soon.

He found a can of Coke in the refrigerator, then sat on the deck with Rusty at his feet, enjoying the cold carbonation on his throat along with the comforting sound of the ocean's waves. He'd eat something later.

After he finished the drink, he sauntered down to the garage, opened one of its three doors, and then leaned on the bumper of his pickup to await their arrival.

Minutes later, Maya's SUV coasted into the driveway and parked, and then Ashlyn launched herself from the passenger seat and scurried over to him.

"Daddy! You won't believe what happened when we went to buy the tables and chairs."

"What was that?" He smiled at her, but the smile felt forced.

"A lady thought Maya was my mom! She said we have the same hair and eyes and look alike. Isn't that funny?" Ashlyn hooted.

Brody nodded and hugged her. "It is." He glanced at Maya as she walked toward the garage with a tentative expression. That comparison must have been awkward for her.

"I'm going to see Rusty and the kitties." Ashlyn spun toward Maya. "Thank you for letting me come over and for dinner. See you soon!" She dashed toward the garage stairs leading up to the house.

Brody stood to his full height and met Maya at the top of the driveway. He spotted several tables and chairs in the back of her SUV. "Looks like shopping went well."

"It did." She motioned for him to follow her back to her 4Runner, then opened the tailgate. "I was able to get all four sets for a great price. And since they have adjustable legs, they'll work for girls of all ages."

"Cool." He raked his hand through his hair as he took in the white furniture with purple accents. They looked almost new. He pivoted toward her, and her smile flattened as concern seemed to flash over her face.

"You look like you had a really bad day."

"You could say that." He cleared his throat, then turned his eyes toward the bright azure sky to avoid her sympathetic expression. "When I was an intern, I got emotional all the time. After a while, I got used to having to deal with a sad situation and then pin a smile on my face before stepping into the next room to examine a happy puppy or kitten. I don't mean telling owners their cats have cancer or putting dogs to sleep doesn't hurt. I just found a way to plow through the rest of the day."

He dropped his gaze toward her SUV's bumper. "But sometimes I still get so drained and overwrought that I don't know what to do with the emotions."

"Brody, what happened to the dog hit by a car?" she whispered.

"He's a four-year-old chocolate Lab named Hershey." He couldn't seem to speak much above a whisper. "One of his owners opened the back door of their house, and Hershey pushed past her and ran right into the street."

He shifted his gaze to his sandals. "I knew the situation was dire as soon as I saw him. I called Cam in to help with the surgery."

His eyes locked with hers and stung with tears. *Don't lose it in front of her!* "I was so afraid Hershey wasn't going to make it, but thankfully, he pulled through. It was touch-and-go there for a while, though." Tears trickled down his face, and he quickly brushed them away as he cleared his throat again. "I'm sorry."

"It's okay." She rubbed his shoulder.

He took a deep breath, and suddenly she stood on her tiptoes and wrapped her arms around his neck. He stilled, and then he enveloped her with his arms, resting his chin on the top of her head. They stood like that for several moments as he tried to get hold of his emotions.

"You saved his life, Brody," she whispered. "I'm sure Hershey's family is extremely grateful for you and Cam."

Closing his eyes, he lost himself in the feel of being held—not by just any woman but by Maya. And he felt comfortable embracing her too—as if his arms belonged there.

He inwardly cringed, then sniffed and stepped back, wiping his eyes with the back of his hand. "I'm sorry," he said again. He forced both a smile and a laugh. "You must think I'm a big dope."

"No." She shook her head. "I think you're an amazing vet who cares deeply for his patients and their families, and that's commendable. Do you want me to stay awhile?"

"No, thanks. I think I just need to decompress." He folded his arms over his chest. "I should let you get home."

"Okay."

"Thank you for taking Ashlyn today."

"We had fun." She started toward the front of the car, but he stopped her with a touch on her arm.

"Maya."

She pivoted toward him.

"I know we haven't known each other very long, but I already don't know what I'd do without you."

She swallowed, and the look in her eyes nearly stole his breath. "You're welcome. Anytime."

He considered telling her he'd like to be more than friends, but he wasn't ready to risk his heart again. He'd never forgotten the pain his former fiancée had caused him. Besides, not only was he focused on Ashlyn now, but Maya was still recovering from an even more recent breakup.

He nodded. "Be safe going home. I'll talk to you soon."

She hesitated but then said, "Okay."

As she approached the driver's side door of her SUV, Maya looked . . . what? Disappointed? Did she want to be more than friends? He didn't think so. After all, she said she was giving up on love. *At least for now*, she'd said. But when he'd encouraged her not to give up on love yet, he hadn't meant he'd be involved.

For her sake, he wished she wouldn't. He just didn't think he was the man for her. And he couldn't be for a long, long time.

⁓⁓⁓

Maya climbed the stairs to her apartment after tucking the tables and chairs into a corner of the party room. She was so disappointed. She'd felt a connection with Brody when they'd held each other, and now as she touched her shoulder and found it still damp from his tears, her heart lurched. He'd relaxed as if he, too, felt their friendship morphing into something more meaningful. When he'd thanked her, she was certain she saw attraction in those blue eyes. But then he'd said goodbye as if that moment together meant nothing.

Well, not nothing. He felt *something* for her, but obviously it was just friendship.

Perhaps she was expecting too much of a compassionate veterinarian who had just nearly lost one of his precious patients. Maybe she was just being selfish to think emotion might make him realize she meant more to him than a friend.

Still, she couldn't stop from being drawn to the depth of Brody's compassion for his patients. That was what she admired most about him—how much he cared about them *and* his daughter. And that was why she'd hoped he might love her one day.

Love?

"Oh no." She groaned and cupped her hand to her forehead. She couldn't allow herself to fall in love with Brody. He'd made it clear he considered her only a friend—almost as clear as Kyle had been about not wanting a relationship with her at all.

When she opened the bathroom door, Tinker Bell bounded out, meowing her disapproval at being locked up for so long.

"I know, I know. I'm a terrible cat mom. You should definitely call the animal welfare society and report me." Maya sighed as she lifted Tinker Bell's food and water bowls.

The kitten continued her rant as Maya refilled the bowls in the kitchen.

"Here you go, girl." Maya set down the bowls, and the kitten happily dove in.

When she leaned against the counter, Maya's eyes moved to the calendar on the wall, and a pang of anxiety hit her. The Fourth of July was only two weeks away.

Yikes! She had to complete the float. But she couldn't advertise her new tea party service without finishing the room for it first. Both deadlines weighed heavily on her mind.

"Simmer down, Maya. You got this," she whispered.

Pulling her phone from the back pocket of her jean shorts, Maya searched for the names and numbers of Ashlyn's friends' moms and then sent a group text explaining she was Brody's friend and why she wanted to ask their daughters to be on her float representing CeCe's Toy Store. Then she headed to the garage.

While she considered what supplies she needed to pull off her tea party theme, she thought about how having a family to call her own was still her heart's greatest desire—no matter what she'd said to Brody or anyone else. She'd always longed for the family she'd never experienced, one with a father. She'd witnessed families like that only through friends, TV shows and movies she'd seen, and the books she'd both read and written.

And now she realized she longed to have that family not with Kyle but with Brody. To belong with him and Ashlyn. She loved them both so much, even though she'd known them for only a short time.

She sagged against the side of Aunt CeCe's purple truck. What a pipe dream. And not just because Brody wanted nothing more than friendship. If she wasn't good enough for Kyle, why would she be good enough for Brody?

Maybe finding Quincy Hamill was the best she could do.

Chapter 11

"W ell, it's done," Maya said to Gayle, "and it's only Thursday afternoon! I thought it would take me at least one more day." Maya gestured around the finished party room.

After realizing the urgency of finishing her projects, she'd decided to burn the midnight oil Tuesday night and placed the castle and bird decals on the far wall. Then yesterday she'd set her alarm for six and got to work affixing the Disney princesses, doing her best to position them symmetrically on the side walls. On one wall, she hung Cinderella, Jasmine, Rapunzel, Anna, and Elsa. On the opposite wall, she positioned Snow White, Tiana, Belle, Aurora, and Ariel. Then she sponged white clouds around the room before giving the tables and chairs a good cleaning.

Finishing had taken all day, and she was grateful Gayle had again run the store alone without complaint. Maya had also met with Sasha Burke, the owner and manager of Beach Bakery, and got her on board to provide the cakes for the parties. She just had to talk to Callie about providing books as party favors. She smiled as she considered how much she enjoyed involving these local businesses in her little venture. It felt as if she were forming a family bond with both the owners.

After lunch, she'd run out to a nearby flea market and purchased a buffet. Already painted white to match the tables and chairs, the buffet had glass doors, and it was the perfect place to store the paper products, tea sets, and serving dishes she'd ordered online on Monday. Gayle had helped her move the buffet from her SUV into the party room when the store had a lull in customers.

She'd considered asking Brody to help. After all, he had offered. But she decided it was best to keep her distance. Analyzing their encounter on Sunday over and over again, she'd come to the same conclusion—she had indeed fallen in love with him, but he didn't reciprocate those feelings. And since she hadn't heard from him since Sunday, she'd come to another heartbreaking conclusion as well. Not only did he not reciprocate her feelings, but he must have felt she'd overstepped their friendship boundary and needed some time away from her.

That realization crushed her soul!

She hated to admit it, but she missed him and Ashlyn so much she ached. All week she'd found herself wondering how they were doing and what they would say about her progress on the room. She longed for their input and approval, but she was wasting such high emotions on them. They would never be more than her friends.

"What do you think?" Maya asked Gayle as the older woman's blue eyes narrowed. She held her breath, hoping Gayle's unfiltered opinion wouldn't burst her already fragile bubble.

A smile broke out on Gayle's face. "It's positively perfect, Maya."

"Yay!" Maya clapped her hands and jumped up and down like a little girl. Then she wrapped her arms around Gayle's neck. "Thank you!"

Gayle gave her back an awkward pat and then backed away. "All right. That's enough." She crossed the room and peered through the buffet's glass doors. "Where did you get those precious tea sets?"

"Mostly online, but I did pick up one set today at the flea market where I found the buffet."

"Huh." Gayle frowned. "I'm surprised you bought glass tea sets. Why didn't you just get plastic ones? You know kids break things, right? I'm still a little annoyed that my grandsons decided it was a good idea to play catch with the dog in the house. They broke three of my mother's Hummels."

"The tea sets were inexpensive. Besides, I think the girls will appreciate the full experience. They want to feel grown up even though Disney princesses are all over the walls."

Gayle shrugged. "Suit yourself. But you might change your mind when someone knocks over that pink teapot and you have a mess on your hands. Have you figured out a menu?"

"Yes. I found recipes for cucumber and cream cheese sandwiches, and Sasha Burke will send me the cakes." She touched her temples where a headache had suddenly begun brewing. "And I need to make up flyers and design an ad for the local paper. I have so much to do. Not to mention finish the float."

Gayle rubbed her arm. "One day at a time, sweetie. You have a little over a week before the parade. It doesn't all have to be done in one day." Her brow furrowed. "How's your writing going?"

"I tried to work on my outline, but I didn't make much progress. I did, however, start working on character sketches and found photos depicting how I see them in my head. I didn't do much else, though. I've been so focused on the store, the party room, and the float. I want to honor Aunt CeCe's memory, and this is all for her."

"Maya, you're honoring her every day by keeping her business running." This time Gayle gestured around the room. "She would be so proud of this."

"You think so?" Maya heard the uncertainty in her words.

"I know so." Gayle touched her cheek. "Your great-aunt was my best friend, and she was so proud of your success as an author. She'd want you to continue living your own life. So don't give up on writing because that jerk chose some job over you. Don't let him steal your talent and legacy. Don't lose sight of your dreams because of a man's stupidity."

Maya nodded as her throat thickened. "Okay."

The bell on the front door of the store rang, and Gayle stepped away. "Duty calls."

"I'll be right there."

"Finish what you're doing. I can handle the customers." She paused in the doorway. "This will be an amazing success. I can feel it."

"I hope so," Maya mumbled as Gayle disappeared.

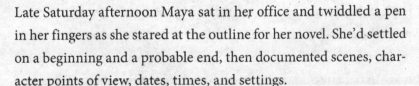

Late Saturday afternoon Maya sat in her office and twiddled a pen in her fingers as she stared at the outline for her novel. She'd settled on a beginning and a probable end, then documented scenes, character points of view, dates, times, and settings.

Now she closed her eyes and tried to imagine her characters

in the first scene. But when nothing came to her, she growled with frustration, then peeked down at Tinker Bell as the kitten rolled around on the floor.

"You know, Tink, you're not helping me with this book. In fact, you're no help at all."

On her back, the kitten kicked her toy mouse with her back claws, biting its head at the same time.

Maya sighed and peered out the window toward the garage. The float was there, just waiting for her to finish it for the parade. Her mind whirled as she again recalled her favorite Fourth of July memories. She'd so enjoyed both watching and being part of that parade.

And then an idea formed in her mind. She'd design a small card advertising her new party room and then staple a snack-size bag of candy to each one and give them out during the parade. She'd just have to find someone to drive her truck while she walked beside the float.

She'd find a driver later. Right now she needed to design the card and send it to the local printer, another way to bring in a local business. She searched her laptop for the sign she'd designed asking customers to keep Tinker Bell from escaping the store.

She copied the store's logo and designed a simple card inviting customers to check out her new tea party service. Then she located the number for the local printing store. She'd ask them not only to print the cards but also to design a banner to hang on all three sides of the float to advertise the tea parties. And she'd order flyers to hang in her store and more cards to include in merchandise bags.

She looked up the store's number, and as she made the call,

she felt a jolt of joy knowing she would be making the most of the Fourth of July to bring more business to her aunt's beloved store.

⁓•⁓

Maya stepped out of Something Sweet carrying a shopping bag with six containers of individually wrapped, assorted candies. A fraction of the tension she'd been feeling released from her shoulders as she checked another item off her mental to-do list—purchasing candy for the parade.

She stood on the corner waiting for the traffic light to change, and her gaze flickered to Beach Reads. She studied the front window display of the latest book releases, and Brody's words floated through her mind: *A book signing might remind you of one of the reasons you create stories.*

Maya's lips ticked down in a frown. She still hadn't contacted Callie to discuss her supplying books for the parties, let alone a book signing. But she suspected Brody was right. A book signing might push her back to writing.

Brody.

She hadn't spoken to him for nearly a week, and she missed him and Ashlyn immensely. Of course, she'd purposely kept her distance, but anguish still spiked through her. If only she hadn't hugged him, maybe she would have seen them a few times this week and wouldn't feel so rejected. The loneliness nearly suffocated her. Kiana was in Charlotte, and although Gayle was a friend, she had her own life. Her own family.

The light changed, and after she crossed the street toward the toy store, she strolled along the sidewalk past couples and families enjoying their evening.

Her phone rang, and when she pulled it from her back pocket, she saw Kiana's name on the display. "Hi. I was going to call you tonight."

"Cool. So . . . I have a question for you."

"Okay."

"I know it's last minute, but how would you like some company for the Fourth of July weekend?"

Maya saw the bench outside Beach Reads was empty and dashed to it. "Oh my goodness. I would love to see you!" She sank down onto the bench.

"I know it's only a week away, but what do you think?"

Maya's heart lifted. "A thousand times yes! It's not last minute at all."

"Okay." Kiana hesitated. "I have another question. Would it be okay if I brought Deacon?"

"Oh." Maya sat back, a little shocked. "Sure."

"You still have both an office and a spare room, right? I could take the spare room, and he could stay in the office on a cot. Would that be okay?"

"Yes, of course. I think there's a cot up in the attic."

"He's super nice, and I really want you to meet him. I promise we'll be good guests. I'll bring a cake and everything."

Maya laughed. "It's fine. You don't need to bring anything. I'm excited to meet him."

"And I can't wait to meet Brody and Ashlyn. Maybe we can all have a barbecue or something."

"Maybe." Maya tried to mask the sadness in her voice as she watched traffic roll by. She had no reason to believe she'd be invited to another cookout at Brody's.

"How's that party room coming along?"

"I finished it today. Now I'm working on the parade float." She snapped her fingers as another idea came to her. "Maybe Deacon can drive the truck pulling my float while you and I give out candy."

"Oh, that sounds like so much fun! Yes, count us in."

"Great."

"What's the float like?"

After Maya shared her plans, Kiana said, "That all sounds amazing. How's writing going?"

"It's not."

"You're still stuck?"

"Yeah, and I'm not sure what to do about it."

"You could visit your books at that bookstore in town. Beach Reads, right? That should remind you why you love writing your stories."

Maya rolled her eyes. "You're the second person to suggest that. And I'm sitting outside the bookstore now."

"Well, stop talking to me and go relive how it felt to see that first one in print. Smell a copy of your latest, and then sign it for whoever buys it. Your next one comes out in September, right?"

Maya huffed out a breath. "It does. And you're right."

"You know I am. Oh, hang on a minute." Maya heard voices in the background. "I need to go. Deacon is here, and we're going out to eat."

"Tell him I said hi and I can't wait to meet him."

"I will. Love you."

"Love you too." Maya disconnected the call, then stood and faced the bookstore. When she pushed open the door, the bell above it chimed as she breathed in the welcoming smell of new books. She glanced at the cashier counter and spotted Callie talking to a customer. Another half dozen people stood in line.

Maya wandered past the nonfiction and young adult sections, then when she reached the fiction section, she turned down the aisle with romance novels. Locating the *R*s, she quickly found her books and pulled out the most recent release—*On a Summer Breeze.* Then she ran her fingers over the colorful cover featuring an ocean-front scene with a sunset before lifting the book to her nose and inhaling its glorious scent.

As she flipped open the cover, she remembered outlining its story and then diving into crafting it. She'd always believed writing her novels fell into two categories. Some seemed to write themselves because the characters never stopped "talking" to her, and she couldn't type fast enough. Those were the best. For others, she had to push the characters through some of the scenes.

Every scene in this novel, however, had fallen into the former category. Once she started typing, the story took off, and the characters kept talking to her long after she wrote the last sentence. If only she could find that kind of inspiration again.

Maya hugged the book to her chest and closed her eyes, doing her best to bring her current characters alive. Then she imagined finishing the manuscript, sending it to her editor, working closely with her to fine-tune the story, reading the final pages, and then holding the finished book in her hands. If only she could get those characters to talk to her.

"I'm going to the children's section, okay?" Ashlyn asked Brody as they walked into the bookstore together.

"You can choose exactly this many books," he said, holding up two fingers. "I'll be over there in fiction." He pointed to the sign. "Then I'll come find you."

Ashlyn nodded before scampering off.

Brody made a beeline for the fiction section and spotted the aisle with the sign that said *Romance*. His plan was to pick up at least one of Maya's five books and read it before contacting her again. He just didn't know which one to read, so maybe he'd buy one of each and decide when he got home.

He picked up speed, scanning the shelves on his way toward the authors with last names beginning with *R*.

He turned the corner and froze when he found a petite woman with a thick, dark brown braid standing in front of the shelf he needed to reach.

When she turned toward him, his lungs squeezed as heat crawled up his neck.

"Maya. Hi." Embarrassed, he raised his hand in an awkward wave.

She blinked at him as a hesitant smile lifted her pretty pink lips. "Brody. What are you doing here?"

"You caught me." He pointed to the book in her hand. "I want to read your books. Which one should I read first?"

She looked suspicious as she handed him the book she'd been holding. "This one is my favorite."

He examined the front. "*On a Summer Breeze.* What a great cover." Then he pointed to the shelf. "I'd actually like to buy them all."

"I have copies back at my place. I can just give you one of each."

"No, I'd rather support you this way." He took a deep breath, feeling self-conscious. He needed to explain why he hadn't been in touch all week, but humiliation trapped the truth in his throat. "I've been meaning to contact you, but the clinic has been chaotic, and Ashlyn has had playdates nearly every evening this week."

"Oh. I totally understand. I've been busy too."

"How are things at the store?"

"Good." She set her shopping bag on the floor. "I finished the party room."

"Really?" More embarrassment gripped him. "That's amazing, but I thought maybe we could help you this weekend."

Maya shrugged. "That's okay. I got it done. Now I just need to write up some advertisements for the paper."

"Have you done any writing for your new novel?"

"Not really, but I'll get there."

"Miss Maya!" Ashlyn rushed down the aisle toward them. She had an armload of books.

"Hi, Ashlyn. What have you got there?"

Ashlyn held out her pile. "A few books by my favorite author."

Maya perused the stack. "These look great."

Brody raised an eyebrow. "A few? I count eight. And I told you two."

"But, Dad, you always say reading is better than watching television. That's why I picked out so many."

Maya put her hand over her mouth, no doubt to cover a grin.

Brody's lips twitched as he tried to stop a grin of his own. "Okay, but those will need to last you a while."

"Are you buying any books, Miss Maya?"

"I just came to visit the books I wrote to see if they could offer me inspiration."

Ashlyn scrunched her nose. "What does that mean?"

"I thought seeing them here might help me write my new book."

Brody pointed to the shelf behind her. "Miss Maya's books are right there."

"Oh, wow!" Ashlyn rushed over, and after setting her books on the floor, she pulled one of each of Maya's novels and held them up. "Dad, you need to get these."

"I was planning on it."

He took the five novels from her. "Do you need to look for anything else?" he asked Maya.

"No. I'm done."

"Will you walk out with us?" Ashlyn asked.

"Sure."

Relief spilled through Brody as Maya followed Ashlyn and him to the front of the store. While they waited their turn in line, she talked with his daughter about the books she'd picked out.

"Hi, Dr. Brody," Callie said when they approached the register. "And Ashlyn." When Callie saw Maya, she gave her a pointed look.

Maya held up her hands as if in surrender. "Okay, okay. Let's plan a book signing when my new release comes out in September. Do you have a few minutes to talk about it now? I have something else to ask you about too."

Callie brightened. "Yes. Let me get Rhiannon to take over." She took care of Brody's purchases, then turned toward the office behind her and called one of her employees to come out.

"I'll be a few minutes. I understand if you need to leave," Maya told Brody and Ashlyn.

Brody lifted his bag. "We'll wait for you outside." He had no idea why Maya looked a little confused as he turned to lead Ashlyn through the door.

Once they sat down on the bench in front of the store, his daughter lifted a book out of her bag, then flipped through it as he drummed his fingers on the wrought iron armrest and tried to pull his jumbled thoughts together. He needed to tell Maya the real reason he'd stayed away from her this week—hopefully without sounding like a complete jerk. Well, one of the reasons.

After several minutes, the bookstore door swung open, and Maya stepped out holding a bag from the bookstore as well as her bag from the candy store. He'd recognized the Something Sweet logo right away. "Well, it was nice seeing you," she said without even slowing down. "Take care." She turned and started down the street.

"Maya, wait," Brody called. When she stopped, he turned to Ashlyn. "Stay here. I need to speak to Maya alone for a moment."

Ashlyn's little brow puckered. "Okay."

Brody jogged toward Maya, who stood staring at him. He couldn't tell if what he saw on her face was anxiety or curiosity. Either way, he had to confess.

As he closed the distance between them, he swallowed against his dry throat. "Maya, I'm sorry."

"For what?" Her voice sounded almost childlike.

His stomach twisted. "The real reason I wasn't in touch this week is I was still embarrassed about how I acted on Sunday. I was a blubbering idiot, crying in your arms like that."

"No." She shook her head. "I didn't think that at all. I was glad I was there to comfort you. I felt bad leaving you when you clearly needed a friend. I wanted to stay, but you told me to go home."

He grimaced. "Why would you want to be friends with an emotional wreck?"

"But isn't that what friends are for? We're the people you can lose it in front of and not be embarrassed."

"Well, I'm grateful you feel that way about me." The heavy brick of anxiety in his stomach began to dissolve. "Could Ashlyn and I come see what you've done with the party room?"

"I'd love to show you."

His heart lifted as he touched her hand. "Great."

Chapter 12

As Maya walked toward her building with Brody and Ashlyn, she breathed in the warm evening air. The streetlights weren't quite on, but they were festive with alternating red, white, and blue stars and hats, shimmering with tinsel. Soon the streets would be full of both tourists and locals celebrating the Fourth.

Happiness bubbled inside her as she recalled how Brody had apologized. All along she'd thought she'd been too forward when she'd hugged him, but he'd been worried he was too emotional with her. She was grateful to have both Brody and Ashlyn back in her life—even if friendship was all she could hope for.

Maya led the two into the back door of her building and into the party room. She clicked on the overhead light, then set her bag of candy and the bag of books from Callie on the buffet.

"Wow," Ashlyn said with a gasp. "It's beautiful."

But Brody frowned, and Maya's shoulders sagged. "You don't like it."

"What?" He angled his body toward her. "Oh no, no. I just feel terrible that you did all this by yourself. I'm sorry I—" He paused and glanced over at Ashlyn, who had crouched in front of the buffet to peek inside.

He took a step toward Maya and lowered his voice. "I should have been here to help you instead of worrying about what you thought of me."

Maya shook her head as appreciation for this thoughtful man swelled in her chest. "You have your own business to run and a daughter to raise. This was my responsibility."

"I still feel like I let you down."

She resisted the urge to place her palm flat on his chest. "You didn't." She narrowed her eyes and lifted her chin. "But you will if you criticize my hard work."

He grinned, and once again his dimple came out to play. "It's amazing. Out of this world. Spectacular. The princesses and castle look great, the tables and chairs are charming, and the clouds and birds are the perfect accent. Girls are going to love it here."

"Yes!" Ashlyn jumped up from the buffet. "I can't wait for *my* party. It's going to be the best one ever!" She spun as if she were a princess showing off a flowing gown.

Maya and Brody shared a grin, and her heart stuttered.

Maya picked up the bag of books from Callie. "What do you think of these stories Miss Callie recommended for goody bags?" She pulled out the books featuring princesses and fairy tales.

"I love them!"

Brody pointed toward the garage. "Have you finished the float too?"

"No. I've started, but finishing it is my next project."

"Would you like our help?"

She shrugged. "I can handle it."

He lifted his eyebrows. "Maya . . ."

"Okay, okay." She waved for them to follow her.

Maya grabbed the keys from her purse, suggested Brody and Ashlyn leave their bags in the hallway, and then took them to the garage. She unlocked the side door, and as they stepped inside, she flipped on the lights.

Brody gave a low whistle as he walked straight to her great-aunt's old Ford pickup. Then he ran his hand over its fender. "This is the coolest truck."

Maya smiled. "I agree."

Ashlyn pointed at the flatbed trailer with its purple stage. "So Tessie, Bailey, Sammie, and me are going to sit up on this float and pretend to have a tea party, right?"

"That's what I was thinking. I have some strong tape to secure the table and chairs and the tea set so they won't fly off. I also have a plastic tea set in the store to use. It's oversize, so the crowd will be able to see it. I've spoken to all your friends' moms, and they've all agreed to you girls wearing your favorite dresses and riding on the float to wave."

Maya stepped closer. "I'll just need to attach the banners on the sides. I don't think I need any other decorations." She spun toward Brody, who was leaning against the truck bed, rubbing his chin. "What do you think?"

"I think you're right." He nodded. "If you add anything else, it might be too busy. Would you like help securing the table and chairs?"

"No, thanks. I've got it." She climbed up onto the trailer.

Ashlyn jumped up beside her. "This will be the best float ever."

Maya smiled. "I hope so."

Late afternoon the following Saturday, the bell above the toy store's front door dinged as Kiana rushed in. What a sight for sore eyes! Her long, light brown hair was styled in two French braids that hung below her shoulders, and as usual, she wore just enough makeup to accentuate her light blue eyes. Kiana stood at barely five-foot-two, and Maya always thought she was adorable with her petite nose and rosy cheeks.

"We're here!" Kiana exclaimed.

Maya squealed as she hugged her best friend. "It's so good to see you."

"You too." Kiana beamed, then pointed to the man standing behind her. "This is Deacon Rollins. Deacon, this is the amazing Maya Reynolds."

Deacon gave Maya a warm smile as he held out his hand. With the promised sandy-blond hair and brown eyes, he had an approachable air about him. He was a few inches taller than Maya, and his broad shoulders and wide chest gave her the impression that he spent time at the gym. Like Kiana in her jean shorts, tank top with a heart on it, and sandals, he was dressed for beach life and had a pair of sunglasses perched on his head.

"I've heard a lot about you," he said as he gave Maya's hand a firm shake.

"I've heard a lot about you too."

Kiana made a sweeping gesture around the store. "This place is amazing, My! You've changed it since I was here last year, right?"

Maya chuckled. "No, not really."

Tinker Bell rushed to Kiana, the bell on her collar tinkling away. Then she gave a loud meow.

"Oh my goodness!" Kiana dropped to her knees and scratched the kitten's ears. "You must be Miss Tinker Bell. I've been so excited to meet you."

Maya glanced at Deacon, and they shared a smile. "Kiana gets excited about things," she told him.

"It's one of the things I enjoy most about her."

Maya's heart warmed at the way Deacon looked at her friend, admiration shining in his eyes.

"Is Miss Gayle here?" Kiana asked as she stood.

"No. She doesn't work on Saturdays."

"Oh. I was hoping to see her." Kiana pointed toward the back. "Let's see the party room."

"Sure. I just have to lock up." Maya flipped the front sign to Closed and locked the door before lifting Tinker Bell and leading Kiana and Deacon to the back room.

Kiana gasped. "Oh, wow. The photos you sent were amazing, but this looks even better in person. Kids are going to love this." She touched the Cinderella decal.

"It'll be a hit," Deacon said, agreeing. "I know my sister's girls would love it."

"Thanks."

"I told Deacon he's going to drive the truck in the parade." Kiana grinned at her boyfriend.

Deacon smiled in return. "It'll be fun."

"I appreciate it," Maya said. "Would you like some dinner? I can make something. Or we can go out."

Kiana took Deacon's hand in hers. "We want to take you out tonight to thank you for hosting us. How about we go to that Japanese place you and I enjoyed so much last summer?"

"That sounds great. Are you parked in the back? Let's get your luggage upstairs, and I'll put this little one where she can't get into trouble while we're gone."

Maya leaned down and kissed Tinker Bell's head. The kitten squirmed, and Kiana and Deacon both laughed.

~~~

"Dinner was amazing," Kiana said as the three of them walked down the boardwalk later that evening.

Maya nodded. Even at low tide, the waves pounded the shore, and the sun was about to set. Maya breathed a sigh of relief. She'd needed her best friend at her side again. The two of them had laughed all through dinner, telling funny stories from high school and college. Deacon had laughed right along with them.

Maya noticed how relaxed Kiana and Deacon were as they shared each other's food, teased each other, and held hands. They seemed like a couple who'd been together for years, not just a few weeks. She was delighted for her friend. Deacon seemed like a wonderful man—easygoing and attentive as he listened to Kiana's stories and contributed to the conversation as well.

"The food was delicious," Maya said. "Thank you so much."

"We should thank you for letting us land on you this weekend." Kiana gave Maya's side a gentle nudge. Then she sighed. "I love it here."

"You're welcome to visit anytime."

Deacon nodded toward an ice cream vendor. "Would anyone like dessert?"

"I would love a cookies and cream cone." Kiana bit her lip and raised her eyebrows. "How about you, Maya?"

Maya hesitated, then shrugged. "Why not? I'll take chocolate chip cookie dough."

"Coming right up." He pointed to a nearby bench. "You two relax."

Maya followed Kiana to the bench, and they sat down and looked out toward the waves.

"Deacon is great, Key."

"Yeah, he is, isn't he?" Kiana smiled, then peeked over her shoulder before scooting closer to Maya. "I know it's still awfully soon, but I think I'm falling in love with him." She held up her hands, palms facing out. "I know what you're going to say, and I'm being careful with my heart. But I can't deny that I feel like we really complement each other. I'm impulsive, and he's levelheaded and thinks things through. I'm outgoing, and he's more of an introvert." She shrugged. "I just have a good feeling about us."

Maya touched her arm. "I do too. You deserve someone who treats you well."

"So do you." Kiana angled her body toward her. "How's Brody?"

Maya fingered the edge of the bench. "He's fine."

"Deacon will be coming back soon." Kiana gazed over her shoulder again. "So tell me the latest. Did you see him this week?"

Maya nodded. "He and Ashlyn came by Thursday night, and we finalized the plans for the float."

"Has he kissed you yet?"

"No. I've told you. We're just friends."

"Are you satisfied with that?"

"No." Maya sighed. "But I'll accept it if that's all he'll give me."

"Are you sure that will be enough to sustain a relationship with him? Mere friendship might be too difficult for you at some point."

"What are you getting at, Key?"

Kiana folded her arms over her waist. "I guess I mean you might eventually tell Brody how you feel because you can't stand it anymore. But maybe you should just do that now. He might be afraid to take a chance on you because he's been hurt by someone else somewhere along the line."

"But he insists Ashlyn is his world, and I respect that. And he's never mentioned having a serious romantic relationship with anyone."

"But if you ask me, he does want more than friendship, and something besides his devotion to his daughter must be keeping him from telling you how he really feels. What if you were honest with him and that truth gave him the courage to be honest with you?"

Speechless, Maya just stared at her.

Kiana suddenly brightened. "I'll let you know what vibe I get when I meet him." She looked behind her and smiled. "Here comes our ice cream."

Deacon arrived balancing three ice cream cones in his hands. "Cookies and cream for you," he said, handing one to Kiana.

"Thank you," she sang.

"And chocolate chip cookie dough for you, Maya." He held out hers.

"Thank you so much."

"You're welcome." Deacon sank down beside Kiana. "This is the perfect dessert on a summer night."

"What did you get?" Kiana asked.

Deacon held up his cone. "Chocolate peanut butter."

"Yum." Kiana looked out toward the waves as she licked an ice cream drip on her hand.

Maya considered Kiana's suggestion that she be honest with Brody about her feelings. Maybe she could find the courage to do that. Her hands began to sweat at the thought of admitting the truth to him. But the possibility of that truth ruining their friendship also scared her.

She turned her thoughts to the Fourth festivities. "Would you both please help me finish getting ready for the parade? I don't have much time left."

"Sure!" Kiana grinned as Deacon nodded.

Maya and Kiana sat at the kitchen table slipping four pieces of candy into resealable, snack-size bags and then stapling them to one of the cards promoting the tea parties. As they dropped each packet into a box, Deacon sat on the sofa in the family room watching a Captain America movie with Tinker Bell happily curled in his lap.

"You'd better tell your boyfriend he can't take my cat home with him," Maya said, teasing.

Kiana gazed into the family room and then gave Maya a look. "And you'd better tell that cat of yours that she can't steal my boyfriend."

Maya laughed. "Touché!"

They worked in silence for a few moments, and then Kiana looked up again. "You haven't mentioned your dad lately. Have you made any progress finding him?"

Maya shook her head. "No."

"May I read the letter your aunt wrote you?"

"Of course." Maya gathered both the letter and her laptop from the office and brought them back to the kitchen.

While Kiana studied the letter, Maya opened her laptop, then accessed her email. She'd been wondering if Kyle had finally answered her. When she found no new messages at all, she turned her attention back to the task at hand.

Kiana's expression was pensive as she slipped the letter back into the envelope. "She said he went by a nickname or maybe a middle name. What have you searched for?"

"Just Quincy Hamill and a few other spellings of Hamill in case CeCe got that wrong. But, honestly, I haven't had time to do much else."

Her best friend reached for the laptop. "May I? I'm pretty good at this."

"Knock yourself out. I'll keep working on these."

After about ten minutes, curiosity overwhelmed Maya. "Okay, Key. You need to show me what you're doing."

"Here." Kiana turned the screen to face Maya and then scooted her chair around the table. She had several personal Facebook profile pages open. "Between Facebook and some cross-references on the internet, I found four family law attorneys in the DC area—a Michael Hamal, Ryan Hamel, Nicholas Hamel, and Leonard Hamel."

"I never thought to look for attorneys like that!" Maya pursed her lips. "Michael and Ryan don't look much older than we are."

"I thought that too." Kiana touched her nose. "So if your dad was almost ten years older than your mom, how old would he be now?"

Maya tilted her head as she contemplated the question. "Almost sixty."

"Well, Nicholas and Leonard look about that old, don't you think?"

Maya nodded and realized her hands were shaking. "Yeah."

"Hey." Kiana bumped her shoulder against Kiana's. "It's okay. You don't have to do anything."

"No, I want to." She closed her eyes and groaned as the truth took hold of her. "But I am scared."

"Why?"

"What if he doesn't want to know me?"

Kiana's eyebrows lifted. "And what if he *does*?"

"You're right." Maya took a deep breath and then, using Facebook Messenger, sent messages to both Nicholas Hamel and Leonard Hamel, explaining she'd like to send a friend request because they might have known her mother.

Then she sighed. "And now we wait."

Chapter 13

Y ou're all the perfect princesses!" Maya exclaimed Monday morning as she stood by her float and admired Ashlyn, Tessie, Bailey, and Sammie.

Sunday had quickly passed as Kiana, Deacon, and Maya spent the afternoon finishing up the candy packets and then making sure the table and chairs were secure on the float. After eating pizza, they'd sat on the beach before deciding it was best to get some rest before the big day.

And now that day was here! It was the Fourth of July, and the parade was about to begin. Maya couldn't stop admiring the stars of her float.

Ashlyn was the perfect Belle in a yellow ball gown, complete with a yellow headband holding her dark hair in place. Sammie made a charming Princess Tiana in her green gown, her dark curls piled on top of her head with a green crown. Tessie's blue Cinderella gown and matching crown were also stunning, as was Bailey's Elsa costume.

The table was covered by a long, disposable purple tablecloth and adorned with the oversize plastic tea set secured to the table. Banners that read *Book Your Birthday Tea Party Today at CeCe's*

Toy Chest and displayed the store's phone number hung on each side of the float.

Maya bit her lip. Had she forgotten anything?

No doubt reading her stress, Kiana rested her arm around Maya's shoulders. "Everything is perfect, My."

"Thank you. You and Deacon have been a tremendous help." She pulled her phone out of her pocket. "Let's get some photos before the parade. You girls all stand together and strike a pose." The girls lined up on the float, and Maya took several shots. "Perfect."

Deacon stuck his head out the pickup's driver's side window. "It's time to roll!"

"Okay, ladies," Maya told the girls. "Your job is to smile and wave." She pointed to the table. "There's a box under there with extra teacups. Feel free to pretend to sip from one, but just have fun and wave a lot, okay?"

"Yes, Miss Maya," the four girls sang in unison.

Kiana opened the pickup truck's tailgate and pulled out a box with half the candy packets. "Let's do this!"

Maya laughed as she grabbed the other box.

Soon the pickup was rumbling slowly down the street, following the high school marching band toward the start of the parade route.

The band members were glorious in their blue uniforms, moving together like a giant centipede as they played an upbeat march. The baton twirlers and color guard performed to the music, and the color guard's blue-and-gray flags shimmered in the bright morning sun. When the parade crowd came into view, the sea of people dressed in red, white, and blue cheered and clapped as they waved American flags.

Pride blossomed in Maya's chest as both she and Kiana handed the cards and candy to children, all while marching to the band's contagious beat. She glanced back toward the float, where the four glamorous little girls waved to the crowd as they moved down the parade route. They were even blowing kisses, and she wondered if that was Ashlyn's idea.

Above them, the sky was a bright azure and cloudless, and a warm breeze mixed with the aromas of salt water, cotton candy, and of course cocoa butter washed over Maya. The sun was bright and hot, and she wiped sweat off her forehead.

The cards and candy lasted almost to the end of the parade route.

"That went super quick," Kiana said as she helped Tessie and Sammie down from the float.

Maya nodded as she helped Ashlyn and Bailey. "All that preparation and it was over in an hour. But it was a lot of fun."

"You were great, Sammie!" The little girl's mom hurried over to her. "My little Princess Tiana."

"Thank you so much for letting Sammie participate, Natasha," Maya told her. She thanked Bailey's and Tessie's moms as well as they collected their daughters.

Deacon came around the back of the pickup truck and sat on the tailgate. "This seemed like a great success to me."

Kiana hopped up next to him, and he looped his arm around her shoulders.

"It was!" she said.

Maya stepped closer to them. "Thank you both. You were a great driver, Deacon."

"Can I sit up there too?" Ashlyn pointed to the tailgate.

"Come on up, Belle," Kiana said.

Maya lifted her up beside Kiana and then pulled out her phone and opened the camera app. "Smile!"

Kiana rested her arms over Ashlyn's and Deacon's shoulders, and Maya snapped a few more photos.

Ashlyn's face lit up as she pointed behind Maya. "There's my dad!"

Brody jogged over, looking handsome in a striped shirt adorned with a flag. Maya introduced him to Kiana and Deacon. He'd dropped Ashlyn off that morning, but he had only enough time to wave to everyone before rushing off to help supervise the clinic's float.

"How'd it go?" he asked after shaking their hands.

"Great," Maya said. "Kiana and I gave out all our cards and candy, and the crowd seemed to love the girls."

"It was so fun, Daddy. We need to do this again next year."

Brody smoothed her hair down. "I guess we'll see."

"How did your float go with the volunteers giving out cat and dog treats?" Maya asked.

"It went well, but we ran out of them. The treats, not volunteers." He picked Ashlyn up, and she wrapped her legs around his waist and rested her head on his broad shoulder. "You look tired, sweet pea. Too much sun already? The day's just started. Do you need a nap?"

"I'm not a baby, Dad." Her face scrunched with a frown.

He chuckled and then met Maya's gaze again. "Are you all still coming over?"

"Yeah." Maya gestured behind the truck. "Thanks again for

inviting us. We just need to drop off the float and truck, get into our swimsuits, and pick up our snacks."

"Great. Cam, his family, and the rest of our staff will be there too. We'll see you soon."

"Maya," Kiana whispered as they walked around the float. "He's gorgeous."

"I know. And wait until you see his house."

Deacon gave a low whistle from the back seat of the 4Runner as Maya nosed her SUV into the driveway at Sandy Feet Retreat, then pulled into Brody's extra parking space. Another four vehicles had lined up closer to the garage—a dark blue Acura RDX SUV, a red Jeep Wrangler, a gray Honda Accord, and a black Chevrolet Suburban.

"This is his house?" Kiana was staring.

Maya slipped the car into Park. "Yup."

"And only Brody and his daughter live here?"

"That's right. Well, along with six cats and a dog."

"Wow," Deacon whispered.

They climbed out of the Toyota and gathered their bags and supplies, then walked up to the front door and rang the bell. Ashlyn appeared with a blond girl who looked a few years younger than she was.

"Hi! This is my friend Melanie." Ashlyn turned to the girl. "Melanie, this is Miss Maya, Miss Kiana, and Mr. Deacon."

The little girl lifted her hand in a wave as the adults greeted her.

"Come on in," Ashlyn told them, and they followed her into the foyer.

Maya could tell Kiana and Deacon were both holding in a gasp as they glanced around the family room on their way to the kitchen.

"Oh my," Kiana whispered low enough that Ashlyn and her friend wouldn't hear. "This place is incredible."

Deacon nodded. "No kidding."

"Wait until you see the view from the deck," Maya told them.

After depositing their bags in the kitchen, they walked out onto the deck, where Brody sat talking with a couple who held hands and looked about his age. An attractive blonde who looked a few years younger than the three and a young man probably in his early twenties sat on either side of them.

Brody jumped to his feet. "Hi. I'm so glad you all made it." He gestured toward each of them as he said, "Everyone, this is Maya, Kiana, and Deacon." Then, turning to the couple, he said, "This is my partner, Cam, and this is his wife, Donna."

Donna stood and held out her hand to Maya. The bright orange straps of a swimsuit peeked from under her blue tank top with a flag on it, and Maya took in her ash-blond hair, honey-brown eyes, and warm smile.

"Hi, Maya. We've heard so much about you from Brody."

Maya shook her hand. "Oh? It's nice to meet you."

Cam also stood to greet them. He was a few inches shorter than Brody, and while they both had dark hair, Cam's eyes were brown, not blue. But they had the same warm demeanor Maya was certain calmed their patients' owners at the clinic. "Happy Fourth! It's great to see you all."

Brody then turned to the blonde. "This is Kim Banks, my vet tech."

Kim gave Maya and her friends a curt nod.

"Hi," was all Maya could manage as she took in the woman's long hair, perfectly straightened and hanging past her slight shoulders. When Kim stepped about as close to Brody as she could get without actually touching him, jealously hit Maya hard and fast, stealing her breath for a moment. Those long, tan legs stemming from her white shorts were gorgeous.

Brody pointed to the young man. "And this is Justin Hayden. He's our amazing receptionist."

"Nice to meet you too," Maya said.

Justin shook her hand. He had a welcoming smile, and his large hazel eyes held a smile behind black horn-rimmed glasses. He wore a white T-shirt with *Coral Cove Veterinary Clinic* on it.

"Let's hit the beach!" Brody said, rubbing his hands together. "Adding to the snacks you brought, we have sandwiches and drinks ready to go, and it's the perfect day."

Maya looked toward the waves, where hundreds of beachgoers seemed to agree.

"Let's do it," Kiana said. "I've been looking forward to this!"

After gathering Brody's coolers and a few beach chairs, they all headed down with their bags and towels. They found an open spot, and Brody set up two umbrellas before he jogged away. The two little girls were already digging in the wet sand near the shoreline, and all the adults except Maya and Donna had uncovered their swimsuits and waded into the water. A flag on a pole indicated that current conditions were safe for swimming.

Maya's heart had sunk as soon as she saw the red string bikini that boasted Kim's perfect figure. She looked like a swimsuit model. Trying to mask her sudden self-doubt, Maya removed her shorts and tank top, then settled into a beach chair and watched the knots of people bobbing in the water. Seagulls swooped by singing their familiar songs, and even more boats than usual passed by in the distance.

It *was* a lovely day.

Donna took a seat beside her and adjusted the straps of her one-piece suit. "I heard your float was a big hit this morning. Ashlyn told me all about it."

"We had fun." Maya grimaced. "I'm sorry we didn't invite Melanie to join us. I wish Ashlyn and Brody had suggested it."

"Oh, it's fine. Please don't apologize. Mellie is a bit shy, so I think she was happier helping me give out pet treats. She would have been too nervous to ride a float without me."

Maya looked toward the water just as Brody dove under a wave, then quickly popped up, shaking his head and pushing his hands through his thick, wet hair. He laughed at something Cam said and then ducked under the water again. Kim plodded over and said something else that made him laugh, and Maya's stomach lurched as jealousy skulked under her skin.

Kiana jogged up the beach. "You don't come to the ocean with me and just sit in a chair, woman. Come swim!" Grabbing Maya's hand, she yanked her out of the chair and pulled her toward the waves, passing the high, wooden lifeguard stand where a young man and a young woman sat wearing sunglasses and red swimsuits, each with a whistle on a cord around their neck. Aunt CeCe had always appreciated the town council funding lifeguards during the summer months. First aid kits sat nearby, and Maya knew the lifeguards were trained to sound an alarm if they spotted a shark. But none had ever been seen at Coral Cove's beach.

"See you later!" Maya called to Donna, who laughed as Maya stumbled in the sand.

Kiana dove into the water, then swam toward Deacon. Maya had just waded to where the surface reached her waist when Brody appeared beside her. She tried not to stare at his tan and muscular chest and abs. "Are you having a good time with Kiana?"

"Yes. It's so great to spend time with her again."

"Deacon seems nice."

"He is. They get along really well." Maya looked over to where Deacon held Kiana in his arms, her head flung back as she laughed, her long hair flowing on the surface of the water. "They seem really happy too." She met Brody's gaze. "Thank you for inviting us over."

"I thought you might want to take advantage of my beach."

"And your super-awesome deck," she said, teasing him. "To see the fireworks tonight, of course."

He chuckled.

"And I guess your amazing grilling abilities too."

He laughed again, shaking his head. "You're something else, Maya Reynolds."

She rested her hands on her hips. "I hope you mean that in a good way."

"Only the best of ways."

"Daddy!"

Brody turned to where Ashlyn stood on the sand with Melanie. She was holding a shovel and a bucket. "Yeah?"

"Would you please help Melanie and me build a sandcastle?"

"One second." Brody pivoted back to Maya. "Duty calls."

"Go build your little princess a castle."

"I'll do my best." When he plodded through the water but then turned back to grin at Maya, her heart felt as though it had just tripped over itself.

~·~

Brody stood on his deck and looked up at the beautiful night sky. The afternoon had flown by as they'd all enjoyed the beach and then devoured a delicious supper of grilled steaks and chicken, salad, and watermelon.

The group talked and laughed as they ate, and Brody enjoyed the fellowship with all his guests. He served cookies decorated with patriotic icing and slices of lemon cake from Beach Bakery for dessert, and then everyone helped with cleanup before heading back out to the beach until dusk.

Now they stood looking out over the ocean, waiting for the fireworks display as lightning bugs presented their own show. To his right, Maya's friends relaxed a few feet away from him, Deacon standing behind Kiana with his arms wrapped around her. Cam and Donna waited just beyond them with Melanie perched on Cam's shoulders. Her little hands rested in his dark hair, and Donna leaned into her husband's side, one arm wrapped around his waist.

Ashlyn stood to his left, and Kim and Justin were somewhere beyond her. Maya had stepped into the space on his right.

Then as "You're a Grand Old Flag" sounded from speakers down on the beach, the first fireworks exploded in glorious, shimmering shades of red, white, and blue. Maya jumped a little and then graced him with a warm smile. His pulse skittered, and he couldn't help himself. Reaching over, he pulled her to his side.

"Are you okay, Maya?"

She looked up at him. "I was just surprised, and sudden loud noises scare me sometimes."

She looked so beautiful with her chestnut-colored eyes sparkling in the low lights still on above the deck. The urge to kiss her nearly overwhelmed him, yet he didn't release her.

More fireworks shot up into the air, followed by an earthshaking *boom* and more luminous colors stretching across the dark sky.

"Wow," Maya whispered as she leaned into him.

Brody looked down at her hand resting on the deck railing, and he covered it with his. She peered up at him again, and the intensity in her eyes sent a shockwave of desire through him. Maybe mere friendship with her wasn't enough. Maybe he'd opened a door he didn't want to close.

The aroma of sulfur filled the air as fireworks continued lighting up the sky. "My Country 'Tis of Thee" rang through the speakers, and everyone on the deck oohed and aahed at the spectacular display.

Brody leaned down to whisper in Maya's ear. "Isn't it beautiful?"

"It is." She returned his smile with a look that took his breath away.

All too soon, the grand finale seemed to fill the universe—"The Star-Spangled Banner" coupled with what looked like hundreds of fireworks exploding simultaneously—causing everyone on the deck to gasp with delight. When the sky cleared, they all clapped and cheered—especially Ashlyn.

Maya stepped back, and disappointment flashed through Brody. The evening had come to a close too quickly.

"I guess it's time to say good night," Donna announced.

Melanie yawned from atop her father's shoulders. "But I'm not tired. I want to play."

"We'll come back again soon," Donna told her.

His guests all gathered their bags, and he and Ashlyn walked down to the driveway to say goodbye. He was pleased when Maya stood at his side.

Cam shook Brody's hand. "We had a great time. Thanks for your hospitality."

"Of course." Brody patted his best friend's back. "I'll see you at the clinic bright and early tomorrow morning."

Then Kim stepped up. "Thank you so much for inviting me, Dr. Brody. I had the best time."

"I'm so glad you came."

"It was nice to meet you, Maya."

"It was nice meeting you, too, Kim," Maya said.

But the look in Maya's eyes didn't seem to say the same thing. What was that about?

Deacon, Kiana, and Justin all thanked Brody and then said good night to Kim and Cam and his family.

Ashlyn wrapped her arms around Maya's waist. "I'll come see you and Tinker Bell this week if Daddy says it's okay."

"I would love that." Maya tapped her nose. "Good night, sweetie."

Brody relished the love between his daughter and Maya.

"Thank you again, Brody," Maya told him with a smile that seemed full of meaning. "Call me, okay?"

He managed to nod before she joined her friends and drove away, but the euphoria of the evening had suddenly drained from his heart and soul. Maya's last words had been a clear invitation.

Attraction or no, the magic of fireworks or not, why had he embraced her that way, letting down the guard around his heart? And why had he made it worse by covering her hand with his? He cared for her, but they had to be friends. Only friends. He owed that to himself and his daughter.

And if he'd just led Maya to believe he had anything more to offer, that was even worse.

Chapter 14

After saying good night to Kiana, Maya took a shower. Then she dropped onto her bed, her emotions high as she recalled her evening with Brody. She'd started having second thoughts about what his actions meant the moment they left his house. And some of her thoughts featured Kim.

Kiana hadn't missed a thing, and she pounced as soon as Deacon had retired to his cot in the office. "Now will you admit Brody's into you?"

"No. You saw how Kim took every chance to be close to him. I simply beat her to the punch before the fireworks started, and when I jumped at the first boom, he probably just took the opportunity to fend her off."

"You don't really think he's the kind of man who would use one woman to deny another one, do you?"

"He might have thought . . . Oh, I don't know."

But that would mean Brody was a great actor. The way he'd pulled her to his side. The look in his eyes, as if he wanted to kiss her . . . That's why she'd asked him to call her. She had to know if he'd changed his mind about a relationship only as friends. But she wasn't ready to tell even Kiana that.

"Let's not get ahead of ourselves, Key."

Now she rolled onto her side and forced herself to think about Nicholas Hamel and Leonard Hamel. She pulled out her phone, opened her Facebook app, and gasped when she saw Leonard Hamel had agreed to accept a friend request. Her heart picked up speed as she sent it.

When she returned from the kitchen with a glass of water, she was surprised to see he'd already responded. Now able to scroll through his full profile, she saw he listed himself as widowed and a senior partner in his law firm in Washington, DC. As she studied his salt-and-pepper hair, long attractive face, warm smile, and milk-chocolate eyes, she looked for any similarity to her own countenance. But everyone always said she looked like her mother.

Then she examined his photos, which were mostly of him and a brown-and-tan German shepherd. Mr. Hamel was fit and seemed to enjoy spending time outdoors with the beautiful canine.

As she stared at his profile photo again, her chest tightened. This man could be her father.

"Well, there's only one way to find out," she whispered, and then she typed another message to him.

Thank you for accepting my request. I think you may have known my mother about thirty years ago. Her name was Vickie Sullivan. If not, I'm sorry for bothering you.

She hit Send and closed her eyes, trying to stop her racing heart. She hoped and prayed Mr. Hamel would respond soon. But at the same time, she feared his response. If he *had* known her mother, what would she learn next? The unknown was terrifying.

When he didn't respond right away, she locked her phone, then settled under the covers, hoping sleep would come despite her swirling thoughts.

~ · ~

Maya stood with her guests in the parking lot the next morning.

"I'm going to miss you!" Kiana pulled Maya into a tight hug, nearly forcing all the air from her lungs. "Promise me we'll get together again soon."

Maya disentangled herself from her friend's arms and nodded. "I would love that. I'm so glad you came. I had a wonderful time." She turned to Deacon. "I'm grateful I got to meet you. Please take good care of my best friend."

Deacon smiled as he pulled Kiana to his side. "I plan on doing just that for as long as she lets me." He shook Maya's hand. "Thank you for having us. I'd love to return the favor in Charlotte sometime."

Kiana hugged Maya once more. "Brody and Ashlyn are great. I think you'll be dating him before you know it."

Maya smiled. *Maybe.* "Be safe going home."

Deacon climbed into the driver's seat of his black Chevrolet Tahoe and Kiana hopped up into the passenger seat. The engine rumbled to life, and Deacon backed the truck out of his parking spot. The tires crunched through the parking lot and out to the street as Maya waved goodbye.

Sad to see them go, Maya headed back into the building, and Tinker Bell met her inside the store. "Are you ready to get to work?"

The kitten meowed and then jogged to the front door beside Maya, her bell tinkling. After flipping the sign to Open, Maya unlocked the door and then hung a flyer in the window advertising her tea party service. The store's phone started ringing as she moved to the counter.

"Thank you for calling CeCe's Toy Chest. This is Maya. How may I help you?"

"Hi. My daughter received one of the cards about your tea parties yesterday," a woman said. "I'd like to book a birthday party for her. She's turning seven."

"Wonderful." *How exciting!* She pulled her new booking calendar from the shelf under the counter. "What date works for you? And how many will be in your party?"

Maya smiled, ready to start her new venture.

"It's been a busy week," Gayle said as she locked the front door late Friday afternoon. "In fact, I think this is the busiest week we've had all summer."

Maya nodded as she leaned against the counter. "I agree. And the exciting news is I've booked three tea parties so far. I think the website update, the ads in the paper, and the advertising we did on the Fourth have been successful. Our first party is in a couple of weeks."

"That's fantastic."

Gayle found the Swiffer in the storeroom and began moving

it around the store with Tinker Bell at her heels. "That silly cat! She's after the mop again. You should have named her Denise the Menace!" Gayle growled.

Maya burst into laughter. "Thank you, Gayle."

The woman's brow crumpled. "For what?"

"For always making me laugh."

Gayle waved her off. "Pshaw."

Brody sat in the parking lot of the clinic, trying to decide what to do after dropping Ashlyn at Sammie's to spend the night. Actually, he'd had the same conversation with himself every night since the cookout last Monday.

Didn't he owe Maya the truth, that although he was attracted to her, friendship was still all he could handle between them? The invitation to call her had been a wake-up call, and he had to stop stalling. He'd call her tonight, suggest they get a bite together, then do his best not to hurt her any more than he had to. He only hoped she'd remain a friend—if not for his sake, then for Ashlyn's.

After Gayle left, Maya dusted and straightened the toys on several shelves before pulling her cell phone from her back pocket. She wanted to see if she had any messages from Brody. He'd never called. Maybe his intentions toward her hadn't changed. Either he really was using her as a shield against Kim or he was just the kind of guy who would hug a friend scared of firework noise. He probably had no idea how much that gesture had made her hopeful—and crazy.

"Let's go upstairs, Tink," she called.

She filled the cat's bowls in the kitchen, and once Tinker Bell was occupied with her food, Maya powered up her laptop and checked her email. Once again, she was disappointed to see Kyle hadn't responded. Maybe she was having a hard time figuring out what was happening with Brody, but she shouldn't have to figure out what had happened with Kyle. He owed her an explanation—one that made sense!

Fuming, she opened a new message.

Kyle,

I'm sure you received my first message and have read it by now. I think I'm entitled to know why you just dropped me. Didn't our relationship mean anything to you?

Please email me back.

Maya

After sending it, she logged into Facebook, and her breath caught when she saw an icon indicating she had a message. Opening it, she found a note from Leonard Hamel.

Maya,

Thank you for your friend request. Yes, I knew your mother, and I remember her fondly. She was very important to me. I look forward to hearing from you again.

Sincerely,

Leonard

Then in a second message, he gave her his email address.

Maya's lungs seized, and she gasped for breath. Then her cell phone rang, and she jumped with a start. She pulled it out of her pocket and read Brody's name on the screen.

"Hey," she managed to say, her voice thick with emotion.

"I just dropped Ashlyn off at a sleepover, and I thought maybe we could get together tonight." Road noise sounded in the background, and she imagined him driving his truck while talking over the Bluetooth. "Have you eaten yet? I'm craving a calzone from Little Italy. What do you think?"

Maya opened her mouth, but no words came out.

"Maya? You still there?"

"Yeah," she said, her voice strained.

"What's wrong?" She could hear the concern behind his words.

"I think I just found my father."

Her eyes filled with tears and spilled over. All the emotions she'd kept sealed in her heart poured down her face, and a sob escaped her throat. She'd found her father! And there was a possibility he'd want to know her. This was an impossible dream come true.

"I'm a block away. I'll be right there."

"I'll unlock the door."

Brody sat across from Maya at her kitchen table while he read the message. He'd arrived only a few minutes after their call, then ordered two calzones, adding two pieces of Italian cake for delivery before she handed him the letter from Aunt CeCe.

While her mind continued to spin like a cyclone, Maya hugged her arms tightly to her chest as she awaited his assessment.

He looked up at her and blew out a deep breath. "Wow."

"I know." She sniffed and gestured widely. "I can't believe I found him after all this time."

"This is amazing, Maya." The compassion in his voice gave her the courage to go on.

"I've spent my entire life believing my father didn't want me, feeling like I wasn't worthy of his love. But the truth is he didn't even know my name. And now that I've found him, I keep wondering what could have—"

Her voice broke, and she covered her face with her hands and sobbed. She heard a chair scrape the floor, and then Brody's strong arms looped around her shoulders as he knelt and pulled her against his chest.

"Hey. It's okay."

His voice was low, his breath warm in her ear, sending chills trilling along her spine. She rested her head on his broad shoulder and let her body relax against him, settling into his embrace.

"You can take your time getting to know him," he whispered. "It sounds like he wants to know you."

"I just don't understand why my mother didn't tell me about him. In her letter, Aunt CeCe asked me to forgive her, but it still doesn't make any sense. She could have told me when I was old enough to understand." She closed her eyes and realized how safe and protected she felt in his arms.

His head bobbed with a nod. "You're right, and now that you know the truth, you can decide what to do with the information."

The doorbell rang, and he stood. "I'll get our food."

She pulled out plates and utensils, and when Brody returned with the Little Italy bag, a delicious aroma escaped to fill the kitchen. They washed their hands at the kitchen sink, and then she poured them each a glass of sweet tea.

They ate in silence for several minutes, her mind trying to take it all in.

"So are you going to answer him?"

Her eyes snapped to Brody's. "Now?"

"Sure." He shrugged.

"I have to think about what I'll say."

His hand covered hers. "Take your time. And I can help you with the message if you'd like."

She looked up at his handsome face, and the empathy she found there comforted her battered heart. "Now my mother never wanting to stay put in one house or apartment makes sense. She was afraid he'd find me, so she felt like she had to keep running." She blinked as fear settled over her. "Do you think she was afraid he'd hurt me?"

"I don't think so, Maya." Brody shrugged again. "But most likely she really was afraid he'd use his clout as a powerful family attorney to get custody of you. She was afraid of losing you."

"Right."

She took another bite of her calzone, then wiped her hands on a napkin and clicked on Leonard Hamel's Facebook page. Brody stood and pulled his chair around the table before sitting down beside her.

She studied Leonard's profile photo and then turned to Brody. "Do you think I look like him?"

"Uh, Maya, that's hard to say." Shaking his head, Brody chuckled. "You're a beautiful young woman, and he's a much older man."

Her heart did a little flip in response to his compliment.

"Show me more of his photos," Brody said.

She scrolled through them. Again, they were mostly of Leonard and his German shepherd.

"Well," Brody began, "his dog looks nice."

Laughter exploded from deep in her throat, and the knots of anxiety in her chest relaxed.

Brody bumped his shoulder against hers as he grinned. "There's that gorgeous smile."

She licked her lips and stared at the computer screen. "I want to answer him, but I really need to consider what to say."

"Don't rush it. In the meantime, why don't we finish our calzones and eat the cake I ordered? Then you can think about all the questions you want to ask him. Maybe make a list of them."

"Okay." She studied his face. "You must think I'm a train wreck."

He shook his head. "No. I know what it feels like when everything you think you know is true turns upside down and inside out. I'm just glad you let me offer you a shoulder."

Maya relaxed as she settled back on the sofa beside Brody, their legs stretched out as they rested their feet on the coffee table and ate the cake and drank decaf coffee. Tinker Bell sat beside Brody on the arm of the sofa and purred as he scratched her head and ear. Maya resisted the urge to rest her head on Brody's shoulder and enjoy the comfort touching him gave her. He was indeed her friend—a generous and caring friend—but that was all. She felt sure of that now.

But Brody's presence didn't do much to distract her from all the questions whirling in her mind about Leonard Hamel. She still felt anxious, unsettled, and confused—yet excited—at the possibility of getting to know her father after all these years.

Soon Brody collected his dishes from the coffee table and stood up. "I guess I'd better get home. Will you be all right, Maya?"

"Yes. Thanks."

She walked Brody down to his truck.

"Are you working tomorrow?" she asked as they stood by the driver's side door.

He nodded. "Yup. It's my turn. Ashlyn will be at day camp."

"Okay." She paused. "Thank you for everything—for supper, for listening, for calming me down."

He pulled her into his arms, and she breathed in his familiar scent as she rested her head on his shoulder. "I'm only a phone call away," he whispered. "Don't ever forget that." Then he kissed the top of her head and stepped back. "I'll check on you tomorrow. Sleep well. And if you need someone to talk to, call me. I don't care if it's three in the morning. My phone is always next to me."

"I will. Good night."

He climbed into his truck and started the engine.

Maya watched him disappear from the parking lot and then headed inside. She took a long, hot shower, pulled on a pair of pajama shorts and a tank top, and then sat down at the kitchen table. She opened a new email message and wrote to the man who was most likely her father.

Dear Mr. Hamel,

Thank you for your message. I'll skip the formalities and get right to the point. I believe you might be my father.

My mother never told me about you—not even your name—but I recently found a letter my late great-aunt left me. She said a man named Quincy Hamill had a brief relationship with my mother when she attended Georgetown University thirty years ago, and I'm the result of that relationship.

Your last name is spelled differently, but you're about the right age, and my aunt said my father, like you, was a DC family law attorney. If you are my biological father, I have many questions to ask you. Please let me know if you're interested in communicating with me further.

Thank you for your time.

Sincerely,

Maya Reynolds

She stared at the letter, doubt creeping in. But then a new confidence surged. She had a right to know the truth, and this man could give it to her—if only he would. She just had to be careful with her heart as Aunt CeCe advised.

She hit Send and then leaned back in her chair. Now she had to wait for a response. She just hoped he wouldn't take too long.

Maya climbed into bed, and as Tinker Bell curled up into a ball at her side, she stared up at the ceiling. With all the questions still roaring through her mind, it might be a sleepless night.

As Brody crawled into bed, he mulled over the turn of events. When he realized Maya needed him, of course he'd rushed right over. All thought of discussing their relationship flew out of his head.

"Did you find everything okay?" Maya asked as a young woman with purple hair and a nose ring set a baby doll on the store's counter the following morning.

The woman nodded as she pulled her wallet from her lime-green tote. "Yeah. I needed a birthday gift for my niece. She'll be six."

"You made a great choice."

Maya heard her cell phone ding as she rang up the purchase. Then she handed the woman her change before slipping the doll and a receipt into a bag, adding one of the cards advertising her tea party service. "Enjoy the rest of your weekend, and come back soon."

Maya glanced around the store, and finding all the customers browsing, she pulled her phone out of her pocket and read a text from Brody.

How are you feeling?

She texted back: Okay.

Did you sleep?
A little.
Good.

Thank you again for coming over last night.

Anytime.

She smiled, and her heart swelled with appreciation for him as she responded: I sent him another message last night.

Did he answer?

Last I checked, no.

Keep me posted. Gotta go. A Labrador is waiting for me.

She grinned as she typed, picturing him with his patient: Talk to you later.

~ ·~

Maya had just finished settling the register for the night when she heard a knock on the front door. She laughed when she found Brody and Ashlyn standing on the sidewalk.

Feigning a frown, she opened the door a crack and said, "I'm sorry, but we're closed. You'll have to come back on Monday."

Brody held up a bag from the Jade Kitchen. "But we brought food. And ice cream!"

"Oh. Then come on in!" The delicious smell of Asian food caused her stomach to gurgle as she opened the door and beckoned them in. Once the two had entered the store, Maya locked the door behind them.

Tinker Bell ran to Ashlyn, the bell on her collar ringing as she rubbed up against the little girl's leg.

"Ashlyn wanted to surprise you." He looked a bit sheepish when he nearly whispered, "And I wanted to check on you."

"May I give Tinker Bell some of the treats you keep for her down here?" Ashlyn asked.

"Of course," Maya told her. Ashlyn bolted to the counter, calling Tinker Bell to follow her.

"Have you heard anything?" Brody asked once his daughter was out of earshot.

"No, but I set up my message so he can let me know if he's at least read it. I'll show you what I wrote." Maya logged into her email, then handed him her phone.

Brody frowned as he read the message. "Hmm. Well, don't give up. I'm sure he'll answer soon."

"I hope so. The suspense might kill me."

He handed her the phone, and she pocketed it.

"Why don't we go eat that scrumptious food you brought?" Maya suggested. "Ashlyn, would you please carry Tinker Bell upstairs for me?"

After eating, they scooped up ice cream for dessert, then settled on the sofa to watch *Tangled*. Later they gathered around her kitchen table and played Uno until Ashlyn couldn't keep her eyes open.

"It's time to go," Brody said. "You look like you're half asleep already, Ash."

The little girl moaned. "But I'm having fun."

"I'm sure your dad will bring you back to visit me soon."

"Go use the bathroom before we leave," Brody told her. After his daughter left the room, he pointed to Maya's phone. "Check again."

When she did, her heartbeat picked up speed. "He read it."

"Awesome."

She frowned. "But he hasn't responded."

"He will."

"How do you know?"

"I just have this feeling."

Ashlyn returned, rubbing her eyes and yawning. "Thank you for having us, Miss Maya."

Suppressing a grin, Maya strode over and kissed the top of Ashlyn's head. "Go home and get some good rest, and I'll see you soon."

"Okay." Ashlyn crouched down and gave Tinker Bell a hug. "Bye, Tink."

Maya turned to Brody. "Thank you for coming."

"Keep me posted." He touched her hand. "Remember, you can text or call me anytime."

"Thank you."

She let them out the back door, then hustled upstairs. She had to tell Kiana the latest news.

Chapter 15

"I need to talk to you," Maya told Gayle as soon as the woman traipsed into the store Monday morning.

Gayle frowned as she dropped her belongings on the counter. "Sounds serious."

"Did you know the truth about my father?"

"The truth?"

"Just answer the question. Please."

"All CeCe told me was that he was a boyfriend of Vickie's who left her before you were born. Isn't that the truth?"

Maya pulled her aunt's letter from her pocket and handed it over. "Read this. Then I'll tell you what happened over the weekend."

While Gayle sat on a stool behind the counter and read the letter, Maya busied herself with straightening a few displays and setting out a few more video games. Then she unlocked the front door and switched the sign to Open. She returned to the counter and found Gayle frowning at the paper in her hands.

When she met Maya's gaze, she shook her head. "Sweetie, I had no idea."

"I was led to believe he abandoned me, when the truth is I was hidden from him."

Gayle held up the letter. "Well, it sounds like Vickie was truly afraid she would lose you."

"But she could have told me everything when I was an adult and let me decide if I wanted to meet him."

Gayle nodded. "That's true."

"I believe I've found him on social media, and we've communicated in writing a few times. An exchange of messages on Facebook, and then I wrote an email."

"Let me see."

Maya let her read all the messages on her phone, including the email she sent. She also showed her Leonard's Facebook profile.

"Well now. He's handsome, and he says he's a widower." Gayle smiled. "Maybe he's a good man and he's delighted to have finally found you after all these years."

"But if he's such a great guy, why was my mom so afraid of him?" A dart of nerves made her stomach clench.

"I don't know, but after she learned he'd deceived her in the first place, she obviously felt she had to protect you."

Maya studied the profile. "I'm anxious for him to respond, but he might not be interested in knowing me."

Gayle tilted her head. "Or he's just as shocked and emotional as you are."

"Why do you think Aunt CeCe kept the truth from me even after Mom was gone?"

"I honestly don't know, although she was one to keep a promise." Gayle shrugged. "At least she left you the letter."

As Maya considered that, the bell above the door dinged, announcing their first customer.

Maya swiped her sweaty hands down her shirt and tried to turn her attention to the job at hand. But anxiety gripped her once again. She wanted to hear from Leonard Hamel, and she wanted him to confirm what she already knew—that he was in fact her father.

The following evening Maya pulled the last new teddy bear from a box and set it on the shelf with the rest. She'd decided to work in the store late to try to wear herself out, hoping that would help her sleep.

Leonard Hamel had finally answered her, and she'd sent him another email in response. Now she couldn't stand just sitting in her apartment waiting to hear from him again. She and Brody had texted briefly earlier, and she'd considered inviting him and Ashlyn over. But she didn't want to appear too anxious to see him. And since this whole situation with finding her father had made her too distracted to write, she figured concentrating on the store was her best option.

When her phone rang and she found Kiana's name on her display, she answered it. "Hi, Kiana."

"What's the latest with your dad?"

"It's gotten pretty interesting. I'll open my laptop and read the latest messages to you."

"Oh! I can't wait!"

Maya rushed upstairs and into her office, where Tinker Bell lay sprawled out on the desk chair. She took her laptop to the kitchen table.

"Okay, so here's what he sent last night, after you and I talked: 'Maya, first, please call me Leonard. Also, I want to say that I've been waiting nearly thirty years for this day. When Vickie told me she was pregnant, I was stunned. I regret the many mistakes I've made in my life, but losing the opportunity to know you is the one I regret most.'"

"Wow," Kiana said. "Just wow."

"I know. Then he said, 'I tried to find Vickie after she left, but it was as if she disappeared. I assumed she moved in with the aunt she talked about so much, but she'd never told me where she lived or her name. Until now I didn't know if she chose to keep you or made an adoption plan or even if you were a girl or a boy. So to answer your first question, yes, of course I'm interested in speaking with you further. And I'm happy to answer your questions. I also have some for you, but ask your questions first. Sincerely, Leonard.'"

"Wow!" Kiana said again. "Oh my goodness. I'm going to cry. It's so amazing that he wants to know you!"

Maya nodded even though Kiana couldn't see her. Why they didn't video chat, she didn't know. "Yes. But let's not get ahead of ourselves. Let me read you my response. It's long, but I have a lot to get off my chest. 'Dear Leonard, thank you for taking the time to respond and for allowing me to ask you questions. As I said before, my aunt wrote that my mother had a brief affair with you. She said when she discovered she was pregnant and shared the news with you, you confessed you were married.'"

Maya took a deep breath. "'You also told her your wife was

unable to give you children, and between that and how you'd deceived her, she was afraid you'd use your money and power as a family lawyer to take me away from her. That's why she left and moved in with her aunt. She also changed her last name to Reynolds, making it harder for you to find her.'

"And then I got to my questions: 'Did you prey on my mother— a young, naive student all alone at Georgetown? Do you have other victims like her? Is that another thing you confessed to her? And what did you do to make her think you might try to take me away from her? I'm not asking you these questions to accuse you. My only purpose is to understand why she felt she had to keep the truth from me. I thank you in advance for your honesty. Sincerely, Maya.'"

She held her breath, waiting for Kiana's response.

"Triple wow," Kiana finally said. "You did get right to the point. Has he read that message?"

Maya sighed. "Yes. But I probably scared him off. I bet my questions lost any chance to hear his side of what happened."

"Give him time. Have you talked to Brody?"

"He called earlier, and I filled him in when he was between patients. But then he had to go because someone came in with an emergency." Maya frowned as her jaw tightened. "I could hear Kim in the background sounding all flirty as she said, 'Dr. Brody, we're ready for surgery.'" She rolled her eyes as she rested her elbow on the table and her chin on her palm. "I'm still convinced she's after him."

"Oh, whatever, My! He was so totally into you when I was there."

"Maybe, but he still hasn't told me he is. I still think he just wants to be friends." *A friend who puts his arms around me when I don't want to be alone.*

"Give him time too."

Maya sighed. "It really doesn't matter. What I need right now is a friend to help me navigate these strange and choppy waters with my father, and he's being the friend I need."

"Oh. I'm sorry I haven't been there for you."

"Oh no, no," Maya said quickly, feeling a stab of guilt. "You've been here for me, and I appreciate that. You're always an amazing support. You're the sister I never had, Kiana." She paused. "I just meant Brody is also being a really good friend, and that's what I care about. I need him as a friend more than a boyfriend right now."

Kiana hesitated. "Well, I hope you hear back from your dad soon. You have to keep me posted."

"I will." Maya smiled. It was good to talk to the friend who knew her best.

～•～

The bell above the door dinged Saturday afternoon, announcing a customer as Maya swept the hallway floor. "Welcome to CeCe's Toy Chest," she called as she entered the store.

"Thank you," Brody said as he and Ashlyn stood by the counter grinning.

Her heart beat faster as she brushed her hands down the front of her shirt and wished she'd done more than put her hair up in a ponytail. Some mascara would have helped too. "Hi. What a nice surprise."

Ashlyn rushed over and hugged her. She was wearing the beaded necklaces and rubber bracelets Maya had given her. "I missed you this week."

"I missed you too." Maya touched her nose.

"I'm sorry we haven't stopped by before now." Brody grimaced. "Work has been crazy. I can't tell you how many emergencies we've had. Both Cam and I have stayed late every day. Kim says we should hire a third vet, but I don't know . . ."

Maya's stomach curdled at the mention of Kim's name. Oh, if only she could get that jealousy under control.

"There's Tinker Bell!" Ashlyn announced before running to the bike section.

"How are things here?" Brody asked, resting one hip against the counter.

"Good. I've booked some more parties, which is great for business." She shrugged.

His brow pinched. "Have you heard from your father since we last talked?"

"No." She heaved out a heavy sigh. "I guess that tells me how serious he is about knowing me." She pulled out her ponytail and tried to fluff her hair without looking like she was primping. "I know I asked him some hard questions, but now I see why my mother wanted to keep him away from me. He's not the man she thought he was when . . . you know."

"Don't give up on him yet."

"How can you say that?" She threw her hands up in the air,

frustration burning through her chest. "I've waited my whole life to learn about my father, and when I finally find him, he bails." She hopped up on a stool. "Maybe I came on too strong, but I need to know the answers to the questions I asked." She rubbed the bridge of her nose. "My tone might have been too harsh, though."

"May I read what you wrote?"

"Sure." She pulled her phone from her pocket, then opened the email for him.

"Miss Maya!" Ashlyn called. "Tinker Bell likes the necklaces you gave me."

"Don't let her break them." Maya looked over at Brody, waiting for his thoughts as she hugged her arms to her middle.

He looked up and handed her the phone. "You weren't too harsh."

"Really?" She gave him a stern expression. "Don't lie to me, Dr. Tanner."

He grinned, and that cute dimple appeared. "I'm not lying, Maya. You said nothing wrong, and if he decides not to answer, then, unfortunately, you'll know he's not really interested in knowing you."

Maya moaned, guilt eating up her insides as she suddenly felt ashamed for being angry with her mother. "That's what my fear is."

"Hey, Ashlyn," Brody called.

She scampered over to them. "Yes, Daddy?"

"You know what? I think we all need to have some fun. What's something fun we can do? Maybe ride bikes or play miniature golf?"

"Let's go to the county fair!" Ashlyn exclaimed.

Brody turned to Maya and lifted his eyebrows. "What do you think, Maya?"

She shrugged, not sure she was up for rides or fair food. But at least she'd be with Brody and Ashlyn. "Sure. Let me just close up the store."

~~~~~~~

Forty-five minutes later, Brody pulled his pickup into the fairgrounds parking lot. After buying their tickets, they strode inside, and Brody scanned the knots of roller coaster riders screaming as the cars zoomed past on nearby tracks. Others stood in line to sample offerings from food vendors.

In the distance, he spotted carnival games, a carousel, a large swinging pirate ship, a stage for shows, and kiddie rides. He breathed in the enticing aroma of popcorn mixed with baked pretzels, cotton candy, and the cocoa butter always present near beach communities.

"So what should we ride first?" he asked.

Ashlyn jumped up and down. "The Screamer!" She pointed to the line leading to a gigantic roller coaster. Then she took Maya's hand in hers and tugged. "Let's go. The line is short right now."

"Oh no, no, no." Maya pulled her hand from Ashlyn's. "No, thank you." She held her hand out to Brody. "I'll hold your phone, your wallet, and your keys. You two go have fun."

Ashlyn shared a look of disbelief with her father and then turned back to Maya. "You're afraid of riding roller coasters?"

"Yes, I am." Maya lifted her chin.

"Have you ever ridden one?"

"Yes, I have, but I don't like them."

Brody held up his hands, palms out. "Wait a minute. You've been to Disney World, and you're telling me you don't like roller coasters?"

"If you remember our conversation correctly, I told you my favorite rides were Pirates of the Caribbean and It's a Small World." She jammed her hands on her hips and looked adorable. "I tried Space Mountain once and almost wound up sick. I had a bad headache the rest of the day too."

Brody and Ashlyn shared another shocked expression.

"Miss Maya, maybe you just rode the *wrong* roller coaster. If you try this one, you might change your mind."

"No, I won't." Maya frowned. "A few of my friends dragged me to Carowinds for a so-called day of fun a couple of years ago. They conned me into going on Fury 325." She shook her head. "Never again."

"Maya, this one isn't as fast as the Fury, and the drops aren't nearly as high. Just give it a chance."

Maya shook her head a second time. "No."

"Pleeease?" Ashlyn whined.

Maya shook a finger at his daughter. "That puppy-dog look won't work on me, Ashlyn."

"What if I promise to hold your hand the entire time?" Brody asked, his heartbeat skipping at the thought.

Maya hesitated.

"I will too." Ashlyn held out her hand. "We won't let you fall out. We promise."

Maya laughed.

Brody grinned. "I think we got her, Ash."

"Let's go before she changes her mind." Ashlyn took Maya's hand and steered her toward the line for the roller coaster.

Maya's smile wobbled and then flattened as they waited in the short line. She peered up at the bright orange metal track as the red roller coaster car zoomed by, its occupants screaming, hooting, and hollering with delight.

"You got this," Brody reminded her, hoping to ease her nerves. "I promise you it's worth it."

When they walked up the steep steps to the coaster's cars, Ashlyn bolted to their row, hopped into the seat, and fastened her safety harness in quick succession.

When Brody looked over his shoulder, he found Maya frozen in place, her pink Birkenstock sneakers cemented to the metal platform. "Maya?" he asked as he stood with his hand outstretched. "Are you coming?"

An expression of pure terror flickered over her beautiful face.

"Ma'am?" A teenage girl with turquoise-streaked hair and an eyebrow ring appeared beside her. "I need you to either get in the seat or leave through the exit. We have to keep moving."

Maya didn't budge despite the warning.

"Please come with us, Miss Maya," Ashlyn called. "Sit between my dad and me so we can hold your hands like we promised."

"You can do this, Maya," he said.

Maya finally moved past Brody and slipped into the seat.

Brody climbed in and fastened his harness. Maya followed his lead, and when she fumbled, he secured hers. "I promise you'll be okay."

The teenage girl made her way down the line, checking all the harnesses and then giving a thumbs-up to a young man sitting in a booth.

"All right," the guy's voice called over the intercom. "Who's ready to scream?"

The roller coaster train jerked to life and then started its journey forward, going up, up, up, up.

"Are you ready, Miss Maya?" Ashlyn called.

Maya kept her eyes closed as she shook her head.

"Maya," Brody said. "Look at me." He held his hand out to her.

She opened one eye.

"Hold my hand."

Maya reached out and threaded her fingers with his, and he relished the warmth of her skin against his.

"I won't let go," he said, intent on the promise.

"Miss Maya," Ashlyn said, holding out her own hand. "Hold mine too."

Maya did.

Ashlyn smiled. "Now you're ready."

"Okay," Maya managed to say.

The roller coaster train came to the top of the hill, hesitated for a second, and then started its plummet. Brody kept his eyes on Maya. She sucked in a breath, opened her mouth, and then screamed.

The roller coaster kept going down, down, down, zooming through twists and turns. Suddenly, Maya's lips turned up in a grin, and then she screamed again as the roller coaster took them upside down—still twisting as it accelerated through more turns.

Brody laughed. She was enjoying the ride after all!

The roller coaster made another dip, and as Maya held tight to

Brody's and Ashlyn's hands, she screamed again. But her expression seemed filled with delight, not fear.

When the roller coaster climbed another hill, Brody looked up just as a flash of light exploded. Someone had taken their photo.

After a few more dips, twists, and turns, the roller coaster slowed down and came back to the station. When the train came to a stop, Maya released their hands.

"What'd you think?" Ashlyn asked as they climbed down the stairs toward the souvenir stand.

Maya grinned. "It was fun."

"Ha!" Brody said. "We told you so!"

Brody looked up at a screen and spotted their photo. The three of them were grinning up at the camera, holding hands. He smiled, recalling the feel of Maya's skin against his.

"Would you like the photo?" he asked her.

"Yes." Maya reached into her pocket.

"Me too!" Ashlyn said.

"I'll get it." Brody looked at Maya. "I'll scan it when we get home and text it to you."

He paid for the photo, and they walked away. But then Maya slowed, and he turned to see her grinning.

"Let's ride it again," she said.

"That was the perfect afternoon," Maya said as she settled back in the passenger seat of Brody's pickup truck. "Thank you so much. This was just what I needed."

"You're welcome." Brody peered into the rearview mirror and smiled. "Ashlyn has already nodded off back there. I think you wore her out."

"What do you mean? She wore me out. My feet are so sore, but other than that, I feel wonderful." She untied her shoes and let them drop onto the floor mat.

She smiled to herself, recalling their jubilant time filled with rides, laughter, sweet treats, and happiness. She realized they'd ridden both of the fair's roller coasters twice each.

Maya's smile faded as she silently scolded herself. She rubbed her forehead, longing to banish all thoughts of Leonard Hamel from her mind. But he'd already taken up permanent residence there, and she was determined to evict him.

Brody gave her a sideways glance. "What's on your mind?"

"You know the answer to that question."

"Have you checked your messages?"

"I'm afraid to."

Silence stretched between them, and the hum of the truck engine filled the cab.

She suddenly sighed, feeling his silent encouragement. "Fine. I will." She pulled her phone from her back pocket and pulled up her email, then stilled when she found a message from Leonard.

Maya,

I've started and deleted my response to you at least a dozen times. But each time I tried to answer your questions and explain what happened, it seemed to come out wrong. I know you don't owe me the benefit of the doubt, but would you be willing to talk to me by phone? If so, then please call me. My cell number is at the bottom of this message.

I look forward to hearing from you. Call anytime.

Sincerely,

Leonard

Maya blinked and then read it again. He hadn't given up on her, and she hadn't pushed him away. In fact, her father wanted to talk to her—to have a real conversation.

"Did you hear from Leonard? What did he say?"

Maya read the message to Brody and then looked at him. "So he wants me to call him."

"Are you going to?"

She nodded. "Yes, I think I will."

"Good." Brody smiled. "Do you want me to be there?"

She felt a sudden flare of confidence. "No, thank you. I've got this."

"You do." Reaching over, he grabbed her hand, the feel of his touch giving her comfort. "And if you need to talk after you speak to him, especially if Kiana isn't available, call me. I don't care what time it is. I'll keep my ringer on."

She smiled, appreciation and affection both coursing through her. "Thank you."

Chapter 16

Maya paced her family room as Tinker Bell watched from the sofa. "Okay, Tink. I'm going to call my dad now." It sounded so strange to say those words.

After Brody dropped her off, Maya had rushed inside, showered, and changed into a pair of yoga pants and a T-shirt. Then she'd stared at Leonard's message while trying to muster the courage to call him.

She could do this. She could face whatever he told her, no matter how painful it was. She was strong and brave.

Taking a deep breath, she slipped in her wireless earbuds and then pushed the number already programmed into her phone.

After two rings, a man's voice answered. "Hello?"

"Hi." She sounded breathless, but she couldn't help it. "Is this Leonard Hamel?"

"Yes."

"I'm Maya Reynolds."

"Maya. Hi. I was hoping you'd call."

She sat down on the sofa beside the kitten, and an awkward pause stretched between them.

"It's good to hear your voice," he added.

"Thank you."

"Well, I looked at your Facebook profile, and I see you're a published author."

"Yes, I am."

"That's amazing. Your books look interesting. I ordered them all. I'm eager to read them."

She smiled. That was unexpected. "Thanks."

"So you sent me some questions to answer. I suppose we should start there."

"Okay." She rested her feet on the coffee table and rubbed Tinker Bell's head.

"You have every right to think the worst of me, Maya. But I promise all I'll ever tell you is the truth." He took a deep breath. "I never meant to take advantage of your mother. When I went into the café the first time I met her, no, I wasn't looking for young college women to use."

Maya pursed her lips as she continued to rub the cat's head.

"I was there looking for a meal after another stressful day at the firm, and Vickie just had a way about her. Yes, I was lonely, but I wasn't actively looking for someone to have an affair with. It just happened. I'm not proud of it, but it happened. I fell in love with your mother."

"But you were married."

He sighed. "Yes, but it's more complicated than that."

"What do you mean?" Maya settled back on the sofa.

"Patrice, my wife, was ill."

Maya's eyes narrowed. "What do you mean by ill?"

"We met in college and married right after I finished law school.

We were happy and looking forward to having a family when she was the victim of a drunk driver, hit head-on during her commute home from work one day. She was a teacher."

Maya gasped, cupping her hand to her mouth. "Oh no. I'm so sorry."

"It was a shock."

"What happened to her?"

"When I met your mother, Patrice had been in a coma for three years. I already felt like a widower even though I was technically married."

Maya considered this. "Is that why you stopped wearing your wedding ring? Were you living your life as a single man?"

"Yes and no. Not wearing my ring avoided awkward conversations. New clients regularly asked about my wife and family, and I hated seeing the pity in their eyes once they learned my story. When I stopped wearing my ring, I didn't have to answer their questions. People assume you have children when you're married and in your later twenties. It was easier to just let them believe I was single. Of course, then I had to deal with some flirty clients, but that was less painful than being forced to admit my wife was in a coma with little chance of coming out of it."

Maya nodded, and she felt her heart softening toward this man who had clearly suffered a tragedy. "That makes sense."

"That still doesn't excuse my having an affair with your mother. She was barely twenty-one."

"And you were twenty-nine? Almost thirty?"

"Yes."

"So you're approaching sixty."

"That's right."

"And you loved my mother?"

"Yes. I knew her for only a brief amount of time, but the connection between us was unmistakable. She was beautiful, sweet, and easy to talk to. When I was with her, I could relax."

"But you weren't honest with her. In her letter, my aunt said when my mom told you she was pregnant, she thought she could quit school, marry you, and raise me with you as a family. She was crushed when you told her you were married. You lied to her, Leonard."

He sighed. "You're right. I made mistakes, Maya, and I'm sorry for that. Losing her and the opportunity to know you is the biggest regret of my life."

Maya blinked, wanting to believe him, but she pushed on, needing to know more. "Were you angry when she told you she was pregnant?"

"I was stunned but not angry. I'd always wanted a family, but at first I was just shocked by the news. After I confessed I was married and mentioned my wife couldn't give me children, I wanted to tell Vickie we'd figure out what to do together. That I wanted to be a part of her life and yours. But she walked out on me, jumping into a cab before I could do that.

"I was afraid to just show up where she lived until she had some time to think. But when I didn't hear from her, I called her apartment and then the café. We didn't have cell phones then. Her roommates and coworkers said she left town, but I had no idea where to even begin looking for her. As I told you before, I assumed she'd gone to her aunt, but Vickie'd never told me where she lived or even what her name was. I wanted to find her and make things right, but I couldn't."

Maya leaned back on the sofa, and her chest tightened as she imagined how life could have been if he'd found her mother. "She made that nearly impossible by changing her name."

"I can't blame her," he continued. "That's my fault because I'd lied to her. I'm sorry for hurting her. I wish I could go back in time. I should have told her the truth from the beginning. Maybe we could have found a way to be together, but it was so complicated with Patrice. She needed care, and I wouldn't have abandoned her."

"How is your wife now?"

"She passed away twenty years ago."

"I'm sorry."

"Thank you."

Maya looked down at Tinker Bell, who had rolled onto her back, revealing her belly. She rubbed it, and the cat purred loudly. "My aunt said your name was Quincy. Why do you go by Leonard?"

"My legal name is Quincy Leonard Hamel—the third. It's a mouthful, right?"

"Yes," she said with a chuckle.

"I loved my father and grandfather, but I hated the name Quincy. So I went by Lenny, and then I decided to use Leonard to sound more professional in law school."

"Oh." She hesitated as more questions raced through her mind. "Your Facebook profile says you're a widower. Were you widowed twice?"

"No. I never remarried."

"Do you have any other children?"

"No." He paused. "You talk about your mother in the past tense. When did she pass away?"

"Three years ago."

"I'm so sorry." His voice had softened with both sadness and sympathy.

"Thank you. My mother was stubborn. She had uncontrolled diabetes and refused to see a doctor. By the time she did, she was already in kidney failure, and she soon wound up on dialysis."

"Oh no."

"It was awful. I quit my job as an office manager and moved in to take care of her. Fortunately, I wound up getting my first book contract about that time, and the small advance helped. But Mom also worked for a marketing firm in Charlotte, and they were generous to her until she received disability.

"She went to the dialysis center three times a week because home dialysis couldn't get her levels where they needed to be. It was a nightmare watching her suffer. It was as if I'd already lost my mother." Maya sniffed as grief once again bubbled up.

"I'm sorry you went through that alone."

"My great-aunt came to help us when she could. Mom was never the same, though. The dialysis sapped her energy, and she was sick all the time. I wanted to be tested to see if I could donate a kidney for her, but she wasn't well enough to undergo the surgery. She developed pneumonia and died from complications. She was only forty-eight."

"So young," he said, sounding wistful.

She sniffed. "Yeah."

"Are you in Charlotte?"

"No, I'm in Coral Cove, North Carolina." She hadn't updated her location on Facebook yet. "This is where my great-aunt lived until she passed away in May. She left me her store here. She was my only family. Well, until . . ." Maya cleared her throat. "Anyway, I decided to move here. I took over her store, and I'm living in her apartment above it."

"What kind of store is it? I didn't read many of your posts. I didn't think I . . ."

Had he been about to say he didn't think he had the right?

"It's a toy store called CeCe's Toy Chest. Her name was Cecelia Reynolds. She was my maternal grandmother's sister. She never married or had any children of her own."

"And she did take in your mother when she left Georgetown?"

"Yes. Mom and I lived here while she finished her degree at a college not far from here. Then when I was four, she got a job in Charlotte, and we moved there. But I have no real ties to Charlotte, and I can write anywhere. So I decided to just move here and honor my aunt's legacy." Maya picked up a pillow and fiddled with its fringe.

"Are you working on a book now?"

She snorted. "I should be."

"It sounds like you have a bad case of writer's block."

"That's an understatement. I have a deadline extension until mid-September, but the story isn't going anywhere." She wasn't ready to share the source of her writer's block—her failed relationship with Kyle—which meant she needed to change the subject fast. "And you're a senior partner in your law firm?"

"Yes. But the firm has expanded quite a bit, and I don't work as many hours as I used to. I'm even considering early retirement. I like to spend a lot of time outdoors and with my dog, Ralph."

"Ralph." Maya laughed. "What a great name. I saw photos of him. He's a handsome guy."

"Thank you. And you have a kitten, right? Tinker Bell?"

"That's right."

"I've enjoyed your photos." He was silent for a moment. "You look a lot like Vickie. She was lovely."

"Thank you."

"I always wondered about you. I used to try to imagine what my daughter or son might look like, and I hoped Vickie had kept you." His voice took on a melancholy tone once again. "I would wake up at night sometimes worrying about you—wondering if you needed anything, if you were cold, hungry, safe . . ."

Maya's eyes stung, and she sucked in a breath, trying to keep the tears at bay.

"Maya? Are you still there?"

"I'm here," she managed, her voice gravelly.

"I'm sorry. I didn't mean to upset you."

"You didn't upset me. I'm just feeling overwhelmed. I've waited a long time for this."

"I understand, and this is a lot to take in." He paused for a moment. "Wow. We've been talking for a long time. I should let you get some sleep. We can talk again. Maybe tomorrow?"

She sniffed and wiped her eyes. "That would be nice."

"I have a question for you."

"Okay." She sat forward on the sofa.

"Would it be possible for me to visit you? I can drive down, get a hotel room, and stay for a few days."

She hesitated as she considered his proposal. "Let's talk for a while first."

"Of course. Well, I'll let you go, Maya."

"Good night."

"Good night."

She disconnected the call and then immediately opened her texting app and shot off a text to Brody: We just hung up.

The conversation bubbles began almost immediately—as if he'd been waiting for news.

How'd it go?

She smiled. Really well.

Great! Want to talk?
How about tomorrow?
Okay. Good night.
Sleep well.

Maya carried Tinker Bell to her bedroom and set her on the edge of the bed. Then she climbed under the covers and replayed the conversation with her father.

Her father!

She couldn't stop the what-ifs from rolling through her mind. What if he had been a part of her life? Would he have taken her to that father-daughter dance, where they could have laughed and danced the evening away?

Would he have visited her on birthdays and holidays? Taken her to Disney World and maybe Paris? Dried her tears after the mean girls at school made fun of her? Covered her cuts with Band-Aids? Read her stories at night and then tucked her into bed?

Told her he loved her?

Maya sniffed as more questions consumed her. What if he had found her mother, eventually married her, and given Maya what she'd always wanted—a family with two parents?

Stop torturing yourself!

Maya picked up her phone and looked at the time. It was after midnight. She considered calling Kiana, but she was most likely sleeping. Brody told her she could call him anytime, but he was probably asleep by now too.

She rubbed her eyes as she imagined Leonard sitting with her mother at Maya's high school and college graduation ceremonies. Then her mind turned to the future. He wanted to visit her. Did that mean he truly wanted to cultivate a relationship with her? And if so, what would that look like?

Maya studied the shadows on her ceiling as the air-conditioning clicked on. She had to turn off these thoughts and try to get some sleep. But until then, why not allow her imagination to run wild? She so hoped Quincy Leonard Hamel—the third—genuinely wanted to know his daughter.

Chapter 17

Monday morning Maya and Gayle stood on the sidewalk look-ing at the new display in the toy store's window. Maya had created a tea party, complete with a child's table and two teddy bears and two dolls sitting in the four chairs. The table was adorned with a pink linen tablecloth, a purple-and-blue tea set, and plastic cake.

Behind the tea party, she'd hung a few of the leftover decals from the party room—a few blue birds and tiaras, a pair of glass slippers, and a tree with bright green leaves. Then she'd hung a poster advertising the tea parties, featuring a castle. The entire scene was finished off with white fairy lights.

Gayle clucked her tongue. "You did this yesterday during your talk with your dad?"

"Yup." Maya nodded. "Well, some of it. We didn't talk too long. I'd planned to update the window, but I hadn't had the time or moti-vation. I thought this would be a great way to advertise our new party service."

"It has a dreamy, magical feel to it."

Maya grinned at her friend. "Did you just use the words *dreamy* and *magical* in the same sentence?"

"Don't get used to it." Gayle wagged a finger at her.

Maya laughed. "You don't think the display is too much?"

"No, it's perfect." Gayle folded her arms over her chest and studied Maya. "So your conversation with your father went well?"

"It did, but I don't know . . ."

"Don't know what?"

"Nothing he's said so far seems wrong, but I still wonder if he wants something from me."

"Like what? Money?" Gayle chuckled as they walked back into the store. "He's a successful lawyer, for crying out loud."

"Sure, he says he's a successful lawyer, but what if he's not? What if he lost his job? Or maybe he was disbarred for inappropriate behavior. What if he has a lot of gambling debt? Or owes back taxes?"

Gayle shook her head. "I can see how that wild imagination of yours makes you an author."

"Well, he could be out of money for some reason. Maybe he thinks I inherited some kind of trust fund and I'm an easy target like my mom was. But I *am* older and wiser. That comes with having your heart broken." Maya slipped behind the counter and started straightening a pile of merchandise bags.

"Do you really think he's after something?"

Maya shrugged. "I don't know. I want to believe in him, but I don't want to be stupid." She sat on a stool as Tinker Bell zoomed by, the bell on her collar tinkling away. "He wants to come visit me."

"Did you agree to that?"

"No. But I talked to Brody about it last night, and he thinks I should let him." Maya held up her hand. "He suggested I offer him the names of a few nearby hotels and meet him for dinner. I won't invite him to my apartment since I don't really know him. Brody said he'd even go with me. But I'm not sure I'm ready for a face-to-face meeting yet. I don't want to set myself up for disappointment."

Gayle smiled. "So you're finally seeing Brody?"

"No, we're still just friends." She frowned. "Good friends, but I think he's seeing someone. Someone I doubt will take no for an answer."

"Who?"

"His gorgeous tech, Kim. She invited him out on her cousin's boat yesterday. Get this. She also suggested Ashlyn would have more fun staying with one of her friends, so he left his own daughter behind. But at least he called me when he got home. He said the boat was practically a yacht." Jealousy wrapped around her chest and squeezed her heart when she pictured the beautiful blonde fawning all over Brody.

Gayle huffed. "You're not kidding about her intentions. What man can say no to a yacht?"

〜・〜

"The party was perfect, Maya," Mrs. Wilson said as they stood in the party room Saturday afternoon. "We loved every minute of it, didn't we, Sabrina?"

The seven-year-old, dressed in a poufy pink party dress with a matching shimmering pink tiara on her head, smiled. "Yes. Thank you, Miss Maya."

"I'm so glad you both liked it."

Maya hoped sheer exhaustion didn't show on her face. Her first tea party had gone well, but it wasn't without its bumps in the road.

In fact, her mind had already formed a list of changes for the next one. First, she'd prepare games so the girls wouldn't just run around, shrieking and chasing each other while they waited for Maya to bring them the cake.

She'd also lock Tinker Bell in her apartment so the girls couldn't chase her around the room, trying to hug and kiss her. She was grateful her cat had found a good hiding place and avoided injury to the girls with those claws—which reminded her she had to get those nails trimmed before she was injured herself!

Maya also toyed with the idea of hiring someone to help her run the parties, but she'd have to consider that when they were profitable enough to warrant hiring an extra set of hands.

Maya smiled at the little girl. "Happy birthday, Sabrina."

"Thank you."

Mrs. Wilson and Sabrina walked out, and Maya wilted as she took in the mess—icing smudged on the chairs, paper napkins and plates strewn about, puddles of spilled tea on the tile floor, and platters of uneaten food on the buffet.

Maya dragged her tired legs to a roll of paper towels and began mopping up the mess. Once the room was clean, she tied the trash bag closed and carried it out to the row of cans behind the building. After depositing the bag in the closest one, she looked up, doing a double take when she spotted a pickup truck that looked like Brody's parked beside Gayle's gold Camry.

She hiked back into the building and made a beeline into the store, where she found Brody standing by the counter, his back to her. Gayle was telling him about the fishing trip her grandson had just taken.

When Gayle finished her story, Maya slipped around to face him. He was holding a tray with two cups and a box from Joe's Donut Hut. "Brody. Hi."

"Hi there." He smiled, and the dimple she loved so much appeared. "I thought we should celebrate your first party—if you're not too tired. And unless you have other plans, of course."

"I would love that. I just finished cleaning up the party room." Maya snuck a look at Gayle, who winked at her. "Is Ashlyn at another playdate?" she asked, ignoring the woman.

"All the way 'til nine. You know her social calendar is always full."

Gayle grabbed her purse and the money bag. "I've already swept up and closed the register." She gave Maya a devious smile behind Brody's back. "Have a great evening."

"See you Monday." Maya shot her a menacing look and hoped Brody hadn't seen it.

Gayle waved with a grin and then disappeared down the hall to the back door.

"Would you like to sit up on the roof?" Maya said, offering a view.

"That sounds great."

~⌒•⌒~

Brody followed Maya up the attic steps to the door that led to the flat part of her roof, next to the attic's rafters. They sat down in two of the folding chairs she kept there, and with no two-story buildings in their way, they could see all the way to the beach. He breathed in the familiar and comforting scent of ocean air.

"I already added the cream and sweetener you like." He handed her a cup, then opened the box. "But I bought a half dozen assorted donuts because I didn't know your favorites."

"Mmm. Thank you. And the coffee smells wonderful."

The late-afternoon sound of traffic and conversations of people walking by below filled the air as Maya sipped her hot drink. "Yes, this is positively perfect, Brody. How did you know I needed this?"

"I'm happy to hear that. I was hoping this would be a nice ending to your day." He was enjoying his coffee too. "So the party went well?"

"Yes . . . with lessons learned." She shared a few of her ideas for making the parties run more smoothly. "I have two more coming up, but I've saved the date for Ashlyn's party. I want to do something special for her."

"Thank you." He was so grateful for the way Maya always thought of his daughter. Maya was truly special—a blessing to both Ashlyn and him.

"Yesterday you texted that you had an emergency at the clinic. How was today?"

He shook his head. "So busy." He grimaced. "I also had to give Kim a ride home because her Jeep was in the shop, and then after I picked up Ashlyn from day camp, I completely lost track of time. Otherwise I would have called you." He settled back in the chair. "Did you talk to your dad again last night?"

"Yes. We didn't talk long, but that makes three times this week."

"Why do I hear another *but* in your voice?"

"I want to trust him, but I'm afraid." She brushed a piece of lint off her jeans.

"What are you afraid of?"

She took a deep breath. "Being let down. Being hurt again. Thinking he cares and then losing him. I'm afraid I'll let him into my heart and then he'll crush it the way Kyle did."

Brody bit into a chocolate-covered donut and tried to imagine how it felt to be in Maya's shoes.

"What do you think?" she finally asked him.

Brody set his cup on the small table between them. "It's hard to say since I haven't spoken to Leonard, but from what you've told me, it seems like he's making the effort. And I think finding a family member might be a blessing now that your mom and aunt are gone."

She nodded.

"You and I have that in common, Maya. We've both lost family, and it stinks. Sure, I have Ashlyn, but I miss the rest of my family. And friends are wonderful, but they're not the same."

"Exactly."

"So if you're asking my opinion, I say give Leonard a chance, but be cautious."

"Okay." She looked at him. "Would you like me to order us some food? We can eat up here."

"Sure, but I'm paying."

She rolled her eyes. "Whatever, Dr. Tanner."

He laughed and then pulled out his phone. He loved her sense of humor. "How about we order from that Greek place? I'd love a gyro."

"Ooh! Yes!"

Later, as they ate on the roof with their chairs turned so they could watch the sun set across the bay, Brody said, "Maya, I've been meaning to tell you. I haven't had much time to read lately, but I finished your first book the other night. It was great."

She gave him a look of suspicion tinged with amusement. "Great? So you love romance novels, huh?"

He laughed. "Okay. You got me. I do prefer mysteries and spy novels. But that doesn't mean I don't appreciate a good story. Your characters are believable, and without that the plot doesn't really matter."

"Well, thank you, sir," she said, tilting her head. "But why don't you save the rest for Ashlyn to read when she's older?"

Soon the sun glowed low in the sky, its luminous colors streaking across the horizon as the lightning bugs began their nightly dance.

Maya leaned back in her chair and sighed.

He lifted an eyebrow. "What's that sigh for?"

"I just relaxed for the first time this week."

"Me too."

Darkness crept in, and Maya popped up and flipped on the white fairy lights strung across the roof. She returned to her chair, and her smile sent awareness zinging through him. Did she have any idea how stunning she was?

"I love these." He pointed above them. "They're the perfect amount of light. They don't take anything away from those beautiful stars above us."

She nodded. "My aunt and I weren't always at the beach. Sometimes we'd sit up here at night and make up stories. She encouraged me to let my imagination run wild, and then I wrote the stories down. She's the reason I never gave up on my dream of holding one of my own novels in my hands. I couldn't wait to see my name on the cover of my own creation. This was our special place, our little hideaway after working in the store all day. We'd watch the sunset and then make plans for the next day."

He angled his body toward her. "Let's do that."

"Do what?"

"Plan something for tomorrow afternoon. Why don't we ride bikes at the state park?"

"Will Ashlyn be up for that after a sleepover? I'd need a nap if I was her."

He shrugged. "If not, we'll do something else."

"Okay."

They gathered their trash, deposited it in the apartment, and then she walked him down to the parking lot.

"So do you think you'll let Leonard come visit?"

She kicked a stone with the toe of her Birkenstock sneaker. "Yes. I think I'm ready to see him. I want to look him in the eye and see if he wants a true father-daughter relationship."

"Why don't you call his bluff if that's what this is? If he doesn't come, then you'll know he's not really interested." Brody touched her hand, feeling protective of her. "And if he does come, I'll join you if you want me there."

"Thank you." Maya nodded slowly as if rolling the idea around in her mind. "I don't have any tea parties next weekend. Maybe I'll ask him to come down then."

"Let me know what he says." He brushed her cheek with a featherlight touch, and the feel of her soft, smooth skin sent his nerve endings zinging.

Then he realized he'd done it again, and he lowered his hand. The look in Maya's eyes was the same as the night they'd watched the fireworks. What was he doing? Ashlyn was still his focus, and he knew only too well that a woman—even a good woman like Courtney or Maya—could break his heart.

"Well, good night, Maya."

"Good night."

And then he turned to leave. He wanted Maya in his life and in his daughter's, but he had to be a lot more careful.

After they said good night, Maya bounded up to her apartment. Once she'd fed Tinker Bell and given her fresh water, she pulled out her phone and dialed Leonard's number.

He answered almost immediately. "Maya, hi. I was hoping you'd call. How'd your first party go today?"

She smiled as she sat down at the kitchen table. He'd remembered that today was a big day for her business. "It went well. But I definitely learned how to make the next party even better."

"Good."

"Listen, I have a question for you."

"Go for it."

"Are you serious about coming to visit me?"

"Of course I am."

She took a deep breath. "How about next weekend?"

"I'd love to. Just let me check with the office. I'll see if I can drive down on Friday and stay until Monday morning. Does that sound good?"

"Yes." Her heart took on wings.

"Would you please text me the name of a hotel you'd recommend?"

"Of course."

"Great. Now tell me about these lessons learned."

As Maya fetched a bottle of water from the refrigerator and started telling her father about the party, she couldn't help but imagine talking with him in person for the very first time.

Chapter 18

Friday afternoon Maya paced around the store, wringing her hands. The day had come—her father would be here soon. But her excitement had morphed into anxiety. Thankfully, the store was empty of customers, which meant she could freely express her doubts to Gayle.

"What if I made a mistake inviting him here?" she said. "What if I hate him? And what if he hates me? Then he'll have driven more than seven hours just to find out he can't stand his one and only child!"

"Calm down, Maya!" Gayle called from the counter. "He won't hate you. You two already have what sounds like a better relationship than I had with my father. That grumpy old coot barely ever looked at or talked to me or my seven siblings." She tilted her head. "Maybe it was because he and Mama had too many kids. I suppose I'd be a grouch if I had eight kids of my own. I'm glad I decided to have only two."

Maya had spent the week preparing for the visit. After enjoying an afternoon of riding bikes at the state park with Brody and Ashlyn on Sunday, she'd set to work making her apartment and the store sparkle. She'd finally finished unpacking and organizing her bedroom, the guest room, and the office, and then she'd cleaned all the windows. After mopping all the floors, she'd even mopped the storeroom.

But now all that effort felt like a mistake, and worry climbed onto her shoulders and dug its claws into her already tight muscles.

Maya halted in front of the counter. "I really don't know him, Gayle. How do I know he's really Leonard Hamel? People set up fake accounts all the time without the real people even knowing theirs has been copied." She cupped her hand to her forehead. "What if Ralph isn't even his dog?"

"Now, listen to me, Maya." Gayle leaned forward and began speaking to her as if she were a toddler. "Stop stressing out. You're jumping to ridiculous conclusions. How would he know so much about your mother if he wasn't the man she knew? Everything will be just fine."

"But what if it's not?"

Gayle took Maya's hands in hers. "It will be. You're going to enjoy getting to know each other this weekend, and then you'll take it from there."

"But what if it's a disaster?"

"Then he'll go home on Monday, and it will be over." Gayle came around the counter and rested her hand on Maya's shoulder. "But it *won't* be a disaster. He's dropping everything and driving seven hours to come here." She pointed to the floor. "He's doing this because he wants to spend time with *you*."

For the next few hours Maya's stomach was tied in a knot so tight she thought she might be sick. She tried to concentrate on her customers, but her mind continued to run through disaster scenarios—a horrific weekend spent with this stranger who said he was her father. She'd been so sure, but now . . .

When five o'clock rolled around, Maya flipped the store's sign to Closed while Gayle closed down the register. Just as Maya was heading to the storeroom to retrieve the Swiffer, her phone chimed with a message. She pulled it from her back pocket and saw it was from Leonard.

> Hi. Just made it to Little Italy. I'm getting a table. Come on over when you can. Looking forward to seeing you in person.

Maya's stomach dipped. "He's here. I need to get cleaned up."

Gayle waved her off. "I'll finish closing down."

"Thank you."

But when Maya hesitated, Gayle added, "Just go, for crying out loud. Relax and enjoy yourself. It's going to be wonderful."

"I hope so." Maya lifted Tinker Bell from the Barbie aisle and hurried upstairs.

After feeding the cat, she changed into a blue sundress featuring little white daisies and pulled her hair back in a French braid before applying a little makeup. Then she pushed her feet into a pair of white wedge sandals, picked up her phone and purse, and hustled downstairs.

She nearly sprinted the two blocks to Little Italy.

"Hi," she told the hostess. "I'm looking for Leonard Hamel."

"Right this way." The young woman led her across the busy restaurant. It seemed nearly every table was full.

The delicious smells of tomato sauce, fresh bread, and oregano filled her senses as the woman led her toward a booth in a far corner.

"Thank you," Maya told her. "I see him." The man had his head down, perusing the menu, but she could still tell this was the face she'd seen on Facebook.

She stood straight and sucked in a breath, then joined him. "Leonard."

He looked up, and his eyes seemed to glisten as he slid out of the booth. He wore a pair of tan chinos and a dark blue collared shirt, and he had the same salt-and-pepper hair, gray eyebrows, brown eyes, and trim physique she'd seen in his profile photo. What surprised her was his height—he wasn't as tall as she'd expected him to be. He was a few inches shorter than Brody.

"Maya. You're even more beautiful in person." He held out his hand and gave hers a firm shake. Then he gestured to the seat across from his. "Please. Sit down."

She slipped into the booth, then deposited her purse on the bench seat and folded her hands on the table. "How was your trip down?"

"Long and boring, but that's not a bad thing." He chuckled.

"Right."

They shared an awkward smile, and then she pretended to study her menu even though she just about knew it by heart.

"So what's good here?"

"Everything." She peeked up at him. "I normally have the chicken parmesan, and Brody has the lasagna." She stilled when she realized what she'd said. She hadn't told Leonard about Brody yet.

Leonard's eyebrows lifted. "Who's Brody?"

She cleared her throat, embarrassed. "Um, he's a good friend." She smiled awkwardly, hoping he wouldn't ask more questions. "But anything on the menu is good here."

They both turned their attention to the menus again, and soon a young man appeared at their table. "May I take your order?"

"Are you ready?" Leonard asked Maya.

"Yes. I'll have the chicken parmesan and a Diet Coke." Maya handed the server her menu.

Leonard looked up from his. "Lasagna and a glass of water."

"Coming right up. I'll be back with salad and breadsticks."

"So," Leonard began, "how was your day at the store?"

Maya fingered the edge of the white linen tablecloth. "It was busy." She told him about one of her challenging customers—a woman who wanted gifts for her teenage twins that were the same yet different. She was sure his eyes would glaze over, but he seemed interested in everything she said. At least her story filled the awkward space between them.

The server arrived with their drinks, salads, and a basket of breadsticks. As they ate, Maya tried to think of something else to say to this man she didn't really know. Phone chats went only so far. This was going to be an uncomfortable evening!

"I've read two of your books this week."

Maya's gaze flicked to his. "Two of them?"

He nodded while wiping tomato sauce from his clean-shaven chin. "Yes. I read *On a Summer Breeze* and *Not a Moment Too Soon*. I really enjoyed them."

She studied him. "Not many men read romance novels. Are you trying to butter me up?"

To her surprise, he laughed, and she appreciated the warm, comforting sound. She joined in and suddenly felt as if the ice between them had broken.

"No, Maya. I'm not. I'm just telling you I'm impressed by your talent. Although I can't take any credit, I'm proud of you."

His words sank through her skin and wrapped around her heart. Not in a million years would she have imagined hearing her father say them.

But then her smile faded as emotion swelled in her throat.

"Did I say something wrong?" he asked.

"No." She shook her head. "You just said the most beautiful thing ever. But . . . but tell me all about your work."

"There's not much to tell. As you know, I work in family law, and not all of it is pleasant."

For the rest of dinner, Leonard told her about his law practice, then about his life in Washington, DC, his condo, a few of his travels, and his German shepherd. They ordered tiramisu and coffee for dessert, and she told him all about spending summers in Coral Cove.

They were both surprised how much time had passed when Leonard paid the bill, leaving a significant cash tip on the table. Maya was impressed by it, although she did wonder if her father was trying to impress *her*.

When they walked outside the sun was still setting, and the air was humid and heavy. But the sky was clear, and the emerging stars shone bright. Clusters of people moved past them on foot and riding bikes. Vehicles motored by, music blaring from some of their speakers.

"Is this a typical Friday evening in Coral Cove?" Leonard asked as he looked around.

"It is. We get a lot of visitors on summer weekends."

"I love it." He paused. "How about we meet for breakfast tomorrow?"

Maya nodded. "That would be great. Then I'll give you a tour of my little town."

"Perfect. What time and where should I meet you?"

"How about nine o'clock at my store?" She pulled out her phone. "I'll text you the address."

"I'll look forward to it. Have a good night, Maya."

"You too."

She waited for him to start toward his car before she took her phone from her purse. Then she called Brody's number as she started back to her apartment.

"How'd it go?" he asked.

"It was awkward at first, but then we had a really nice talk. We're going to meet for breakfast tomorrow, and then I'll give him a tour of Coral Cove. He'll come to the store first."

"That's great." Brody paused for a moment. "Have you made plans for tomorrow evening?"

"No. Do you have something in mind?"

"Well, you once told me you liked my super-awesome deck and my amazing grilling abilities."

Maya couldn't stop a grin as she crossed a street. "Are you suggesting we come to your house for a cookout?"

"Maybe." She could almost see his own grin with that charming dimple on his chin. "Well, what do you think? I figure you'll want my expert opinion on your father."

"I love that idea, but I should bring what we grill."

"My freezer is always stocked."

"How about this?" She stopped at the next corner and waited for the light to change. "Leonard and I will pick up the groceries, and then we'll use your super-awesome deck and your amazing grilling abilities."

"Perfect."

"Thank you for inviting us." The light changed, and she stepped into the street. "And of course I want your opinion of him."

"It's a plan. Just text me and let me know what time. Ashlyn and I will be ready."

"Thank you, Brody." Her heart warmed at the thought of seeing him tomorrow.

"I'm so happy for you."

"What do you mean?" she asked as her building came into view.

"I'm glad you had a good time with your father and that the weekend is off to a good start. That's what I'd hoped when you told me he was coming to see you."

"I appreciate that." Maya heard Ashlyn calling for him in the background. "You'd better go see what your daughter wants."

"Okay. Have a good night."

"You too. And give Ashlyn a kiss for me." She disconnected the call and walked around to the store's parking lot, then unlocked the back door, glad for a well-lighted area.

After greeting Tinker Bell upstairs, she pulled off her shoes and flopped onto the sofa. Then she called Kiana and told her best friend all about her first meeting with her father.

"I think he's here," Gayle called as she stood behind the counter at the store.

Maya headed for the front door just as Leonard stepped in. "Good morning."

He gave her a wave. "I'm a little early."

"That's fine." Maya gestured toward Gayle. "Leonard Hamel, this is Gayle Hughes. She was my great-aunt's best friend. She's been working here ever since the store opened."

Gayle shook his hand. "What she's trying to say is that I'm older than dirt. Nice to meet you, Leonard."

Her father laughed. "It's a pleasure to meet you too." He glanced around the store. "This place is great. Give me the twenty-five-cent tour."

"I'd love to." Maya steered him around the store, pointing out the different aisles and telling him about her time there as a child and a teenager. When she led him over to the counter, she picked up the framed photo of her with her mother and great-aunt. "Aunt CeCe always kept this photo here. It's one of my favorites."

She handed him the frame, and his smile faded as a faraway look flickered over his face.

"She was just as lovely then as she was the day I met her."

A bell tinkled, and Tinker Bell pounced onto Maya's shoes from behind the counter. She looked up, yawned, and then took a step to rub Leonard's shin.

He set the photo on the counter and smiled down at her. "This must be Tinker Bell. How are you, Tink?" He crouched down and rubbed the cat's ear.

"I call her Stinker Bell. She's a menace," Gayle quipped. "She's always trying to trip me."

Leonard chuckled as the cat purred. "Now, I won't believe that for a second. You're a good kitty, right?"

Maya shook her head. "Gayle, I guess that means you want me to put her upstairs before I leave."

"Yes, please."

Maya picked up the cat. "Would you like to see the tea party room?"

"Of course," Leonard said.

Maya took him into the hallway and opened the door to her new creation.

"Wow. I saw the photos on the store's Facebook page last night, but this looks even more spectacular in person. You did a wonderful job." He walked around and studied the decals. "I love these clings. They look great."

"Thanks. They say they're removable and won't ruin the paint, but I'm not going to test that out."

"They look perfect where they are."

"Let me just put Tinker Bell in my apartment and grab my purse. I'll be right back." She hurried upstairs and left the cat locked in the bathroom with food and water. She still didn't trust her to roam around the apartment alone. Then she picked up her purse and zipped down to the store, where she found Leonard and Gayle chatting about their favorite places in North Carolina. She'd have to ask her father where he most liked to vacation in the state. Maybe he preferred the mountains to the beach.

"I'm ready to go." Maya looked at Gayle. "Thank you for running the store today."

"Don't worry. You'll owe me." Gayle winked. "Enjoy yourselves. Again, it's nice meeting you, Leonard."

Her father held the door open for her as they stepped out onto the sidewalk. "So where are we going for breakfast?"

"How about Pancake Palace? It's right around the corner from here."

"Sounds delicious," Leonard said as they strolled toward the crosswalk.

"We've been invited for a cookout at the beach tonight."

"I love cookouts."

Maya stopped at the corner and waited for the light to change. "Great. We'll go to the grocery store later. I want to provide what we grill."

"Okay. Who's hosting?"

"My friend Brody. He has this enormous beach house. Wait 'til you see it."

"Ah. Brody the friend." He smiled kindly.

"Right," she said as they crossed the street.

"May I ask if you're dating anyone?"

"You can ask, but I'm not. I was supposed to get married next month, but my fiancé decided to take a job in the UK and broke our engagement. He didn't ask me to go with him. He just said, 'I'm going to Europe. Don't wait for me.' I won't lie. That hurt."

"Ouch. What a jerk."

Maya laughed. "Yes. I said something to that effect."

"I'm sorry he betrayed you like that."

"Thank you." She looked at him. "Why did you never remarry?"

"I dated some after Patrice passed away, but I never found anyone who seemed like the right fit."

She nodded toward Pancake Palace. "There's our destination. Then we can walk around town, maybe hit a few shops and find a fun place for lunch."

"Sounds great," he said with a smile.

Chapter 19

"Sandy Feet Retreat," Leonard repeated as Maya parked her SUV in Brody's driveway. "I love the name."

Maya smiled. "I do too."

The day had flown by as Maya enjoyed spending time with her father. After eating too many pancakes, they'd walked all around Coral Cove's downtown area, with Maya pointing out her favorite places and telling Leonard more about her summers with Aunt CeCe. They'd visited several shops, walked along the boardwalk, and eaten lunch at a new café close to the beach.

During the afternoon, they'd taken off their shoes and walked along the shoreline while Leonard told her about growing up in New Jersey, then attending Princeton. She wondered if he had other family members still living, but she'd decided to let his story unfold without too many questions from her.

Later, they visited the grocery store to pick up food for the cookout. She couldn't wait for Brody to meet Leonard and to see how they interacted.

Each taking a grocery bag, they headed for the front door and rang the bell. As if on cue, Ashlyn appeared at the door with Rusty.

"Miss Maya! You're finally here!"

"Ashlyn, this is Mr. Hamel. And, Leonard, this is my little buddy, Ashlyn Tanner."

"Hi, Mr. Leonard."

"Hi, Ashlyn. Who's your friend?"

"This is Rusty."

"Nice to meet you, Ashlyn and Rusty." Leonard's smile was wide and warm.

Ashlyn led them into the foyer, and Maya watched Leonard's expression as he scanned the large family room. For all she knew, he was used to places like this. But she could see he was in awe as much as she'd been during her first visit.

"Welcome, Leonard!" Brody came out of the kitchen with his hand extended. "I'm Brody Tanner." He shook her father's free hand.

"Your house is exquisite."

"Thank you. We like it." Brody reached for his bag. "May I help you with that?"

Leonard nodded toward Maya. "I'm good. Why don't you take hers?"

Brody took Maya's bag, and when their hands brushed, electricity skipped up her arm.

"Leonard, did Maya tell you she just uses me for my super-awesome deck and amazing grilling abilities?"

"I thought I'd already made that clear. Why else would I want to come here?" She snapped her fingers. "Oh, right! To see Ashlyn."

He shook his head and grinned.

Ashlyn pulled on Leonard's arm. "Why don't you put your bag in the kitchen, and then me and Rusty will give you a tour!"

"I would love that."

"I'll take it." Maya took her father's bag from him.

Ashlyn seized the opportunity to grab Leonard's hand and tow him toward the sofa. "Come meet our kitties."

Maya followed Brody into the kitchen, where they deposited the bags on the island.

"So how's it going?" Brody asked as they both leaned back against a counter.

"Great. We spent the day sightseeing and talking. I can honestly say I've had a great time."

"I had a feeling you would. " Brody took both her hands in his and rubbed his thumbs over the back of her hands. "I'm so happy for you."

Thrilled to have her hands in his, Maya barely got out a thank you.

He let go and turned toward the bags. "What did you bring?"

Leaning toward him, she lowered her voice. "Leonard picked out the best chicken and steak kabobs for you to grill. He also insisted we bring chips, dip, macaroni salad, and a peach pie for dessert. It's like he's trying to make up for lost time." She tried to ignore how much she enjoyed the fragrance of Brody's spicy aftershave—almost as much as the handholding.

"That's awesome."

"I just felt so strange letting him insist on buying the food when he drove seven hours to get here and then had to pay for a hotel room."

"He's a lawyer, Maya. He can afford it."

"Sure, but he's my guest."

"He's missed out on thirty years of your life. Let him feel like he's giving you something for once."

"And this is our kitchen," Ashlyn announced as she and Leonard appeared with Rusty at their heels.

Maya stepped away from Brody. She didn't want her father to catch them looking like more than friends.

"I enjoyed meeting all six of your cats, Brody," Leonard said. "Rusty too."

"Did you catch all the cats' names? We'll have a quiz later," Maya said, and they all laughed at her joke.

Ashlyn touched her father's arm. "Mr. Leonard has a German shepherd named Ralph. He showed me photos on his phone." Turning to Leonard, her little brow crinkled. "Who's taking care of him while you're away?"

"My neighbors. They have two dogs Ralph likes to play with."

"Oh good. I was afraid he'd be hungry."

Leonard smiled down at her. "I made sure he was taken care of."

Maya's heart seemed to turn over in her chest as she took in Leonard's warm expression. Was he imagining her as a little girl of eight when he looked at Ashlyn? They did have similar coloring.

Brody had been taking food out of the grocery bags, and now he rubbed his hands together. "Why don't we cook up these delicious kebabs?"

"Ashlyn, would you please help me set the table?" Maya asked.

Soon they were eating their delicious meal out on the deck. Maya took in the beautiful symphony of the ocean, enjoying the sight of colorful umbrellas spread across the sand.

"I can't get over this view," Leonard said.

Maya nodded as she lifted her glass of sweet tea. "I keep saying that as well. I never get tired of it." She smiled. "That's another reason I keep coming back."

"Oh, it *is*?" Brody's expression challenged her. "Are you sure it's not for the superb adult company?"

"Yeah, I guess that too. But I told you earlier. I mostly come to see Ashlyn. Oh, and Rusty and the kitties." She loved teasing him.

Brody put one hand to his chest. "You got me right in the heart. You're killing me."

"You're silly, Dad!" Ashlyn giggled, and they all laughed.

"So, Brody," Leonard began as he picked up his steak kabob, "Maya mentioned you're a veterinarian and you and your best friend own your practice."

Brody nodded as he dropped a handful of chips onto his plate. "That's right."

"I suppose you stay busy with both locals and tourists."

"We do."

Brody kept pace answering as Leonard peppered him with questions about his work. Maya enjoyed watching the two men fall into an easy conversation. They seemed like old friends, and their comfortable camaraderie was like a dream.

Later, they enjoyed pie and coffee on the deck, the three adults sharing memories from trips they'd taken as children.

While the men were talking about fishing, Ashlyn reappeared. She'd been excused to spend time with her pets.

"Miss Maya?"

"Yes?"

"Could I show you something?"

"Of course." Maya excused herself before Ashlyn pulled her inside.

～·～

"Your daughter is precious," Leonard said once Ashlyn and Maya had left.

Brody smiled. "Thank you. She's the light of my life." He fingered his glass. "Maya said you're enjoying your visit."

"I am." Leonard leaned back in his chair. "I'm sure she told you about her mother and me. I've always regretted how things ended between us. I dreamed of finding my child, but I never imagined it would really happen. I'm hopeful we can develop a close relationship. Having her in my life is a privilege, and I want to make up for lost time." He closed his eyes. "I'm so grateful Maya's giving me the chance to know her."

"She's special," Brody said.

"That's an understatement. She's beautiful, talented, and sweet. But Vickie gets all the credit for that."

Brody looked at the ocean as his feelings for Maya swelled like the waves marching toward the shore. "She's been a wonderful friend to Ashlyn and me. I'm grateful to have her in our lives. You can see how Ashlyn has taken to her, and I enjoy watching them together."

"And you care for Maya too." Leonard gave him a knowing smile.

Brody took a sip of iced tea. He had a decision to make. Would he tell Leonard the truth? That he'd come to the conclusion that he couldn't hide his feelings for Maya much longer? Or continue on the path of denial and fear he'd been on ever since he met her?

He looked at this man he'd just met and felt a solidarity with him. He trusted Leonard.

"I do care for her. Deeply."

"Have you told her?"

"Not yet."

"What are you waiting for?" Leonard held up his hands. "Sorry. None of my business."

"I don't mind answering." He paused and licked his lips. "I suppose I'm waiting for the right moment."

"Don't wait too long. Women like Maya don't come around often. You don't want to regret letting her slip through your fingers."

Brody nodded, suddenly understanding more of Leonard's own experience. "I know. I've just been afraid to move too quickly. I've been burned in the past."

"Yet something tells me you and Maya might have a bright future."

Brody's heart swelled at the notion. "I hope so."

~·~

Ashlyn stepped into her bedroom closet and pulled out an aqua-blue party dress with lace and beads on the top, a bow at the waist, and tulle on the bottom. "What do you think about this? Do you like it?"

Maya's breath came out in a rush as she ran her fingers over the beading. "It's beautiful! I love it. Where did you get it?"

"My dad took me to the mall today to get my watch fixed." Ashlyn flipped the cover on the Hello Kitty watch Maya had given her. "We dropped this off last week, and we had to pick it up today."

"Wow. It works."

"Yeah, the man had to replace something on it, but he got it working. When we went to the mall, I saw this dress and asked Daddy if he'd buy it for my birthday party."

"It's perfect."

Ashlyn held it up to herself and looked at her reflection in the full-length mirror on her closet door. She swayed back and forth, and the tulle moved and shimmered under the ceiling light. "Would you please braid my hair for my party like you do yours?"

"I'd love to." Maya came to stand beside her. "We can find some ribbon that matches the dress and braid it into your hair."

Ashlyn's eyes opened wide. "I love that idea!"

"It will look beautiful." Maya touched the little girl's thick, dark hair, so much like her own.

"My dad doesn't know how to do girls' hair."

Maya laughed.

Ashlyn looked up at her. "He told me Mr. Leonard is your dad."

Maya nodded. "That's true. I didn't know him when I was your age. I just found him."

"I like him."

"I do too." Maya touched Ashlyn's shoulder. "We should get back."

Ashlyn hung the dress in the closet, and Maya couldn't help but notice the men's conversation stopped as soon as she and Ashlyn walked onto the deck.

"Are we interrupting something?" Maya asked.

Brody lifted his glass. "No. We've just had some guy talk."

"Oh really." She'd have to ask Brody for details later. She turned to Leonard. "I guess we should get going."

Leonard stood and shook Brody's hand. "It was wonderful meeting you."

"I enjoyed meeting you too."

Leonard moved on to Ashlyn, shaking her hand and thanking her for her hospitality. When his back was to Maya and Brody, she shot Brody a look, trying to ask what they'd discussed. Brody just winked and gave her a thumbs-up, but she was dying to learn more.

Then Brody and Ashlyn walked her and Leonard out to the driveway.

Brody looked up at the sky. "What a gorgeous summer night."

"Yes, it is. I can see why you all love it here." Leonard raised his hand to both Tanners. "Take care now." Then he climbed into the front passenger seat of Maya's SUV.

She touched Brody's arm. "Thank you for everything."

"You're welcome."

Maya hugged Ashlyn and then hopped into her 4Runner, started the engine, and backed down the driveway. "That was fun—and delicious."

"It was." Leonard seemed to study her. "And I can tell you like Brody as more than a friend."

She frowned. "Am I that obvious?"

He chuckled. "You're not obvious, but your feelings for Brody are."

"What was your guy talk about?" She gave him a sideways glance.

"We talked about how special you are."

Heat crept up her neck. "What did Brody say?"

"He said he thinks you're amazing."

Oh, she wanted the details, but she was too embarrassed to ask.

When they reached her building, she parked next to Leonard's BMW SUV.

"I have something for you." Leonard climbed out and walked over to his vehicle, then popped the tailgate open.

She followed and found him scooting a cardboard box closer to the car's edge. "What's this?"

"Open it." He took a step back.

Maya found the box full of envelopes and small boxes. Confused, she turned toward Leonard again. "I don't understand."

"Open one." He picked up a blue envelope and handed it to her.

On the front, someone had written *Happy Birthday*. She opened the envelope and found a birthday card that said *It's your birthday!* in bright colors on the front. Inside was a $50 bill and the printed words *Hope your birthday is as special as you are.* At the bottom, *Love, Dad* had been written in a slanted handwriting.

Maya blinked and shook her head. "I'm sorry, Leonard, but I still don't know what this means."

"These are gifts I bought and saved every year just in case you ever contacted me. Since I didn't know if you were a boy or a girl, I bought neutral cards for birthdays, Christmas, Valentine's Day, Easter . . ."

He sifted through the envelopes and pulled out one that said

Happy High School Graduation on the front. "I even bought a gift for the year I assumed you graduated from high school and the year you might have graduated from college. I just kept collecting them in case you found me someday, and I'm so grateful you did."

Maya's head seemed to be spinning as a lump swelled in her throat. She dropped the card into the box and covered her face as long-held emotions erupted. And then she sobbed, bending at the waist, trying to stem the intensity of those emotions from dragging her down, down, down . . .

"Maya," he said, his voice close to her ear, "I'm so sorry. I shouldn't have brought this with me. It's too much."

She felt him push a tissue into her hand, and she fought to stop crying. But it was too much. Learning that he'd cared for her all along was so unexpected. So overwhelming. So wonderful!

She wiped her eyes and nose, taking deep, shuddering breaths.

He touched her arm but then pulled his hand back. "I never meant to upset you."

"It's not that." She shook her head. "I've always believed you didn't want me."

"That's not true. It was quite the opposite." He paused. "I never would have taken you from your mother, but I did want to be part of your life and help care for you. I just didn't get the chance. Maya, don't ever believe I didn't want you, because I always did, and I never forgot you." He pointed to the box. "You can see you were always on my mind."

Tears filled her eyes again, but she swallowed back the emotion. "You have no idea how much this means to me. My whole life I've believed my father didn't want me, which made me feel unlovable. Then my fiancé further proved I wasn't lovable by breaking our engagement and leaving me."

Leonard took a deep breath. "Maya, I can tell you one thing for sure. You *are* worthy and deserving of love. I've learned that in a short time, but it's true."

She touched his arm. "Would you like to come in for a cup of decaf?"

"I'd love to."

Leonard carried the box up to Maya's apartment. Then he played with Tinker Bell while she made the coffee and pulled out mugs. They sat at her kitchen table, and she opened each card and gift in the box—all just for her. By the time she finished, she had a pile of money and family photos along with trinkets and mementos her father had gathered for her as he traveled around the world. When she tried to give him the money back, he told her to put it in her savings account for a rainy day.

Leonard pointed to a photo of a man, a woman, a little boy who resembled him, and a young girl. "Those are my parents, and that's my sister."

"You have a sister?" Maya asked.

Leonard nodded. "She's younger than me and married, and she and her family live in Vermont. She has two grown daughters and four grandchildren."

"So I have an aunt and cousins?"

"And an uncle. My sister's husband is a great guy. Maybe we can plan a trip to meet them all."

"Oh, I would love that."

"Have you ever skied?"

"No."

"Don't worry. I'll teach you."

They talked for hours, and Maya retrieved several of Aunt CeCe's photo albums so she could illustrate her childhood. When they talked about her mother—the young woman Vickie Sullivan was when he met her—Leonard shared how much he'd loved her. Seeing her mother so lovely through his eyes meant the world to her.

Maya showed him a photo of Kyle, and her heart clenched with a mixture of anguish and anger. "This is my ex."

"Again, I'm so sorry he hurt you." Leonard frowned but then brightened. "But I believe Brody truly cares for you."

Maya sighed. "He's focused on raising Ashlyn, and he's made it clear he doesn't have room in his life for a relationship. Not that a certain blonde hasn't been trying to make her way in."

"I don't think you have to worry about whoever that is. Just give him time. I think his focus may change."

Leonard patted her hand, then looked at his watch. "Hey, it's almost midnight. I should let you get some sleep. How about tomorrow we do things I didn't get to do with you when you were growing up?"

She smiled. "I'd like that. Tomorrow's the last day for the county fair. Would you like to go?"

He touched her hand. "I'll even buy you cotton candy. Let's enjoy our last day to the fullest."

"I can't wait," Maya said. And she couldn't.

Chapter 20

Maya sat across her table from her father Monday morning. "How's your breakfast?"

"Delicious." Leonard grinned as his dark eyes took in the platters of waffles, scrambled eggs, bacon, and fresh fruit. "But I feel like you forgot to invite a few people to help us eat it all."

"I guess I overdid it, but I didn't want to send you on the road hungry."

Maya smiled as she recalled their perfect Sunday together. They'd arrived at the county fair when the gates opened and stayed until they closed. They rode every ride at least once, some twice, including the roller coasters. Leonard also bought her ice cream and cotton candy, and they laughed—a lot! Then he came back to her apartment and they talked late into the night.

Yes, it had been the perfect day, and now she had to prepare herself to say goodbye to her father. She already missed him, which seemed crazy.

"I had a wonderful weekend with you," he said.

She picked up her coffee mug. "I enjoyed it too. I'm so glad you came."

"Maybe you, Brody, and Ashlyn can come up to see me sometime. Or we could all go up to Vermont this fall to see my sister and her family. The foliage in New England is spectacular that time of year."

"I'd like that." Her heart beat faster at the idea of traveling with Brody and Ashlyn—like a family. Perhaps that would be a possibility.

They talked about their plans for the week, and then he helped her clean up before they walked out to his BMW.

"Thank you so much for coming to see me," she said. She took a step toward him. "Would it be okay if I hugged you?"

"Of course." He chuckled.

Maya stepped into his arms, and he patted her back.

"And is it okay if I call you Dad?" she asked when she stepped out of his embrace.

His dark eyes shimmered with tears. "I would like that very much."

"Thank you . . . Dad." The word felt funny on her tongue, but saying it filled her with joy. "Be safe going home. Text me when you get there."

"I will, Maya. Take care."

Her heart lifted, and she waved as he drove away.

~·~

"I just can't get over it," Maya gushed that evening as she and Brody walked a long pier leading to a gazebo on the bay side of Coral Cove. "I was afraid my father's visit would be a disaster, but it was better than I imagined, even in my wildest dreams. He was sweet, kind, easy to talk to, and just everything I always wished a father would be to me."

It was a lovely early August night. The air was humid, the sky was clear, and the stars seemed to sparkle just for them as they looked out over the bay. Cicadas sang and lightning bugs flickered by as if giving her and Brody their own personal fireworks show.

After making sure Brody and Ashlyn were available, she'd arrived at Sandy Feet Retreat with takeout from her favorite Japanese hibachi restaurant. They'd eaten with Ashlyn, and then after dropping her off for the night at her friend Bailey's house, Brody suggested they visit Coral Cove's bay side.

Now the sun had set, and she and Brody had a chance to talk alone. He lightly touched the small of her back and steered her into the gazebo, where they sat down to the chorus of frogs.

"I feel whole again, you know?" she continued.

"Whole again?" Brody turned toward her, his brow puckered and his blue eyes gleaming under the lights strung along the edge of the gazebo. "What do you mean?"

She looked down at her worn jean shorts and pulled at a loose thread to avoid his gaze. "I always felt fractured, like a piece of me was missing because I didn't have a father. Worse, my mother led me to believe he didn't want me, which meant he didn't love me, so from an early age I thought something must be wrong with me.

"But now I know Leonard just didn't know where to find me. He didn't even know I was a daughter and not a son. And he's always cared about me. He loved me so much that he bought me gifts and wrote out cards for me in case he ever found me—or I found him. I'm still amazed to learn my father has always loved me."

"I don't see how that's hard to believe, Maya."

She smiled as a spark of hope ignited deep in her heart. She also felt a tug deep in her soul. She wanted to be more than friends with Brody. After the cookout with her father, she'd realized a friendship with Brody would never be enough to sustain her, just as Kiana had predicted.

"What did you and my dad discuss during your 'guy talk'?" She made air quotes with her fingers.

"We talked about how amazing you are. He said he always wondered what his child was like, and he never imagined you would be so beautiful, talented, and sweet. He told me he's grateful you're giving him a chance." Brody smiled. "I think he's the real deal, Maya. He really cares about you and wants to be a part of your life."

She nodded as joy radiated through her chest.

They both looked out toward the bay again, and when she looked back toward the shore, she took in the beautiful tall grass swaying in the light breeze.

"Thank you for being such a wonderful support to me, Brody. I'm so grateful Tinker Bell brought you and Ashlyn into my life. I don't know how I would have handled finding my father without you." A surge of confidence swelled in her chest, and she continued, "You and Ashlyn are important to me."

"You're important to us too." He angled his body toward her, then placed one hand on each of her cheeks before brushing his lips over hers.

Maya leaned into the kiss. She felt dizzy and warm all over, and a shiver of wanting vibrated through her body. When he broke away, she felt disoriented. Had that really just happened?

"I care about you, Maya." He took her hand. "I have for a long time. I've just been afraid of getting in too deep, too fast. I want to be with you, but we still have to take it slow."

She nodded as excitement pulsated through her. Brody cared for her! She felt as if she were floating on a cloud. Then a vision of him and Kim in the water together on the Fourth and the look in her eyes as she told him good night filled her mind.

She frowned. "Aren't you seeing Kim?"

"No." He scoffed, looking confused again. "Why would you think that?"

"I know you went out on a boat with her and you've given her rides home after work. But there's nothing going on between you?"

"No. Nothing. I have feelings for one woman, and that woman is you."

Her heart thudded against her rib cage, his words music to her ears.

"But you need to understand, Maya." He took a deep breath. "I have to be sure about a relationship because of Ashlyn. She not only comes first in my life, but I can't take the risk of having her hurt if she believes a woman I'm seeing could be her mother someday and then it falls through."

Maya nodded. "I understand. But I love Ashlyn." *And I love you.*

"I know you love her." He smiled and trailed his fingers down her cheek.

"I'll be patient, but only as long as you invite me over to sit on your super-awesome deck."

He laughed and threaded his fingers with hers. "You're still something else, Maya Reynolds."

"So are you, Dr. Tanner."

His head dipped, and her breath hitched as his lips again met hers. She wrapped her arms around his neck and pulled him closer. He deepened the kiss, and it sent a fire burning through every cell in her body.

When he pulled back, he faced the bay once again, and Maya rested her head on his shoulder, closing her eyes as happiness opened in her like a flower.

Brody had kissed her! She didn't think she'd ever stop smiling.

~·~

Brody steered his pickup truck into the parking lot behind Maya's building. The evening had been both surprising and amazing as he and Maya had walked along the beach kissing, talking, and then kissing some more.

His head still buzzed with euphoria as he recalled brushing his lips against hers. She'd lit a fire in his soul that was nothing like he'd felt with Courtney. For months he'd wondered what it would be like to kiss Maya, and tonight he'd finally found the courage to do it.

And now as they sat in his truck outside her building, it was hard to leave her.

Slow down, Tanner! He couldn't hurry this. He and Maya were more than friends now, but that didn't mean he was ready to make a commitment. He never thought Courtney would break his heart, but she did. He wasn't ready.

"I had a really great time tonight." Maya released her seat belt and shifted toward him. "That pier by the bay is beautiful. We need to go back there soon."

He turned toward her. "The bay is beautiful, but not as beautiful as you." He pushed a tendril of her gorgeous hair behind her ear. When his fingers brushed her cheek, she leaned into his touch.

Once again the urge to kiss her came over him. He leaned down, and as she deepened her kiss, she wrapped her arms around his neck and he threaded his fingers through her hair. He breathed in the flowery fragrance of her shampoo as fire burned through his veins.

When she pulled back, she smiled up at him, her chestnut-colored eyes sparkling in the dome light above them. "Call me tomorrow, okay?"

"I can call you when I get home if you'd like."

"Nah." She gave his arm a playful push. "I do need a break from you sometimes. You're just a little too clingy."

"Clingy? I beg your pardon," he said, teasing in return. "You're the one who's using me for my oceanfront view."

She laughed as she pushed the door open. "Good night."

"Wait." He leaned over, pulled her to him, and kissed her one last time. "Now you can go."

She sighed. "If you say so."

He laughed.

"Good night, Dr. Tanner."

"Good night, Miss Reynolds."

She climbed out of the truck, and he waited until she unlocked the back door, waved, and then slipped into the building. As he eased his truck out of the parking lot, he smiled and imagined kissing Maya again and again and again.

Brody sat next to Maya on her rooftop two weeks later, taking in the nighttime clouds drifting above them.

Maya lifted her glass of iced tea and sighed as she glanced at him. "It's another beautiful Saturday night."

He nodded and stretched his long legs out in front of him. "I'm glad you suggested we come up here."

"Well, after Ashlyn fell asleep on the sofa watching *Sleeping Beauty*, I thought we could sneak up here for a little while before you take her home." She grinned at him. "It's pretty up here, but it's not as nice as sitting on your super-awesome deck."

He chuckled and shook his head. He would never grow tired of her teasing.

He relaxed and considered how the past couple of weeks had flown by. Not only had he and Maya been in touch nearly every day, but they'd also managed to spend several evenings alone. They took turns cooking and enjoyed snuggling on a sofa and walking on the beach.

They'd also visited the bay a couple of times. He was enjoying every minute of getting to know this woman, but he was also grateful she'd agreed to move slowly. He just couldn't risk his heart—or Ashlyn's. What if Maya only thought she was over Kyle? No. She'd told him not only that Kyle had refused to explain his behavior but also that she no longer cared.

Maya sighed, and when he turned toward her, he spotted what looked like pure contentment on her face.

Brody gave her arm a gentle poke. "What's on your mind?"

"I was just thinking about something."

He tilted his head. "I hope it was about me."

"Believe it or not, not everything is about you, Dr. Tanner." She smiled. "My dad suggested a trip to see his family in Vermont this fall. Well, I suppose I should call them my family too. I'd like to go."

"You should. You've waited a long time to find your dad, and more family is a bonus."

"I have waited a long time." Maya hesitated. "I was thinking maybe you could go too. Ashlyn as well, of course. She'll have a fall break from school, right?"

Brody brushed his shirt, sweeping away an invisible speck of lint, hoping to mask the alarm bells going off in his head. "I don't know about Ashlyn and me, but you should definitely go."

Her brow wrinkled. "Don't you want to go?"

Brody rubbed his elbow and searched for a viable excuse. Unbidden, memories of Courtney destroying his heart suddenly swarmed inside his head. He'd visited her family, developed a real relationship with them, and then . . .

"Well, it all depends on what's going on at the clinic."

"You're one of the owners. Can't you take vacation time just about whenever you want?"

"It's not that simple. I'd have to see what Cam had going on, and I doubt we'll have hired another vet by then." He worked to keep his expression even.

"Then we'll plan a trip for whenever it works for you. I want to include you and Ashlyn."

"We'll see." Brody stood, more abruptly than he'd intended. "We've been up here for a while. We should check on Ashlyn."

Maya seemed to study him. "Okay."

He held out his hand. "Come on. I don't want her to wake up and think we left her."

She took his hand and allowed him to pull her to her feet.

Seeing concern in her eyes, he kissed her before gathering their cups and heading for the door that led to the stairs. As they walked down together, he hoped he could somehow tamp down Maya's expectations. He didn't want to lose her, but he still wasn't ready to advance their relationship—like traveling as if they were a family. Two hearts were at stake—his and Ashlyn's.

Chapter 21

Have you heard from your dad?" Kiana's voice sounded through the speakers in Maya's 4Runner the following Thursday evening.

Maya smiled as she steered her SUV out of the grocery store parking lot. "I have. We talk or text just about every other day. We're discussing a possible trip to Vermont for me to meet his sister and her family in the fall, which is crazy! Just over a month ago, I didn't even know who my dad was. Now he's in my life, and I have cousins too!"

"I'm so happy for you."

"Thank you. How's Deacon?"

"He's great." She could hear Kiana's smile. "And how's Brody? You guys have been dating for a while now."

Maya's heart lifted as she thought of all the time she and Brody had spent together since he'd told her he cared for her. She'd relished their late-night talks on his deck, their text messages throughout the day, shared meals . . . And all those amazing kisses. The memories made her lips burn. Brody's touch was nothing like Kyle's. It was as if he'd made her heart come alive!

If only . . .

"Brody is fine," Maya said as she merged out into the intersection. "Ashlyn's birthday party is this Saturday, and I'm just about ready. Her gift finally arrived yesterday. I was getting so nervous, afraid it would be late. I told you about the special doll I ordered, right?"

"You did. I can't wait for you to send me photos."

"I will. I have something else planned for her too—a surprise gift. Oh! And I've been writing! I finished my outline last week, and I'm up to chapter 5 in the novel. The new story is finally flowing! I feel like I can't type fast enough. My deadline is coming soon, though, so I'll really have to hit it hard after the party."

"That's so great." Kiana paused. "How long have I known you?"

"Since you asked to borrow a pencil in Mrs. Zoch's ninth-grade Spanish class. What's your point?"

"You brushed over my asking about Brody pretty fast. I get the impression you're keeping something from me."

Maya shook her head. "What are you talking about?"

"*Brody.*" Kiana's tone held a hint of annoyance. "I asked about him and you told me about Ashlyn's birthday party. So what gives?"

"Brody and I are fine, and the party is what's on my mind right now. That's what gives, Key."

"Fine, huh?"

Maya frowned as the light turned green and she motored through the intersection. Her best friend could always read between the lines and detect the unsaid worries on Maya's heart.

Something was missing with Brody. But she didn't want to admit it out loud. If she did, that would make it true.

"You still there, My? Or did you hang up on me?"

"I'm here." Maya slapped her blinker on and turned right, heading toward her street. "Things are good. They could just be . . . better."

"What do you mean?"

"I feel like . . . well . . ." Maya pressed her lips together. "Fine. Something is off. It's as if he's holding himself back from me. More than just taking things slow." She hated saying those words aloud!

"Why do you think he's doing that?"

"I don't know. But when I brought up the idea of going to see my dad's family in Vermont this fall and suggested he and Ashlyn go along, he said, 'We'll see.' I remember my mom using those words whenever she didn't want to come right out and tell me no."

"Maybe he's just not a planner."

"No, it's not that. It's as if he doesn't believe we'll still be together in the fall."

"Don't say that. He cares about you. And he did tell you he wanted to take things slow . . . because of Ashlyn. Maybe taking a vacation together just isn't slow enough for him."

Maya steered her SUV into the lot behind her building. "The night we started dating, I was the one who started the conversation, telling him he and Ashlyn are important to me. He kissed me, but then he made a point of telling me he wanted to take it slow, and he's told me more than once that Ashlyn is his focus. I get all that. But I feel like he's not just going slow but deliberately holding back—to the point I don't know if he'll ever truly open up. I find myself wondering if he'll break my heart like Kyle did."

"Don't compare him to Kyle, Maya. Brody is nothing like him."

"I know." Maya agreed with her, but the worry growing in the pit of her stomach for the past week felt like it was expanding.

"What if you just flat out told him you're ready to make a commitment?"

Maya steered into her usual spot by the door, cut the engine, and held her phone up to her ear. "You think that's a good idea?"

"Sure. Maybe he's hoping you'll confirm your feelings first because he doesn't want to appear too vulnerable. If you say it first, it might give him the strength to give 100 percent to the relationship."

"But what if it backfires? What if I scare him off?"

"Then you'll know his true feelings."

"Okay." Like water from a fountain, excitement bubbled up in her chest. "I'll do it."

"Awesome. Oh, I have to go. I think Deacon is knocking on my door. Call me soon."

"I will. Bye!" Maya disconnected the call and stared at her steering wheel. She was going to tell Brody how she felt, and maybe, just maybe, he'd tell her he was ready to make a commitment too.

Maya stood in the doorway to the party room Saturday afternoon and smiled. She'd spent all morning specially decorating and was finally done.

Pink mylar balloons featuring flowers and the words *Happy Birthday* were tied to the chairs and happily bobbing in the air. The tables set for ten were adorned with pink tablecloths and plates and utensils one shade darker.

A platter of tiny cucumber and cream cheese sandwiches sat on the buffet beside the pink and baby-blue tea sets, waiting for Maya to bring the tea from the kitchenette. The goody bags featuring Disney princesses and filled with a book from Beach Reads and candy from Something Sweet were assembled and stowed in the buffet. All Maya needed now was for the guest of honor and her friends to arrive.

Her heart gave a little bump as she imagined seeing Ashlyn and Brody. Over the last couple of days, she'd realized she, too, had been holding back from her relationship with Brody. Deep down she'd been afraid of getting hurt because of Kyle. She'd also been afraid she really wasn't worthy of Brody's love. But now, after experiencing her father's love, she believed she was.

Last night she'd decided today was the day she'd tell him she was ready for a committed relationship. She just had to find the right time to do it.

The back door opened, and the scent of rain drifted in. Maya hurried out of the party room just as Brody and Ashlyn appeared carrying bags and umbrellas.

"There's the birthday girl!" Maya rushed over to Ashlyn and hugged her. "Happy ninth birthday!"

"Thank you." Ashlyn beamed.

Maya looked up at Brody. "Hi there."

"Hi to you too." He kissed her cheek.

"Is it raining?" Maya asked.

"It just started. The clouds look pretty ominous, but we won't let it ruin our day, right, Ash?" He touched his daughter's head.

"That's right." Ashlyn held up her tote bag. "Miss Maya, would you please help me get ready? Like I told you, Daddy doesn't know how to braid. Did you get the ribbon that matches my dress?"

"I did. Let's go upstairs." Maya led them up to her apartment, where Tinker Bell met them at the door with a loud squeak.

"Hi, Tink!" Ashlyn said, then turned to Maya. "She told me 'Happy birthday'!"

"Of course she did." Maya motioned for them to follow her into the kitchen, where a large gift bag decorated with Rapunzel, Cinderella, and Belle sat on the table.

"Ooh! What's this?" Ashlyn rushed to the bag as if it were a magnet and she was wearing a metal shirt.

Maya shared a smile with Brody. "Why don't you open it?"

Ashlyn yanked out the tissue paper before pulling out the custom-ordered doll. With its dark hair, dark eyes, button nose, and beautiful smile, the doll resembled Ashlyn. And Maya had even chosen an aqua-blue dress for the doll, closely matching the dress Ashlyn was wearing to her party.

Gasping, Ashlyn looked up at Maya. "She looks like me, and her dress matches mine!"

"Maya, what a gorgeous doll." Brody stepped closer to her and lowered his voice. "You shouldn't have."

She turned toward him and shrugged. "She's worth every penny." Then she looked at Ashlyn. "Do you like her?"

"I love her!" Ashlyn wrapped her arms around Maya's waist. "I'm going to call her Maya after you."

Maya's eyes stung. "Thank you."

Ashlyn held the doll up for Brody to see. "Dad! Doesn't she look just like me?"

"She does, baby." Brody beamed at his daughter. "That's one special doll."

Maya pointed to the bag. "There's something else in there too."

"More?" Ashlyn pulled out the Western Barbie and horse named Dallas that had once belonged to Maya's mother. "You found them!"

"I did."

Ashlyn's face pinched. "But you said they belonged to your mom."

"I know, and now they belong to you."

"Maya," Brody began, his voice again low, "you don't need to give those away."

"I want her to have them."

Brody frowned and started to say something, but Ashlyn cut him off. "Thank you so much, Miss Maya. I promise I'll take good care of them."

"You're welcome, sweetie. And I know you will." She touched Ashlyn's nose. "Happy birthday."

Ashlyn wrapped her arms around Maya's waist again. "I love you."

Maya's heart swelled. "I love you too."

Brody touched his daughter's back. "Ashlyn, your guests will be here soon. You'd better get ready."

"Oh!" Ashlyn pulled her dress from her tote and darted toward Maya's bedroom. "We'd better hurry!"

Brody jammed his thumb toward the door. "I'll go downstairs and wait for her guests. Do you need me to do anything?"

"Just kiss me."

Brody grinned, but at the same time he looked . . . what? Conflicted? Did he think she'd been too extravagant with her gifts? She hoped not. They'd come from her heart.

"I can handle that." He brushed his lips over hers, sending her stomach into a wild swirl.

She released a quiet sigh as warmth soared through her entire body. "Thank you."

He touched her face. "That's *my* pleasure." Then he headed for the door.

"Brody," she called after him.

He spun to face her.

"Can we talk sometime later? I want to talk to you about something in private."

"Okay."

"Miss Maya! I need you!" Ashlyn hollered from the bedroom.

Maya grinned. "Duty calls." Then she rushed off to help the birthday girl prepare for her party.

"Everything is perfect," Brody whispered to Maya as they stood in the party room doorway and Ashlyn laughed with all her friends.

Maya's chest swelled with pride. Brody was right. The party had gone off without a hitch. Once Ashlyn's friends arrived, Maya and Brody served the tea and sandwiches as the girls—all wearing adorable, pastel-colored party dresses—sat around the tables.

Then Maya brought out craft sets, and the girls created beaded necklaces and bracelets. She was grateful a couple of the mothers had offered to stay and help, allowing her and Brody more freedom to move in and out of the room as needed.

Maya checked her watch, and only forty-five minutes remained before the party was scheduled to end. "Should I get the cake and then she can open her gifts?"

"Good idea. I'll come with you. The moms can hold down the fort for a few minutes."

Raindrops drummed a loud cadence on the windows as Maya entered the kitchenette and crossed to the refrigerator. When she reached for the door, Brody took her arm and gently pulled her back.

"Wait," he said.

She turned to face him. "What?"

"We're alone. What do you want to discuss with me?"

"Oh." Nervous flutters filled her stomach. "I want to tell you something."

"Okay. I'm listening." Now his expression seemed open and curious.

Her throat thickened as the rain suddenly seemed louder. Or maybe that was her heartbeat.

He lifted an eyebrow. "Maya?"

"I'm just going to say it." She cleared her throat. "Brody, I love you. Actually, I love you *and* Ashlyn, and I'm ready to make a commitment to both of you."

His eyes widened, and she went on.

"I can't hide how I feel. Oh, I would never ask you to put me first. I just want you to know I'm ready for the long haul when you are. I want a family, and I believe you and Ashlyn are my future."

She reached for him, but he took a step back, a look of panic flickering across his face. She felt the happiness drain out of her as a coldness crept in, and the truth smacked her in the face. He didn't love her, nor did he envision a future with her.

I've made a huge mistake! Why did I listen to Kiana? Brody doesn't love me any more than Kyle did.

"Brody, I—"

"Whoa, Maya. Just hold on." He held up his hand. "I-I told you I need to take it slow. I can't rush things. I care for you, but I can't commit right now. It's too soon."

His words felt like a punch to her heart, but she tried to mask the pain as her hands shook. Sharing her heart with him had backfired, and she'd ruined everything. The room was closing in on her, and she had to get out of there before she started to cry. She couldn't let him know his words had broken her.

"Right," she managed to say, her voice too high and quaky. She opened the refrigerator, retrieved the box with the cake, and then gathered the candles, lighter, knife, and cake server before starting for the door at a quick clip.

"Maya!" he called after her. "Wait. Let me explain—"

With her heart sinking, Maya pinned a smile on her face and returned to the party room, Brody right behind.

"Okay, ladies," she sang, hoping her voice wouldn't betray her misery. "It's cake time! Let's sing to the birthday girl."

The girls cheered as Maya carried the cake to where Ashlyn sat. With her heart shattering, she lit all nine candles. Somehow she'd keep her emotions in check until the party was over and Brody and Ashlyn were gone. Then, once she was alone, she'd allow herself to dissolve in the heartache threatening to drown her.

Chapter 22

"Thank you for coming." Maya hoped her forced happiness was convincing as she smiled at Tessie's mom, the last mom still at the party.

Renee touched Maya's arm. "This party was so fun. Tessie's birthday is in October, and I'll call to get on your schedule next week. I don't want to miss my chance to book here."

Maya nodded. "Great."

It turned out Maya was stronger than she'd thought since she'd somehow managed not to curl up in a ball and cry her eyes out. Instead of succumbing to heartache after Brody rejected her declaration of love, she'd sung "Happy Birthday" to Ashlyn along with the rest of the party attendees, oohed and aahed as Ashlyn opened her gifts, and handed out goody bags.

But she'd also avoided making eye contact with Brody, who repeatedly tried to get her attention. She'd felt his stare throughout the remainder of the party, but she'd done her best to ignore him.

Now, as Renee and Tessie turned to leave, Maya knew the inevitable was about to happen. Brody showed no signs of leaving, and she'd have to face him and his rejection. Yet she'd already accepted the truth in her heart. He didn't love her, and she'd fooled herself into believing he did.

"Mom, can Ashlyn come over to play?" Tessie asked Renee.

Maya muttered, "Excuse me," and then started gathering the used plates and utensils before dumping them into a large trash bag.

"No, sweetie, not today," Renee said.

"Pleeease?" Tessie whined.

"Another day, okay?"

Maya kept working, boxing the leftover cake before she rolled up the disposable tablecloths and pitched them into the trash bag.

"Daddy, can Tessie come to our house?" Ashlyn asked.

"Not today, Ash." Brody sounded tired. Or maybe distraught. This couldn't be easy for him. She knew he cared about her. He just didn't love her.

"Okay," Ashlyn said, relenting. "Bye, Tessie. Bye, Mrs. Gillespie."

"See you soon," Renee called. "Thanks again, Maya. I'll call you."

Maya kept her back to Renee. "Sounds good. Bye."

"Ashlyn, why don't you go show Miss Gayle your favorite gifts?" Brody said.

"But I want to help Miss Maya clean up."

Maya bit her lip. *Please stay, Ashlyn. I don't want to face your father. I'm humiliated enough!*

"Ashlyn, I need a minute with Miss Maya. Please go talk to Miss Gayle, all right?" Maya could hear the strain in his voice.

"Okay." Ashlyn picked up a few of the gift bags. "I'll come back and help you when I'm done."

Maya touched her shoulder. "It's okay. I can handle it."

Ashlyn walked out of the room, her gift bags rattling away. A moment later, Maya heard the door to the store open and close, announcing that she and Brody were alone. Her back stiffened as she fetched a bleach wipe and began cleaning the sticky chairs.

"Maya."

She kept her back to him.

"Maya, please look at me."

When she felt his hand on her back, she stilled, closing her eyes, wishing the pain in her heart would just go away.

"I never meant to hurt you."

Brody's voice was close to her ear, and she hated the chill it sent shimmying down her back. She straightened and turned, but at the same time she backed away from him. "Just go, Brody." Her words scratched out, as both sadness and regret pounded her like waves against the shoreline.

"No, we need to talk about this." He looked forlorn. "I'm just not ready for a commitment."

She tossed the used bleach wipe into the trash bag as an unbidden bitterness gripped her. "So I guess this is my fault because I misread your feelings?"

"Maya, I told you from the beginning that I needed to take things slow, and you know it's only been a few weeks."

"Don't patronize me." Her voice quavered.

"I'm not. I didn't mean to . . ." He took a deep breath. "There's something I haven't told you."

She stilled. "What?"

He rubbed his hands together. "I was engaged once. A long time ago."

"Engaged? Why didn't you tell me?" She tried to swallow past the knot that suddenly appeared in her throat.

His shoulders sagged. "It's not a happy story. I met Courtney when we were in vet school together. I fell head over heels for her, and when I proposed, she said yes. I was certain we'd be together forever."

"What happened?"

"Then my mom passed away, and when I took full custody of Ashlyn, Courtney said she didn't want a ready-made family. She gave me the ring back, and it was over. I was completely blindsided. I thought Courtney loved me enough to accept Ashlyn as a part of our family, but she didn't. I was crushed, and ever since then I've had a hard time trusting. That's why I haven't dated much."

He took a step toward her. "And that's why I told you I need to take it slow. Before I make a commitment to someone, I need to be sure that person is on board with Ashlyn and me. My daughter and I are a package deal. I have to put her welfare first. And I don't want to be hurt again if things don't work out. Haven't you been afraid to be hurt again?"

Anger swelled in Maya's chest. "I was for a while. But then I trusted you. I can't believe you're just now telling me about Courtney when I've poured out my soul to you about my family, Kyle, my father . . ."

"I'm sorry."

"You're sorry?" She scoffed. "We both suffered through broken engagements, but you didn't think you needed to share yours with me?"

"It's not easy for me to talk about Courtney."

"But I'm *not* Courtney! You know me, Brody. You know everything about me."

"And I'm not Kyle, but you can't seem to understand what I'm trying to tell you. You talk about traveling together, and then you go overboard giving my daughter extravagant and highly personal gifts—"

Shaken, she held up her hand. "Just stop talking." She took a deep, shuddering breath as her mind cleared. "I think we're done." Her words scraped out of her throat, nearly suffocating her.

His mouth opened, then closed. Finally, he said, "You don't mean that."

"Yeah, I do." The words tasted bitter, but a block of ice had formed in her chest.

He took a step toward her. "Maya, I didn't mean to be so harsh just now. I care deeply for you. Can't we just see where our feelings lead?"

"I think you and I have different ideas about what that means. When I asked if you and Ashlyn would go to Vermont with me this fall, you said, 'We'll see.' What does that mean exactly? I have an idea, but I'd like for you to tell me."

He pinched the bridge of his nose. "It means we'll see where we are in the fall. I don't know if I'll be ready for trips together by then. I don't want Ashlyn to jump to conclusions about us."

"Brody, Ashlyn loves me. She said so." She narrowed her eyes as her body shook with exasperation. "I don't think she's the one with the commitment problem. You are."

He blanched as if she'd struck him.

"I want a family, Brody," she continued, her voice creaking. "I've been ready to take that leap for a long time. But now I see you're too busy telling yourself you have to be the best father for Ashlyn and all women could be like Courtney. You're so busy worrying about making a mistake that you're missing what's right in front of you—someone who truly loves you."

"Maya, I'm only suggesting what I think is best for now. Especially for Ashlyn."

She shook her head. "If you don't think I have Ashlyn's best interest in mind, then maybe you don't know me after all. Stop using her as an excuse to keep me at arm's length. And if you can't acknowledge the truth, then we should break up."

He looked crestfallen. "So it's goodbye?"

"I guess so." Her voice sounded pinched as her eyes filled with tears, and she held her breath as Brody gathered the rest of Ashlyn's gifts.

"Don't forget the cake," she told him.

When he walked out of the room, she closed the door, leaned back against it, and slid to the floor. Anger gone, anguish wrapped around her chest, squeezing the air from her lungs as tears trickled down her cheeks.

She felt gutted.

~~~

Maya flipped the store's sign to Closed and stared out the window as the rain pounded the sidewalk.

"I'm telling you he looked distraught when he told Ashlyn it was time to go," Gayle said. "He clearly loves you. He's just too stubborn to admit it."

Maya sniffed, her grief sharp as a blade. "Thanks for your encouragement, but I really think it's over. At least I know now before I got in too deep." She closed her eyes. Who was she kidding? She was already in too deep, and she had no idea how she'd go on without Brody and Ashlyn in her life.

"Oh, sweetie." Gayle walked over and cupped her cheek. "Brody is a good man. He proved that when he stepped up with his niece after his mother died." She tilted her head. "Have you considered that maybe he's right? That you *should* take it slower?"

"What do you mean?"

"Perhaps you've been moving fast in your own heart because you want a family more than anything."

Maya opened her mouth but then closed it as her insides twisted.

Gayle shook her head. "It's okay. It will all work out. Just give Brody some time. He'll realize he can trust you."

Maya cleared her throat. "It's past time for you to go home."

"Do you want me to stay?"

"I appreciate the offer, but I'll be fine."

Gayle's eyes narrowed. "You sure?"

"Yes. Now go." Maya waved her off. "Shoo. I'll see you Monday."

Gayle gathered her purse, keys, and umbrella and headed for the back door.

Once the older woman was gone, Maya paced up and down the aisles as the rainfall intensified. She felt cold, lonely, and hollowed out. Hugging her arms to her middle, she leaned back against a display of stuffed sea creatures and tried to stop her heart from shattering completely. But she had no idea how.

A knock sounded on the front door.

Maya blinked and listened. Had she imagined it? Perhaps it was only the rain.

The knock sounded again, only louder.

"Hello!" a familiar voice called. "Is anyone in there?"

Maya crept toward the door, and her stomach dropped when she spotted her ex-fiancé peering through the glass. She scurried back into the aisle and sucked in a deep breath.

The knocking continued, and Maya rubbed her brow with confusion. Was she dreaming? Finally, she walked back to the door.

"Maya!" Kyle called when he saw her. "Please let me in. I'm soaked."

Against her better judgment, she unlocked the door and yanked it open.

"Thank you. Finally." He stepped in, and she closed and latched the door behind him as he pushed his hands through his drenched hair. "Do you have a towel or something?"

She slipped into the breakroom, took an old blanket from the worn wing chair, and carried it out to him. He dried his face, hair, and chest as she stood back and scrutinized him. Kyle looked the same—tall, fit, and handsome with dark hair cut short, brooding dark eyes, wide shoulders, and a wide chest. He wore tight blue jeans and a red T-shirt.

Happy memories of their time together surfaced in her mind— walking along Coral Cove's beach, holding hands at the movies, laughing with friends. Sitting on the balcony at her mother's apartment and watching the sun set, driving around Charlotte Motor Speedway and drinking hot cocoa while enjoying the colorful light displays at Christmastime.

And now Kyle was standing in front of her.

"I thought you were overseas." She hugged her arms to her chest as if to shield her already battered heart.

His lips tipped up in a smile. "I was, but I'm back. I returned to the States last week."

"What are you doing *here*?" She pointed to the floor.

He ran the blanket over his jeans. "My friend Trevor told me he'd heard your great-aunt died and you'd moved to Coral Cove. I'm sorry about your aunt. She was a nice lady."

"Thanks."

An awkward silence filled the store, and the rain seemed even louder.

Kyle suddenly smiled. "So you're running this place now? What about your writing?"

"I'm doing both, but what do you care? You still haven't told me why you're here, Kyle. When you left, you made it clear we were over, and you didn't respond to either of the emails I sent you."

"I quit my job over there and got my old one back."

Why couldn't she get a straight answer out of him? Fine, they'd take the long way around.

"Why? You said it was your dream job. And apparently it mattered more to you than the future we'd planned."

"I quit because I missed you, My." He took a step and placed his hands on her forearms. "I know I messed up, and I want to make things right. Give me a chance to prove it."

She smacked his hands away and took a step back. "When you left, you made it crystal clear you didn't want me. So why are you *really* here?"

"Maya, please just listen." His face crumpled with a deep frown, but was it genuine? She couldn't tell. After all, she'd believed he loved her right up until the day he left her.

"I know I hurt you, and I'm so sorry. But I'm here now to apologize and tell you I'm ready to commit to a future together. It took leaving to realize how much I need you. You're the best thing that's ever happened to me, and I'm here to prove I'm ready to put you first."

She rubbed her forehead as a headache brewed behind her eyes. She'd started the day with a boyfriend, and now she was single with her ex-fiancé insisting he wanted her back. Even more confusing, Kyle was offering her what her heart had been craving—a commitment. And he was offering it to her right now.

It was too much. She needed some time alone.

Kyle appeared beside her, and he had the nerve to look concerned. "You okay, My? You look a little green. I think you should sit down."

"And I think you should go," she snapped.

He moved away from her.

"Look, Kyle, it's been a long day. I'm exhausted, and I don't have the emotional strength to deal with you right now."

He cupped his hand to the back of his neck. "I know this is sudden, and I understand if you're still angry with me."

"Oh, do you?" She snorted.

He held up his hands as if to calm her. "Just listen, okay? I'm staying over at Ocean Breeze on Atlantic Avenue. Why don't we meet for brunch tomorrow at that Pancake Palace and talk? But not too early, if that's okay. I still have some jet lag."

"Fine. Be there at nine."

"Nine it is." He brightened. "I'll see you then."

Kyle walked out the door into the rain. Maya made sure the door was locked, then headed up to her apartment, checking the back door on her way.

After feeding Tinker Bell, she stepped into the shower, and as the hot water soaked her skin, she closed her eyes and let her emotions pour out. Visions of Ashlyn and Brody assaulted her mind, and she again wondered how she'd go on without them.

Tomorrow she'd see what Kyle had to say. She didn't think he held the key to the future she craved, but if he did, it was a future she'd never have with Brody.

~•~

"You okay, Daddy?"

Brody turned toward his daughter beside him on the sofa and found her little forehead creased with a worried frown. He'd thought she was watching *The Little Mermaid*, not him. "I'm fine."

"No, you're not." Ashlyn pointed to his face. "You're sad. You didn't answer me when I talked to you on the way home, and ever since we got back from Miss Maya's store, you've been staring out the window."

He reached over and touched her shoulder. "I'm sorry. I'm listening to you now."

"What's wrong?"

He pushed himself up from the sofa, and Rusty jogged over, his collar tinkling. "I'm fine, Ash. Are you hungry? Would you like another piece of cake?"

"Cake for dinner?" She cackled.

"Why not? It's your birthday."

"Okay!"

Brody hurried out to the kitchen, and every one of their pets followed him. While the cats began a chorus for their supper, he filled their bowls before adding kibble to Rusty's.

Then, admittedly despondent, Brody gripped the counter and dipped his head. He'd never expected to lose Maya today, and that reality rocked him. He'd been stunned when she told him she loved him and was ready to make a commitment. The truth was he loved her, too, but he wasn't ready to admit it. Once he did . . .

But now he couldn't seem to quell the regret that grabbed him by the throat as he and Ashlyn exited Maya's store. Had he made a mistake? The last thing he'd wanted was to wind up with a broken heart. He'd hoped to never again experience the depth of anguish Courtney had caused him. Yet here he was trying to cope with losing a woman he loved, which meant that was exactly what he was experiencing. His heart was broken.

But it was too soon. Why couldn't Maya see that?

"Daddy! Where's my cake?" Ashlyn called.

He stood straight. "Coming. I was just feeding the herd."

Opening a cabinet, Brody found two plates and then retrieved the leftover chocolate cake from the refrigerator. While he cut two pieces, he continued to contemplate how his relationship with Maya had crumbled so quickly. He should have made himself wait until Ashlyn was much older to involve himself with a woman. Yes, that would mean Maya wouldn't be in his life as more than a friend, but at least she would be in his life.

He stowed the rest of the cake in the refrigerator and then balanced two plates and forks on his way back to the family room.

Ashlyn set her new doll from Maya on the sofa beside her and clapped. "Yay! You cut pieces with lots of icing!"

"Here you go, birthday girl," Brody said as he handed her a couple of napkins.

"Thank you, Daddy." Ashlyn turned her attention back to the movie.

Although Brody's appetite had evaporated as soon as Maya told him they were through, he nibbled on the sweet icing and watched as Sebastian and his chorus of friends instructed Prince Eric to kiss the girl. If only relationships were that easy.

"When is Miss Maya coming over?"

Brody faced his daughter. "What?"

"When is Miss Maya coming over? She comes over on weekends or we go to her house, right? Why isn't she here?"

"I-I don't know when she's coming over."

Ashlyn looked incredulous as she set her plate on the coffee table. Then she picked up his phone from the sofa and handed it to him. "Text her and ask her to come over."

Brody stared at the phone. He'd half expected a message from Maya, hoping she'd want to talk, but he saw nothing on the screen.

His heart sank. But then he realized he couldn't give her up without a fight. She meant too much to him. She had to give him another chance to explain where he was coming from. Somehow, he'd try to make her understand.

"Take it, Daddy. Text her." Ashlyn pushed the phone into his hand. "Or I can do it if you're too tired."

Brody took the phone and set it down beside him on the sofa. "I'll text her later. Let's finish the movie."

"Okay." Ashlyn picked up her plate and scooted closer to him.

He'd give Maya time to cool off, and then he'd contact her. And somehow he'd convince her to at least talk to him. He couldn't let her go so easily.

Chapter 23

Maya yawned as she sat across from Kyle at Pancake Palace the following morning. Her eyes burned from tossing and turning all night as grief, confusion, doubt, regret, and anger all pummeled her bruised heart.

She'd spent those hours analyzing her heartbreaking conversation with Brody while puzzling over what she could have done differently to save their relationship. Perhaps Brody and Gayle were right. Maybe she'd been trying to push her relationship with Brody too far too fast.

Then she considered calling him and begging him to take her back. At one point she'd even unlocked her phone and started to text him. But then she stopped when she realized dating him without a commitment would never satisfy her. Still, the thought of life without him and Ashlyn sent her spiraling into a state of painful loss.

She'd also pondered Kyle's return and what it meant. Finally, around five in the morning, she'd fallen asleep. But then her alarm had woken her at eight, and she'd smacked the snooze button three times before dragging herself into the shower. She'd hoped the water would energize her despite a yearning to crawl back into bed, cover her face with a pillow, and sleep the day away.

Maya looked out the front windows of the restaurant, and the cloudless sky seemed to mock her as the usual groups of weekend visitors, looking happy and well rested, moved past on the sidewalks. None of them knew the depth of her confusion and grief. Nor did they care.

"Did you hear what I said, Maya?"

"What?" Maya's gaze flitted to Kyle's.

Leaning forward, he took her hand in his. "I said I care for you, Maya."

"Oh." She pulled her hand away. He'd claimed that before. Why should she think he meant it now?

A middle-aged, portly woman approached their table dressed in the restaurant's usual old-fashioned blue uniform. She was chewing gum and holding a notepad as she pulled a pencil out from behind her ear. "What can I get ya?"

"Coffee and the pancake special with bacon, please," Kyle said.

The woman smacked her gum and scribbled. Then she turned to Maya. "And you, miss?"

"Um . . ." Food was the last thing on her mind. In fact, the idea of eating nauseated her. "I'll have the same."

"Coming right up." The woman headed toward the kitchen.

"So as I was saying," Kyle continued, "I'd like us to make a life back in Charlotte. I got my old job back, and I've already been working on finding us a place to live."

Maya tried to comprehend his words.

"Are you listening, Maya?" He leaned toward her again. "I want to marry you, have a family with you, and grow old with you."

She narrowed her eyes. "If that's true, why did you break our engagement and leave me?"

An unreadable expression flickered over his face. Had she caught him off guard?

He quickly recovered but looked sheepish. "I was selfish, immature, and foolish. I was thinking about my own aspirations instead of our future."

"Interesting." Now she leaned forward, her lips twisting as she challenged him. "But if you cared about me, why didn't you at least invite me to go with you? After all, I'm an author and can work anywhere. I had nothing tying me to Charlotte."

The server approached the table and set their coffee mugs in front of them. Out of the corner of her eye, Maya noticed Kyle's expression relax as if he were grateful for the interruption.

The woman left again, and Kyle began adding cream and sugar to his mug.

"You didn't answer my question, Kyle. Why didn't you ask me to go to the UK with you if you care so much about me?"

Kyle stared at his mug for a moment and then looked up at her. "I already told you I was immature and thoughtless."

"That doesn't make sense." She shook her head. "You can be immature and thoughtless and also in love. And to want to marry someone, you should be in love. Do you love me or not?"

He leveled his gaze with hers. "I'm here to beg for your forgiveness and another chance. Will you give me another try, Maya?"

Maya pulled a deep breath in through her nose as she stared at him.

"Why didn't you answer my emails?" She tapped her finger on the table for emphasis.

"Because I wanted to talk to you in person. I want to give you the things you've always wanted. Didn't you say you wanted to be married by the time you're thirty? And you said you wanted to be a mom by the time you're thirty-one. Well, your thirtieth birthday is only a few months away. I can make those dreams come true for you."

Her hands shook as she stared at Kyle. How dare he talk as though he was her sole escape from old maidhood? Yet he was right. She had said those things. Maybe he deserved a second chance. Didn't everyone? And what choice did she have if she wanted a family of her own?

Then she realized she did have a choice—between waiting for who knew how long for Brody to make a commitment and getting the future she longed for from Kyle, not someday but now.

Kyle reached for something in his pocket and then pushed back his chair. He came around the table and dropped down on one knee, then pulled out a ring box, opened it, and held it up. In it was the ring she'd worn for nearly a year—a princess-cut diamond. The ring that once meant the promise of a happy future.

"What are you doing, Kyle? Stop," Maya hissed as her heart slammed against her rib cage. "Get up!"

"Maya Elizabeth Reynolds," he said loudly, "will you do me the honor of becoming my wife?"

Oh no! No, no, no! This can't be happening!

A woman nearby gasped. "Look! He's proposing!"

Maya's cheeks felt as if they would spontaneously combust as people around them pulled out their cell phones and pointed them at her. She was frozen in place, panic grabbing her by the throat and squeezing the life out of her.

"Say yes! Say yes!" someone yelled.

Maya scanned the crowd, and the room seemed to spin. She was going to be sick!

"Hey, Maya." Kyle gave a little laugh. "Uh, don't leave me hanging here."

She felt the weight of the world pressing down on her shoulders. She just wanted this humiliating moment to be over, and she could end it only by accepting his proposal. With her whole body vibrating, she looked down at him. "Yes," she croaked.

The crowd clapped, hooted, and hollered as Kyle slipped her former engagement ring on her finger.

"Thank you," he said breathily. "I won't let you down this time." Then he brushed his lips over hers as the crowd continued cheering.

When he broke the kiss, she stared at him, hoping for an explosion of emotion, fireworks, anything.

She felt *nothing*.

Kyle's kiss had never felt like Brody's, and it didn't now.

"Congratulations!" Callie Lewis appeared at their table. She lifted Maya's left hand and examined the ring, then grinned. "Great rock," she told Kyle. Then she held her hand out to him. "I'm Callie Lewis. I own the bookshop here."

"Kyle Bishop," he said, shaking her hand.

Callie turned to Maya. "And all this time I thought you were dating Brody Tanner. Ha! What did I know?" She leaned down. "Don't forget to stop by so we can finalize a date for your book signing." Then she called, "Enjoy your day!" over her shoulder as she walked to the counter.

"Who's Brody?" Kyle asked.

Maya looked toward the cash register, and her chest heaved when she spotted Kim Banks wearing burgundy scrubs and holding a tray of coffee cups. She was staring at Maya, her eyes wide and her mouth hanging open. Their gazes locked, and Maya felt as if she couldn't breathe.

"Who's Brody?" Kyle asked again.

Maya turned and found him watching her just as intently. "He's a friend."

The server reappeared with a tray, then set plates with a mountain of pancakes and bacon in front of them. She also presented a large piece of chocolate cake and two dessert forks.

"Congratulations on the engagement. The cake is from me," she announced.

Kyle grinned. "Thank you."

The server disappeared, and Maya stared at her pancakes. The nausea had worsened—especially since Kyle was now talking a mile a minute.

"We can get married right away at the justice of the peace and just have a small reception with a few friends. Then we can rent a place until we're ready to buy." He smothered his pancakes with butter and syrup. "By the way, how are your novels going? Do you have more contracts?"

"I'm working on one now. I have to finish out this contract before my agent can ask for another one."

"Oh, that makes sense. So Trevor told me about this house in his neighborhood that's for rent. It's a little two-bedroom, but it will do for now. I need to find out how much the security deposit and first month's rent will be."

Maya huffed out a breath, her stomach in a knot. "What about my store?"

"Sell it. It's prime property here." He took a bite of bacon and shrugged. "Maybe that cranky old lady who worked for your aunt can buy it. What was her name?"

Maya's eyes narrowed to slits as she glowered at her repeat fiancé. "Her name is Gayle, she still works there, and she's not a cranky old lady. She's a wonderful person and an even better friend."

"Right. Anyway, maybe she'd like to buy the building from you. Or even better, a real estate investor might want the land."

Kyle continued talking, but his words were only noise in Maya's buzzing head. Her world had spun out of control, and she couldn't make sense out of it. *I've always wanted the promise of a future, a husband, a home, and a family, and Kyle's offering it all to me right now. So why does this feel so wrong?*

"We can start tracking down real estate investors right now. You have internet at the apartment, right?"

She covered her face with her hands.

"Maya? Maya."

She peeked at him through splayed fingers.

"You're not saying anything. What's wrong?"

She snorted. He'd finally noticed she'd been quiet.

"This is what you wanted, right?"

She licked her lips. "Kyle, when you've finished your breakfast, we need to go somewhere private to talk."

~•~

"Dr. Brody?"

Brody looked up from the report he'd been trying to write and found Kim standing in his office doorway. "Kim. Hi."

She gave him a tentative expression. "May I come in? I brought coffee." She held up a tray with four cups, and the delicious smell wafted over him.

He stood from his desk. "Of course. Thank you."

She stepped into his office. "Here you go."

Brody took the cup she offered and immediately sipped from it, hoping the warm drink would bring him some comfort. But it did little to heal his broken heart. He'd been awake most of the night, staring at the ceiling and trying to find the right words to apologize to Maya and ask her to give him another chance. If only they could just talk—

Kim's words brought him back to the present. "Justin texted that you and Dr. Montgomery didn't need my help with the Gilleland cat's emergency surgery after all, but since I was already on my way, I stopped and picked up coffees for us."

Brody held up his cup as if to toast her. "I appreciate it. I was just typing up the report." *Or staring at it.*

"You're welcome. I'm glad Oatmeal will be okay." She started for the door but then stopped and gave him a strange expression.

"Something wrong?" Brody sat on the edge of his desk.

Kim hesitated. "I got the coffee at Pancake Palace."

"Okay . . ."

"I saw something there, and I'm not sure if I should tell you."

"Kim, I'm sorry, but I didn't get enough sleep last night to solve riddles. Please just explain what you're trying to say."

"I saw Maya Reynolds there with a man."

Brody's stomach plunged. "What do you mean?" He set the coffee cup on the desk and stood.

Kim grimaced.

"Just say it."

"She was having breakfast with this guy. Then he got down on one knee, pulled out a diamond, and proposed to her. And she said yes." Kim looked pained. "I'm so sorry, Dr. Brody. I know you've been seeing her."

Brody's insides twisted, and he was certain he was going to be sick. "Who was he?" he managed to ask.

"I didn't recognize him, but I saw Callie Lewis talking to them. So when she walked over to where I was standing, I asked her who he was. She said his name is Kyle Bishop."

Brody felt like the floor had collapsed beneath him. "Kyle?"

Kim nodded.

"You're certain she said Kyle?" Surely he'd misheard her.

"Yes, I'm positive."

Brody dropped down on the desk and rubbed his eyes with the heels of his hands. Maya had ripped out his heart and then rushed right back into Kyle's arms. And now she was going to marry him.

Marry him!

This had to be some sort of nightmare.

"Dr. Brody? Are you okay?"

Brody cleared his throat and turned toward the doorway. Kim stood watching him with concern on her face. "I will be."

"You look like you need some sleep. If you want, I can keep Ashlyn this afternoon, and you can go take a nap."

"Thanks, but she's at a friend's house."

"Well, you look like you could use some rest."

"I'll be okay," he told her, but that was a flat-out lie. He wouldn't be okay for a long time.

Kim nodded. "All right." Then she disappeared into the hallway.

Brody picked up his phone and stared at it. He couldn't let Maya fall for Kyle again, not after that man had destroyed her. She may not want Brody anymore, but he couldn't let her ruin her life. He cared about her too much.

He shot off a quick text to her: Can we please talk? Then he held his breath and waited for conversation bubbles to appear.

"Come on, Maya," he whispered. "Answer me! Don't let Kyle hurt you again."

After a few moments he tried again: Please, Maya. I need to talk to you.

He waited for the conversation bubbles again, but none appeared.

There was only one thing left to do. Go to her and hope she'd talk to him when he stood in front of her.

Brody picked up his keys and then headed out of his office. He would tell Cam he was leaving and then get to Maya's apartment as fast as he could.

Maya sat on the sofa while Kyle examined a line of framed photos on a bookshelf in the family room. She'd picked at her pancakes while waiting for him to finish his and then they'd walked back to her place. Although her stomach was still in knots, she thought the few sips of strong coffee she'd managed to take had helped her get a better handle on the situation.

"Who's Brody?" he asked again as he stared at a photo of Maya and her mother. They were at her high school graduation.

"I told you, he's just a friend."

He looked over his shoulder at her. "That woman at the restaurant thought you were dating him."

"It didn't work out." She felt a muscle flex in her jaw.

He pointed to a second photo of her posing with her father— a selfie she'd taken on the beach with him. "Who's this?"

"That's my father."

Kyle spun to face her, his expression stunned. "I thought you didn't know your father."

"It's a long story."

"What happened?"

She gave him an abbreviated version.

"That's great." He grinned. "And he's a lawyer, huh? Lucky you."

Nodding, Maya cut her gaze to the diamond ring. At one time it had been her most prized possession, but now it didn't even seem to fit her finger. It felt too loose and uncomfortable. In fact, at the moment, nothing felt right. Yet Kyle was in her apartment offering her the life she wanted.

As if finally sensing her anxiety, Kyle sat down beside her. "Maya, talk to me. What's on your mind?"

"This is all so sudden."

"Yes, but it makes sense. We make sense." He gestured between them. "I'm sorry for hurting you. I promise I'll do better this time. I'll do everything in my power to make you happy and glad you gave me another chance."

Maya popped up from the sofa. "I'm going to make coffee."

She walked to the kitchen, wishing she knew what to do. Confusion dulled her mind as she readied her coffee maker, and soon it belched to life, flooding the kitchen with its glorious aroma. She searched for two mugs and set them on the table along with sugar, sweetener, and creamer.

When her phone dinged, the screen lit up with Brody's name followed by a text message: Can we please talk?

Her stomach dipped, and her eyes stung.

She locked her phone and stuck it back into her pocket.

When her phone dinged again, she pulled it out and read a second message from Brody: Please, Maya. I need to talk to you.

She unlocked her phone, and her fingers hovered over the tiny keyboard, ready to type . . . Her fingers froze in place. Ready to type what? She'd never felt so conflicted in her life.

Kyle ambled into the kitchen. "So how's your aunt's business? Is it profitable?"

She locked the phone and sniffed before pasting a smile on her face. "Well, profits could use a boost. So I started hosting tea parties for little girls' birthdays, and it's going well."

"Tea parties?"

"Yes. The girls love them."

Maya told him about her new venture while she poured their coffee, but she could tell he wasn't really interested.

She joined him at the table. "So how was London?" she asked when she ran out of things to say about the parties.

He shrugged. "It wasn't what I expected."

"What do you mean?"

Kyle fingered his mug handle. "I decided it was best to come back to the States."

She opened her mouth to ask what he was talking about when the doorbell rang.

"Are you expecting company?"

"No."

Maya stood and then loped down the stairs to the back door.

When she pushed the door open, she found Brody wearing blue scrubs with *Brody C. Tanner, DVM*, embroidered over the breast pocket. Maya felt a heaviness around her heart as she took in his frown and the dark circles under his tired blue eyes. Had he also had a sleepless night? Or perhaps he'd lost another precious patient. After all, he was dressed for work on a Sunday, which meant he'd been called in for an emergency.

But she still didn't want to talk to him.

"What do you want?" The gravel in her throat manifested in the rasp of her words.

"You didn't answer my texts," Brody said. "I need to talk to you."

"There's nothing left to say. You said it all yesterday."

Brody took a step toward her. "No, *you* said it all yesterday. You didn't give me a chance to explain."

"This isn't a good time. I have company." Maya lifted her chin and hoped she sounded more confident than she felt.

Brody looked down at her left hand, and dismay seemed to flicker across his face. Or was it regret? He pointed to her ring. "So it's true, then?"

Her stomach twisted, and she pushed her left hand into the pocket of her jean shorts.

She heard footfalls behind her. Kyle. When he reached the doorway, he took a step outside and gave Brody an arrogant look. "Hi. Kyle Bishop." He held out his hand. "And you are . . .?"

Brody's eyes narrowed, and then he stared at her. "Explain something to me, Maya. I'm confused." His voice seeped with sarcasm. "You break up with me and then get engaged to your ex the next day? Is that how this works?"

"This wasn't planned," she whispered even though his tone was so accusing. This was the last thing she needed—*two* men adding to her confusion.

Brody divided a look between her and Kyle. "I thought this guy was in the UK."

"I'm back." Kyle pointed at Brody's shirt. "So you're the infamous Brody. Well, you lost out." He tried to pull Maya into his arms, but she pushed him away.

Brody gritted his teeth. "Maya, may I *please* talk to you?"

"I'm sorry, Brody, but it's not a good time." She tore her gaze away from his and then spun toward the stairs, her heart breaking with each step.

"Maya," Brody called after her. "I'm sorry. I messed up, and I want to fix this."

"It's too late," Kyle said. Then he placed his hand on Maya's back before slamming the door in Brody's face.

Chapter 24

"So I guess this is goodbye for now," Kyle said as they stood next to his Ford Explorer that afternoon.

Maya nodded. While she'd watched, Kyle had searched the internet for more houses and apartments to rent in Charlotte in case the one Trevor found didn't work out. Then they'd landed at one of Kyle's favorite restaurants in town for a late lunch. He talked incessantly about plans as if they were making them together, which they weren't. Maya only half listened while contemplating what Brody said. Again, she pushed more food around her plate than she ate.

She kept trying to comprehend what Brody's words and demeanor had meant. He said he wanted to explain, that he'd messed up and wanted to fix it. But that could just mean he wanted to repair their friendship, not promise her a future. What did it matter, though? It all seemed too little too late when Kyle was here promising her marriage and children *now*. Yet cold grief seeped into her heart as Brody's anguished face filled her mind.

"I'll be back in time for that Labor Day Festival next weekend, okay? You can run that tea party Saturday, and we'll go to the festival that night. Then maybe we can drive to Charlotte on Sunday and sign the lease for the house we like best. Sound good?"

"Sure." She didn't know what else to say.

"I'll call you when I get to Trevor's." Kyle took her hand and towed her to him before kissing her.

Once again she waited for any sign of fireworks . . . but felt nothing.

"Be safe," she told him.

She waited for him to drive out of the parking lot and then made her way back to her apartment. Dropping down onto the sofa beside Tinker Bell, she turned on Netflix as her mind continued to churn.

When her phone dinged, her heart lurched. A message from Brody: Maya, I'm so sorry. You took me by surprise when you told me how you felt. Let's talk about it, okay?

I need some space.

Tell me you're not marrying Kyle.

That's none of your business.

But he hurt you.

She started to respond but instead opened her phone app and called Kiana.

"Hi, My! How was your weekend?"

"Eventful." Maya rubbed her forehead. "I have so much to tell you."

Taking a deep breath, Maya told her everything from the disaster at Ashlyn's party to Kyle's proposal, then ended with Brody appearing at her back door. When she finished, Kiana was silent.

"Just say what you're thinking, Key. I can take it."

"Do you really want me to be honest with you?"

"Yes. You're my best friend. I expect you to be honest with me."

"Kyle hurt you—a lot. I remember how you sobbed on the bathroom floor the day he told you he was going to Europe and didn't want you to come with him. How can you possibly just forgive him for that and agree to marry him?"

"He says he's changed."

"And you believe him?"

"I-I don't know." Maya stared down at the ring. "My head is spinning. You know I've always wanted to get married and have a family, but Brody isn't ready to commit to a future with me, and I don't know if he ever will be. Kyle, on the other hand, is offering me everything I've wanted right now." She absently spun the ring on her finger. "I'm confused."

"Maya, maybe you should give Brody a chance to tell you what he wants to say. After all, you said you had a real connection with him."

"But I don't know if he'll ever marry me. While we were arguing, he admitted he was engaged once." She told Kiana about his ex-fiancée, Courtney. "I'm devastated that he never trusted me enough to share that story. And after the way I reacted, I doubt he'll ever trust me enough to let me prove I love him—and Ashlyn—enough to never hurt them."

Then something hit Maya like a ton of bricks, and she gasped. Kyle claimed he cared about her, but when she asked if he'd ever loved her, he hadn't said. And he didn't even ask if she loved him. Maybe he did care for her on some level, but without love, how could they build the marriage and family she wanted?

"What?" Kiana asked.

"Nothing."

"Listen, Maya, maybe you need to give yourself time to breathe and think."

Maya nodded. "You're right. I need to take a few days and mull all this over." She sniffed. "Tell me how you are. How's Deacon?"

When their conversation ended, Maya leaned back on the sofa. She longed for life to settle down, but that might happen only by throwing herself back into plans for a future with Kyle, whether or not he loved her. She'd sell Aunt CeCe's business and building, marry him, and move back to Charlotte, trusting that he would love her someday. Then she'd get over Brody—and Ashlyn. She'd have to.

But she didn't have to make a final decision tonight.

"Are you really considering selling the store?" Gayle asked Maya the next morning, right after she gave her an abbreviated version of what happened over the weekend.

"I don't want to, but I do want to get married and have a family. I'll be thirty in November."

Gayle frowned and touched Maya's shoulder. "Sweetie, marriage is hard enough without rushing into it. You need to take a breath and let your heart lead you. Don't feel pressured to marry the first man who asks you. Plus, you shouldn't settle for anyone who makes you give up what you love, and you love this store, right? Think long and hard about marrying Kyle."

For the next hour, Maya busied herself with stocking the Hot Wheels and Matchbox aisle in order to avoid talking to customers.

When her phone dinged, she looked down and found another text from Brody: I know you told me to give you space, but it's killing me. Will you please talk to me?

Her fingers hovered over the keyboard as she considered what to say. When the light glinted off her diamond ring, she closed her eyes and considered Kiana's and Gayle's advice. Then she typed: I need time to think. I'll contact you when I'm ready to talk.

Okay. I'll be ready when you are.

For some reason, disappointment flooded her. She wanted him to show up at her door again but this time sweep her off her feet. Instead, he'd agreed to silence.

And the silence was deafening.

Maya sat at her desk and stared out the window Wednesday evening. She couldn't stop thinking about Brody and Ashlyn and how much she missed them. She kept hoping they would show up at the store and invite her to go out to eat with them, but Brody was respecting her request to give her space. His text messages had stopped, perhaps proving he'd decided to give up on her.

A chasm of disappointment opened in her chest as she looked at the photo of them on the roller coaster, holding hands and screaming together like a happy family. But they'd never be a family, not with the wall around Brody's heart. He and Ashlyn would just be two people she used to know. People she would always miss.

She turned to stare at her laptop screen. She hadn't written a word since she and Brody broke up, and her manuscript was almost due. She'd have to call her agent and ask her to negotiate another extension. She frowned as anxiety once again gripped her. Her editor was great, but she would not be happy.

Her phone dinged with a text message, and she saw Kyle's name on the screen: Hey, babe! Thinking of you and looking forward to the weekend. Work is good, and I found a couple more houses to look at. They look even better than that first one.

Okay.

Gotta go! I've got work to finish up.

Good night.

Maya managed to write a couple of sentences, but she was just as glad when her phone rang and she found her father's number on the screen.

"Hey, Dad."

"Sorry I haven't called in a few days. It's been hectic here. How are things?"

Taking a deep breath, she unloaded and told him everything—from her disastrous breakup with Brody to her unexpected engagement to Kyle. Her father listened quietly, and when she finished she felt as if a weight had been lifted from her chest.

"So what do you think?" she asked.

"Well, here's a question. Why did you accept Kyle's proposal if he's let you down before and you're not even sure if he loves you?"

"Because I want a husband and family."

"Maya, not only do I hear hesitation in your voice, but you're a young, beautiful, smart, successful, independent, and courageous woman who deserves to be loved and adored. And I'm not just saying that because I'm your dad." He paused. "Patrice and I had a good marriage before her accident, but I've known a few guys who felt trapped in unhappy marriages. My advice is don't get married unless you're certain you've found the love of your life. If Kyle isn't that guy, then don't marry him. Don't settle because you're afraid the right person won't come along."

Her eyes filled with tears. "Thank you, Dad. I'll think it over."

"You're welcome. When are you going to see Kyle again?"

"He's coming back on Friday. This weekend is the Labor Day Festival. He said he'd go with me and then we'd make more plans."

"Also think long and hard before you agree to sell your store. I can tell you love it, and I don't want you to rush into a decision you'll regret the rest of your life. Promise me you won't make a snap decision."

"I won't, Dad. Thank you."

They talked about his work for a few minutes, and then he said he'd let her go.

"Let's make plans to see each other soon, okay?" he said. "I miss you."

"I miss you too."

"Let me know what you decide."

"I will. Good night."

She was so grateful to have her father in her life.

~·~

"Hey, beautiful." Kyle handed Maya a dozen pink roses as he walked into her apartment Friday evening. "I missed you."

"These are lovely. Thank you." Maya took the box and walked to the kitchen counter. As she arranged the roses in a vase, her mind wandered through the last couple of days. She still hadn't heard from Brody, and she missed him so much her heart hurt.

She glanced at Kyle and found him staring at his phone. She had to face the truth. Was she trying to convince herself she wanted to marry Kyle only because she wanted a family and Brody wouldn't commit?

Kyle pocketed his phone and then walked over to Maya, wrapping his arms around her waist. "How about we go out to eat? We can hit that Japanese place over on Laskin Road."

She stepped out of his embrace and set the roses on the kitchen table. "I'd rather have the food delivered. It's been a long week."

"Oh." He seemed surprised. "Okay. I'll place an order."

"Thanks."

He pulled up the menu on his phone, and they each chose a meal before he made the call.

Maya leaned against the counter while he placed the order. She felt so unsettled. She needed to get some issues off her chest before she agreed to give up her life in Coral Cove for him. First and foremost, she had to know if he truly loved her.

When he ended the call, she pointed to the kitchen table. "Let's sit and talk while we wait for the food."

"Uh-oh. This sounds serious." He grinned, but when she just stared at him, the grin faded. "What's wrong?"

"My heart breaks when I think about selling everything my

great-aunt built and just leaving here. I may have been back only a short time, but I have friends here. This place also holds a lot of wonderful memories, and giving that up wouldn't be easy."

"Maya, this is your past. We have a whole future to plan. I want to start over." He hesitated. "Your aunt was never married, right?"

"No, she wasn't."

"And she didn't have any kids or other heirs, right?"

"Right."

He leaned forward, and a strange expression overtook his face. "Did she leave you any money?"

She blanched as if he'd struck her. "She left me some, but I put it in savings."

"Really? How much?"

For a moment she didn't know what to think. But then she sat back in her chair as all the times she'd lent—no, given—Kyle money flashed through her mind. She thought about how he told her the job in the UK meant a huge salary and lots of expensive perks. How he'd always wanted the latest car model, the finest furniture, the best of everything. How all his friends, especially Trevor, were the same way.

How could she have been so stupid? Kyle didn't love her; he wanted her money! Hadn't he proposed to her shortly after she told him her agent thought she'd get a bigger advance on her next contract? He was only using her, he'd always used her, and she deserved so much better!

As if he'd read her mind, panic seemed to flash over his face, and he started talking faster than he had after she'd stupidly accepted his ring in the middle of Pancake Palace. "Of course, we'll look for a house with good schools. I know you want kids, and we can start trying right away . . ."

Maya's jaw tightened as outrage swirled in her chest like a swarm of angry hornets. She'd been a fool to think Kyle was a good man, let alone that he'd changed since dumping her!

She was about to tell him so when the doorbell rang, announcing that their food had arrived. Kyle jumped up and jogged downstairs. Maya fed Tinker Bell, trying to calm herself and decide exactly how to end this ridiculous dance with Kyle.

When it seemed he'd been gone too long, she started down the stairs to the back door, noticing it was open a crack. She breathed in the smell of Asian food as she heard Kyle's voice. Who was he talking to?

Tiptoeing toward the door, she peeked outside. He was talking on his cell phone, the delivery bag at his feet.

"Yeah, the job wasn't what it was cracked up to be. The boss was a hothead. He didn't like me from the start, and then he actually fired me and told me to go back to the States where I belonged. He said I wasn't a good fit. Can you imagine that?"

Maya gasped. He'd been fired? He'd *lied* to her!

"Yeah, I'm lucky Jerry rehired me. I ran out of money in London. Guess I did too much partying." He snickered. "So now I'm here in Coral Cove trying to work things out with Maya. She just inherited property and money from her great-aunt. She has this ridiculous toy store, which is a waste of prime property. I think she can get a pretty penny for it. It's two blocks from the ocean, and I'm sure some investor would knock down this dump and put up something classy or turn the building into a couple of vacation condos.

I'm trying to convince her to sell it so we can invest in a nice place in Charlotte. Maybe somewhere like South Park or even Myers Park."

He paused as whoever was on the other end responded, and Maya was tempted to storm outside then and there. But she wanted to hear what else Kyle said.

"Uh-huh. And guess what else. She also found her long-lost father, and he's a successful lawyer up in DC. I looked him up. Since he's never been a part of her life until now, I wonder if we can get some guilt money out of him. He can help me get back on my feet too."

His words were like a knife to Maya's soul, and white-hot fury boiled under her skin. Kyle cared only about himself and what she could do to improve his situation! For all she knew, he'd break their engagement again if it suited him—after bleeding her dry.

Then she realized she hadn't missed Kyle at all. She'd only missed having a companion in her life. Her father was right— marrying Kyle would be a huge mistake. She needed to kick him to the curb now!

She pushed the door open so hard that it swung toward the creep with a *whoosh*. He jumped, his eyes wild as he spun toward her, tripping over the bag of food. When he recovered, he said, "Hey, Austin, I have to go. I'll call you soon. Bye." He disconnected the call and stared at her. "You almost got me with the door. What's your problem?"

"What's my *problem*?" She spat the words at him. "I heard what you said. I was so stupid to think you came back to the States for me. You were fired!"

He opened his mouth but then closed it, reminding her of a fish out of water.

"Now I know the truth. You came here because you need money, and you thought you'd get it from me. And why not? I don't even know how much I've given you before." Her body vibrated as she shook a finger at him.

He held up his hands, caught in his own untruth. "No, I honestly missed you."

"I don't think so. You saw me as a dumb woman willing to forgive you and basically give you all her money—even her property—because she was so desperate for a husband and a family, right?"

He pursed his lips, and the air between them sat heavy and stale.

"Tell me one thing, Kyle," she began, her voice trembling. "Did you ever love me?"

He shrugged. "Sure."

"You're a lying, scheming, lousy excuse for a human being." Her nostrils flared as she gritted her teeth and breathed in. "Kiana tried to warn me not to get involved with you again, but I was fool enough to believe you might have changed. But you were just using me." Her voice was as sharp and cold as glass. "I deserve to be treated better. I deserve a man who truly loves and respects me and isn't just after my resources. You're not worth my time. Get out of here and never come back. I never want to see you again."

"But, Maya. Wait."

She took the ring off and threw it at him. It hit him in the chest and then bounced to the ground. "I'll stay here in my ridiculous store and my dumpy building. I don't need you or anyone else to make me happy. I can find happiness by myself. Have a good life, Kyle."

She barreled back inside and locked the door behind her. He could have the food for all she cared.

She felt relief as she heard Kyle's Explorer rumble to life and then move out of her parking lot. But as she climbed the stairs, she realized that relief wasn't enough. Her heart longed for Brody. She loved him. If only he felt the same about her. A fresh crush of sadness enveloped her as she envisioned him telling her he was sorry, but even though he cared for her, they could only be friends.

Perhaps she'd get over her anguish someday, but that just didn't seem possible. She'd have to separate herself from Brody and Ashlyn just to survive, and that thought sat cold and heavy in her heart.

Chapter 25

"L ook at all those people out there," Gayle said, locking the front door of the store the following evening. "This Labor Day looks more like the Fourth of July."

Maya's shoulders sagged as she closed out the register. "It certainly was busy today. I felt bad that I couldn't help you out here, but I had the party to run. I think I need to hire someone to either run the parties or help you in the store."

She covered her mouth with her hand as a yawn overtook her. All day long she'd fought against the exhaustion that threatened to knock her off her feet. She'd spent the night tossing and turning while berating herself for falling for Kyle's lies and empty promises. He'd never been the man for her. She'd just overlooked his faults for the future she wanted.

She'd also checked her phone throughout the night hoping to find a text from Brody. Why did he have to be such a gentleman, respecting her request for space? Perhaps he had given up on her. After all, as far as he knew, she was still engaged.

She pressed her fingers to her forehead and groaned. When she felt something rub against her shin, she glanced down at Tinker Bell, who squeaked out a meow. Well, at least she still had her cat.

"Are you going to the festival fireworks tonight, Maya? I hear they'll be just as fantastic as they were in July."

She turned to Gayle, who was gathering her belongings. "I don't know. It's no fun going alone."

"So come with my family and me. You know my grandkids think you're the coolest author on the planet. Of course, you're the only author they know." Gayle chuckled and touched Maya's arm.

"Thanks, but I think Tink and I will just watch some Netflix."

Gayle harrumphed. "Suit yourself, but don't sulk too long. You're too young to be holed up in your apartment eating bonbons and feeling sorry for yourself." She ambled toward the hall. "I'll see you next week."

"Enjoy the long weekend," Maya called after her.

After locking the store, Maya picked up a squirming Tinker Bell and ascended the stairs to her apartment. She fed the cat and then heated up leftover macaroni and cheese. She stood by the front window and ate while watching the sea of people walking toward the oceanfront to enjoy the food trucks, music, and fireworks.

Maya turned toward her television set, and as she picked up the remote, Gayle's words echoed through her mind: *Suit yourself, but don't sulk too long. You're too young to be holed up in your apartment eating bonbons and feeling sorry for yourself.*

She set the remote back on the end table. Gayle was right. She was too young to sit at home alone. After all, she lived at the beach, and she needed to take advantage of it.

After pulling on a pair of jean shorts and a pink tank top, she pulled her hair up in a French braid. Then she slipped on her favorite sparkly pink Birkenstocks, grabbed her wallet, keys, and phone, and headed into the humid evening air.

～·～

"Why don't you text Miss Maya?" Ashlyn whined as she took Brody's hand in hers. They were heading to the boardwalk.

Brody shook his head. "I already told you. She said she needs some space."

"Because you two had a fight."

"Yes." He sighed. "Because we had a fight."

"Well, why don't you just say you're sorry? That's what I do when me and Tessie have a fight."

He smiled down at her. "It's a little more complicated than that."

"If you want, I'll tell her you're sorry. Will that help?"

Brody stopped walking and his throat thickened as he looked down at his sweet daughter. "Thank you for offering, Ashlyn, but Maya and I need to work this out by ourselves."

"I miss her."

"I know you do." Brody touched his daughter's hair. *I do too.*

"If I see her at the festival, I'm going to run up and hug her."

"I'm sure she'd like that."

Above them, the sun was just starting to set, bringing nature's spectacular nightly light show. He breathed in the comforting scent of their beloved ocean, coupled with delicious aromas from the street vendors' offerings. Pastries, burgers, fries . . .

When they reached the boardwalk, he scanned the crowd,

taking in the families, couples, and teenagers as southern rock music rang from speakers farther down. He searched the faces for Maya's. The silence between them had been pure torture. He'd checked his phone a hundred times every day hoping to find a text inviting him to come over and talk. He feared she'd already left town with Kyle, even closing down the store, but he held on to the hope he could still fix things between them.

When they stepped onto the boardwalk, memories of the times he'd spent with Maya washed over him—laughing on his deck, talking on the beach, kissing under the gazebo by the bay, talking on the roof of her building, working to care for the rescue cats. If only she'd give him another chance, he'd make her understand!

"Dad! There's Miss Maya." Ashlyn took off running toward a bench where Maya sat eating a pretzel and looking out at the beach.

He rushed after Ashlyn but halted as soon as she hopped up onto the bench and wrapped her arms around Maya's neck, almost knocking the pretzel from her hand.

"Miss Maya! I've missed you!" Ashlyn rested her head on Maya's shoulder as Maya hugged her back.

Brody's eyes stung as he witnessed the tender moment between his daughter and the woman he loved. How could he have thought Maya's love for his daughter would ever change? He'd been so worried about Ashlyn—and his own heart—that he'd lost the second best thing that ever happened to him. He needed to find a way to win Maya back before it was too late—and not just as a friend.

He glanced around the boardwalk looking for Kyle. He didn't see him, but that didn't mean anything.

Ashlyn sat back on her heels, facing Maya. "Daddy said we had to give you space, but I didn't want to. I wanted to check on you every day."

Maya brushed a thick lock of Ashlyn's dark hair away from her face. When she looked up, her eyes locked with Brody's, and his heart felt as if it might beat out of his chest. She looked so beautiful as her eyes sparkled in the light of the setting sun, and his body ached with renewed grief and regret.

"Hi," she said.

"Hi." He took a step closer to the bench, then glanced around the boardwalk. "Where's Kyle?" A muscle in his jaw jumped when he said the man's name.

"Gone."

"For now? Or for good?"

"For good. He was just using me, so I told him to leave and never come back."

He pointed to the ring finger on her left hand. "So it's over?"

"It was over a long time ago."

Relief threaded through him, and he felt the muscles in his shoulders relax. He still might have a chance with her! Now he had to get her alone so they could talk.

He nodded in the direction of his house. "I have a great view of the fireworks from my deck. Would you like to join us?" He held up his hands. "No agenda, I promise. Just a friendly, super-awesome place to watch them."

Maya hesitated, and he held his breath awaiting her response.

"Please, Miss Maya? Please?" Ashlyn asked, a hint of a whine in her voice. "I've really missed our talks."

Maya looked over at Brody, and he held his breath.

"Okay."

Brody released the breath as Ashlyn cheered. Maya dropped the last piece of her pretzel into a nearby trash can, and then Ashlyn threaded her fingers with Maya's and steered her toward the house.

A plan came together in his mind as he followed behind them. He just hoped he could pull it off!

Maya's pulse galloped as she and Ashlyn wove through the crowd toward Sandy Feet Retreat. Ashlyn talked about her adventures during the last week, including news about the two rescue cats they'd placed in homes.

Maya tried to concentrate on her words, but her mind was too busy whirling with questions about Brody. Why had he invited her to his house? Probably to apologize. But he'd still tell her he and Ashlyn would just be her friends. She cared too deeply for him to pretend a friendship would be enough, though. She should go home, but she didn't want to disappoint Ashlyn.

When they reached the steps of the house, Maya followed the two Tanners up into the family room, where she greeted Rusty and the tuxedo cats.

"Have you eaten?" Brody asked. "I mean, besides the pretzel?"

"Yes, I had a nutritious meal of leftover mac and cheese."

When he smiled, his dimple made her knees wobble. "A drink, then?"

"Sure. Thanks."

He brought two glasses of iced tea from the kitchen before they walked out to the deck. Darkness had started to creep in, bringing along the familiar song of cicadas.

Maya stood at the end of the deck and looked out over the ocean, trying to think of something to say to the man who, like Kiana, was her best friend. Oh, how she missed him! If only he loved her like she loved him. She needed more.

Her grief ran deep, and she held her breath, trying to keep her emotions at bay.

"Have you heard from your dad?"

She turned and found Brody standing near the railing a few feet away. "Yes, I have." She was grateful to find her voice calm. "We talk nearly every other day."

"Good." He sipped his tea. "The clinic has been busy. How about the store?"

"It's been busy too. I had a party today. Gayle said the customers never stopped coming in. She had to eat a sandwich at the counter. I think I might need to hire someone to help her on party days."

"That's a good thing, right?"

"Yeah." She studied his pleasant expression.

Ashlyn appeared in the doorway. "Dad, I can't find those glow sticks we got yesterday. I want to show them to Miss Maya and use them during the fireworks. Where did you put them?"

"Did you try your room?"

"Oh! I was looking in your room." Ashlyn rushed off.

"I'll come help you." He looked at Maya. "Excuse me. I'll be right back."

As Maya leaned on the railing, she spotted the shadows of families sitting together on the beach, waiting for the fireworks to begin, and the familiar longing for a family of her own swirled through her. Then, taking a long drink of her iced tea, she wished the cold liquid could wash away her loneliness.

After several minutes, she heard footsteps, and she spun toward the door as Brody walked out of the house. His baseball cap was gone, and it looked as if he'd taken the time to brush his hair.

"Maya, I need to tell you something."

The intensity in his blue eyes made her shiver despite the humidity. She set her glass back down on the table.

"I'm such a fool." He rubbed his chiseled jaw. "When you told me how you felt, I was stunned, but I was also scared. I was afraid of getting hurt, and then I wound up hurting not only you but me. I'm sorry I never told you about Courtney. You were right when you said I was wrong not to share everything about my past after you poured your heart out to me. I'm sorry for that. I built a wall around my heart when Courtney left me, and I was afraid to let anyone else in. You're nothing like her, and I should have trusted you. I never should have compared you to her. I was so wrong."

"Brody, wait." She held up her hand. "I'm the one who was wrong, and I owe you an apology. I was so focused on having a family that I pushed you to make a commitment. I should have respected your wishes to take our time in our relationship. I didn't know about Courtney, but I did know about Ashlyn. I'm sorry for pressuring you, and I hope you can forgive me."

He shook his head. "But everything you said to me was true. When I lost my sister, I blamed myself for not being there for her. And when my mother died, I made it my goal—no, my *purpose*—to be the best father I could for her child. I think I felt I would somehow make up for not being there for Julia by putting Ashlyn first in my life. But that was so shortsighted."

He paused and looked out toward the ocean. "When Courtney rejected a life together because of Ashlyn, I thought I'd never find someone who would want me and my daughter as the package deal we are. Courtney's rejection made me even more focused on Ashlyn, and I convinced myself she was all I needed."

He huffed out a breath. "But, Maya, you made me realize how blind I've been. You showed me that family is more than just having the same bloodline. And I thought Ashlyn wouldn't need more than one parent, but I was wrong."

Maya gasped, and her lip quivered.

"The truth is I love you, Maya. I've loved you for a long time, but I was too afraid to admit it even to myself. I want to be with you. No, I *need* to be with you. Ashlyn and I both do. It just about killed me when Kim told me she saw you get engaged." He paused and took a deep breath, and the tenderness in his eyes made her light-headed. "You're my best friend. You're the one I want to tell about my day, to share my dreams with, to plan a future with."

Her eyes burned, and she wiped them with the back of her hands. Yet his words were a balm to her soul, and she felt her heart starting to heal. "I love you too, Brody. I'm so grateful you're willing to give me another chance. Let's start fresh. We can take it as slow as you want. We can date and get to know each other better."

"But I don't want to date you, Maya."

She took a step back. "I-I'm confused."

"You, Ashlyn, and I are already a family. And I plan to put you both first. I've done a lot of thinking this week. I want to plan that trip to Vermont in the fall. I want to take you and Ashlyn on vacations and make memories with you both." He grinned. "She's been bugging me about Walt Disney World ever since the day we discussed our favorite rides."

Then his expression grew intense again. "You've become my family, and I'd like to make it official—if you'll have me."

"What are you saying?" she whispered.

He reached into his pocket, and something glinted in the deck lights. When he held up a ring, Maya cupped both hands over her mouth as tears streamed down her face.

"My mother gave this to me years ago. It belonged to her mother, and she instructed me to save it for the love of my life." He swallowed as he took her left hand in his. "You're the first and only woman I've ever offered this ring to, because Courtney picked out the ring she wanted. Now I know she wasn't the right woman to receive this ring anyway. Honestly, I was sure I'd never meet a woman who would love both Ashlyn and me, but a runaway calico kitten led me to you. And now that I've found you, I don't want to let you go. Will you be my wife and give me the honor of loving you for the rest of my life?"

She sniffed and nodded. "Yes. Yes, I will."

Brody slipped the ring on her finger, and she gazed down at the antique, emerald-shaped diamond surrounded by smaller diamonds in a white-gold setting.

She shook her head. "Oh, Brody, it's the most beautiful thing I've ever seen."

He traced a finger down her cheek, and she tipped her face toward him. "But you're the most beautiful thing *I've* ever seen, Maya.

You're the most beautiful, brilliant, talented, courageous, and amazing woman I've ever known, and I'm so grateful that I'll be able to call you my wife."

He studied her face, and the air around them felt charged, as if it would explode if they struck a match. His mouth dipped, and when he kissed her, she was certain she was dreaming. But the heat rushing through her veins was as real as the feel of his lips against hers.

Happiness blossomed inside her as Brody deepened the kiss, and she wrapped her arms around his neck. To the depth of her bones she knew this man was her true love, the one who held the key to her future.

"Hey. What's going on?"

Brody's lips smiled against Maya's before he pulled away. "Ash, didn't I tell you to wait in your room until I called you?"

Maya turned to where the little girl stood in the doorway holding two green glow sticks.

The little girl shrugged. "I was waiting for a long time, and then I didn't want to wait anymore." She looked up at Maya. "Daddy said he had a special question to ask you. What was it? Did he ask if he could kiss you?"

Maya turned to Brody. "This wasn't a plan between the two of you?"

Brody leaned against the railing and shrugged. "Yes and no. The idea hit me when we were heading here from the boardwalk, but I needed an excuse to get the ring out of my safe. When Ashlyn asked where her glow sticks were, I realized I had the perfect reason to leave the deck. But then I had to convince her to stay in her room so I could talk to you alone."

"You were taking too long. I want to spend time with Miss Maya too. But what was the question, Daddy?"

"I asked Maya to marry me."

Her eyes grew wide. "You did?"

"And she said yes."

"Yay!" But then she studied Maya. "When you marry my dad, will you be my mom?"

The little girl's words burrowed deep into Maya's heart. "Would you like me to be?"

"Yes. Maybe you could even adopt me. Sammie's mom adopted her, you know."

Maya met Brody's warm expression. "Is that what you want?"

"I meant it when I said I want to be a family. And that means you being Ashlyn's mom as well as my wife. You two are the most important people in my life."

He opened his arms wide, and Maya and Ashlyn both stepped into them. Maya closed her eyes, trying to hold back more tears.

Just then a *whoosh* was followed by a loud *boom*. Maya jumped and then laughed at herself. They all turned as fireworks exploded in the sky. Brody pulled her against his side as Ashlyn wrapped her arms around Maya's waist.

"Wow!" Ashlyn exclaimed as more fireworks flared. "Look at that one!"

"I love you," Brody whispered in Maya's ear, sending shivers cascading down her back.

Maya looked up at him. "I love you too, Dr. Tanner." Deliriously happy, she rested her head on his shoulder.

"I'm so glad you came to my super-awesome deck tonight." His lips twitched. "I promise I will love you and cherish you for the rest of my life."

She ran her fingers over the stubble on his chin. "I never expected to be swept off my feet like one of the characters in my books, but that's exactly what you did. My father told me I was worthy of love, and you and Ashlyn have helped me see that's true. I can't wait to start a new life with you both."

As she leaned against Brody, Maya knew she'd finally found her family. And it was perfect.

Epilogue

"Thank you for coming today, Alexis." Maya handed a book to the pretty young woman. "I hope you enjoy it."

Alexis took the book and hugged it to her chest. "I'm so excited to read it!"

Maya turned to the next woman in line and then surveyed the half dozen people still waiting in Beach Reads to get her autograph on their copy of her newest novel, *Written in the Sand*.

She looked toward the back of the line and smiled when she saw Brody and her father standing together, Brody laughing as her father spoke. When Brody met her gaze, he winked, and his dimple made its grand appearance. Ashlyn sat on a stool behind the counter next to Callie, who was selling copies to the customers. Tinker Bell sat at Ashlyn's feet as Ashlyn held a leash in her hand. Amazingly, the cat would let Ashlyn take her anywhere.

Maya glanced down at the white-gold band sitting behind her antique engagement ring and felt a dizzying happiness as she recalled all the wonderful events during the past year.

After getting engaged Labor Day weekend, she and Brody

immediately began planning their wedding. She hired two part-time employees to help Gayle run the store and to handle the tea parties in order to free up her time. Not only did she need to organize their nuptials, but she had to finish her overdue novel.

Maya was grateful that her literary agent was able to negotiate one last extension for the book, and with the help of her new inspiration and belief in true love, she quickly changed the story. It was about a young woman who moved to a beachfront town and met the love of her life, finding herself along the way. Then after she sent the manuscript to her editor, Maya focused on her new life with Brody and Ashlyn.

Brody had suggested they marry on New Year's Eve. "Ashlyn and I have been alone too long, and I can't wait to start our life together. Let's start the new year as a family."

They were married in a small ceremony at Brody's church—now her church as well—with only their closest friends in attendance. Maya's father gave her away, and Kiana was her maid of honor. At nine, Ashlyn made the perfect junior bridesmaid. Of course, Cam was Brody's best man. Maya was also thrilled that her aunt, uncle, and cousins from Vermont came to celebrate as well.

Not only did Brody and Maya take vows that day, but in a separate, private ceremony the pastor declared Maya and Ashlyn mother and daughter. From that day on, Ashlyn called Maya "Mom," and Maya would never get tired of hearing that name.

The three of them celebrated with a reception at an oceanfront hotel and then rang in their new year as a family before going to Walt Disney World for a week. Ashlyn got special permission to miss school.

When they returned, Maya and Tinker Bell settled into their

new home at Sandy Feet Retreat, and life seemed perfect as Maya enjoyed her new routine. She was still a business owner and author, but now she was a wife and mother too. Brody and Cam had also invited a third veterinarian to join their practice, giving Brody more time to spend with "his girls." Maya had never liked being called a girl, but when it came from Brody or her father, she did.

She placed her hand on her rounded abdomen with joy. In a couple of months, she and Brody would welcome another member to their family—a son—and she could hardly wait.

Sitting up taller in her chair, Maya chatted with the readers as they moved through the line.

After the last customer left, Brody set a copy of her new book in front of her, a smile pulling up the corners of his lips. "I bought several of your novels more than a year ago. You were with me when I bought them, but you didn't sign them. Would you please sign this one for me?"

"Oh goodness. I completely forgot about that." She picked up her Sharpie. "I'm happy to sign this one for you. What's your name again? It's slipped my mind."

He grinned. "Dr. Brody C. Tanner."

"Oh right." She snapped her fingers as she played along. "I thought you looked vaguely familiar."

Then, opening the book to the title page, she wrote,

To Dr. Tanner,

Thank you for sharing your love and life with me. And thank you for giving me the family I've always dreamed of. I can't wait to see what's in store for us throughout the year. I love you, Ashlyn, and our baby boy.

Yours forever,

Maya

Maya looked up as Callie walked over.

"It was a great book signing. Let's do this again when your next book comes out."

Maya smiled as she stood. "I'd love to." She came around the table and threaded her fingers with Brody's as she handed him the book. "I'm glad you came today."

"Well, I did want to get the author's autograph." Brody kissed her cheek. "I'm so proud of you."

"Grandpa!" Ashlyn rushed to Maya's father, who quickly bent down to hug her. "Let's go out for pizza."

Dad rubbed her back. "I love that idea." He looked at Maya and Brody. "What do you think, Mom and Dad?"

"You lead the way," Brody told him. He looped his arm around Maya's shoulders as they followed Ashlyn and her grandfather out the front door.

She leaned into him. "I love you, Brody."

"And I love you, Maya," he said, his voice a little husky.

She pointed to Tinker Bell. "And to think we owe all this to that little cat up there."

Brody grinned. "Thank goodness for that little calico."

Maya grinned back. Her future was here, and she couldn't be happier.

Acknowledgments

A s always, I'm thankful for my loving family, including my mother, Lola Goebelbecker; my husband, Joe; and my sons, Zac and Matt. I'm blessed to have such an awesome and amazing family that puts up with me when I'm stressed out on a book deadline.

Thank you to both my mother and my dear friend Maggie Halpin, who graciously read the draft of this book to check for typos. I'm so grateful for your precious friendship!

To my dear friend DeeDee Vazquetelles—our lunchtime chats were such a tremendous help as I plotted out this story. I appreciate how you always listen to me talk on and on about my books. Thank you also for volunteering to proofread. I'm sorry for all of the horrendous typos. Your friendship is a blessing! I don't know what I'd do without your daily texts and endless emotional support.

To my dear friend Kris Matthies—thank you so much for your help with my research. You are a blessing to me!

To Mikala Steele—thank you for taking the time to tell me about your cat and dog rescues! You are the coolest "crazy cat lady" I know! I'm in awe of all you do for the Lancaster (SC) SPCA. I truly appreciate the time you took to share information, and your stories inspired Brody's cat rescue.

To Melissa Rios, DVM—thank you for taking time out of your busy day to answer my questions. You are a blessing to your patients at Sun Valley Animal Hospital, especially my herd of crazy cats! We all appreciate you so very much.

I'm so grateful to my wonderful church family at Morning Star Lutheran in Matthews, North Carolina, for your encouragement, prayers, love, and friendship. You all mean so much to my family and me.

Thank you to Zac Weikal and the fabulous members of my Bookworm Bunch! I'm so thankful for your friendship and your excitement about my books. You all are amazing!

To my agent, Natasha Kern—I can't thank you enough for your guidance, advice, and friendship. You are a tremendous blessing in my life.

Thank you to my wonderful editor, Laura Wheeler, for your friendship and guidance. Thank you for all you've done to help me improve this book. I'm so excited to work with you, and I look forward to our future projects together.

I'm grateful to editor Jean Bloom, who helped me polish and refine the story. Jean, you are a master at connecting the dots and filling in the gaps. I'm so thankful that we could work together on this book.

I'm grateful to every person at HarperCollins Christian Publishing who helped make this book a reality.

To my readers—thank you for choosing my novels. My books are a blessing in my life for many reasons, including the special friendships I've formed with my readers. Thank you for your email messages, Facebook notes, and letters.

Thank you most of all to God—for giving me the inspiration and the words to glorify You. I'm grateful and humbled You've chosen this path for me.

Discussion Questions

1. Maya is shocked to learn that her father didn't abandon her and had hoped to find her someday. She fosters a close relationship with him and is happy to learn she also has an aunt and cousins she never knew. Do you have special family members with whom you're close? If yes, why are you close with them?

2. Throughout the story, what does Brody learn about himself? How does his past influence his desire to be the best father he can be for Ashlyn? How does that desire influence other areas of his life?

3. Maya's mother, Vickie, kept the truth about Maya's father from her. Do you think Vickie's reasons were valid? Why or why not? Would you have made the same decision?

4. When Kyle arrives in Coral Cove, Maya is in an extremely vulnerable place and tries to give him the benefit of the doubt. How would you have felt and behaved in Maya's shoes?

5. By the end of the story, Maya finally believes she's worthy of love. What do you think caused that change?

6. When Maya finds the letter detailing facts about her father,

she's shocked to learn her great-aunt knew about him but kept the truth from her. Why do you think CeCe wrote the letter but didn't share the truth with Maya while she was still alive? Would you have made the same decision? Why or why not?

7. Ashlyn lost her mother when she was a toddler and so has no memory of her. As a result, she dreams of having a mother figure in her life. Were you close to your biological mother? If not, did you have another mother figure in your life? What difference did your mother or mother figure make?

8. Have you ever visited a place like Coral Cove? If you could go anywhere for vacation this weekend, where would you choose to go?

9. Maya moves to Coral Cove after her great-aunt, her last living relative, passes away. Have you ever experienced an overwhelming change in your life? If so, how did you adapt to that change?

10. Maya and Kiana have been friends since their freshman year in high school. They're each other's support, especially during tough times. Do you have a special friendship like that? If so, what do you cherish the most about that relationship?

Bestselling author Amy Clipston transports readers to a picturesque lakeside town in this heartwarming contemporary romance.

Available in print, ebook, and audio

Follow four cousins and their journeys toward love and happiness while working at the local market!

About the Author

Amy Clipston is the award-winning and bestselling author of the Kauffman Amish Bakery, Hearts of Lancaster Grand Hotel, Amish Heirloom, Amish Homestead, and Amish Marketplace series. Her novels have hit multiple bestseller lists including ChristianBook, CBA, and ECPA. Amy holds a degree in communication from Virginia Wesleyan University and works full-time for the City of Charlotte, NC. Amy lives in North Carolina with her husband, two sons, and six spoiled rotten cats.

Visit her online at AmyClipston.com
Facebook: @AmyClipstonBooks
Twitter: @AmyClipston
Instagram: @amy_clipston
BookBub: @AmyClipston